SO WRONG

SO WRONG

Blurb

No wrong moves.

Those were the words the first boy I ever loved whispered in my ear on graduation weekend.

Naively, I believed him. Now those three little words feel like a bad omen I can't escape.

Every move I've made since I returned to South Chapel hurts my ex-boyfriend, Greedy. But it's for his benefit. That's what I tell myself. Intentionally hurting him is for the best.

It has to be. I said goodbye to the possibility of forever with him the moment my mom and his dad "introduced us" at their engagement dinner.

Three years have passed, but that doesn't matter to Greedy. He's hell-bent on making sure I remember it all.

On my darkest nights, the memories win. Since his bedroom is just two doors down, he's the anchor I seek when it all feels like too much.

But now Greedy's best friend is back in town, and he and I are "dating" to get his meddling mother off his back. Not only is Levi my new fake boyfriend, but he's also our new roommate, too.

No wrong moves, Greedy assured me years ago.

What if there are no right moves either?

Paperback Copyright

Copyright © 2024 by Abby Millsaps
All rights reserved.

paperback ISBN: 9798988800354

No portion of this book may be reproduced, distributed, or transmitted in any form without written permission from the author, except by a reviewer who may quote brief passages in a book review.

This book is a work of fiction. Any resemblance to any person, living or dead, or any events or occurrences, is purely coincidental. The characters and story lines are created by the author's imagination and are used fictitiously.

Developmental Editing by Melanie Yu, Made Me Blush Books
Line Editing, Copyediting, and Proofreading by VB Edits
Cover Design © Silver at Bitter Sage Designs

Contents

Dedication	VIII
Content Warning	1
Author's Note	2
1. Hunter	4
2. Hunter	11
3. Hunter	26
4. Greedy	30
5. Hunter	37
6. Hunter	44
7. Hunter	48
8. Hunter	55
9. Greedy	59
10. Levi	63
11. Hunter	70
12. Levi	73
13. Greedy	76

14.	Levi	81
15.	Greedy	87
16.	Hunter	93
17.	Hunter	100
18.	Hunter	106
19.	Hunter	113
20.	Levi	119
21.	Hunter	127
22.	Hunter	137
23.	Hunter	142
24.	Hunter	148
25.	Hunter	154
26.	Hunter	158
27.	Levi	164
28.	Hunter	170
29.	Hunter	177
30.	Hunter	184
31.	Greedy	189
32.	Greedy	196
33.	Hunter	199
34.	Hunter	205
35.	Hunter	209
36.	Hunter	215

37. Hunter	220
38. Hunter	224
39. Hunter	228
40. Hunter	234
41. Hunter	238
42. Hunter	245
43. Hunter	252
44. Hunter	257
45. Greedy	259
46. Levi	272
47. Levi	275
48. Hunter	279
49. Hunter	285
To Be Continued	292
Afterword	293
Acknowledgments	294
About The Author	295
By Abby Millsaps	296

To the readers who love a country boy *and/or* a star athlete *and/or* a British billionaire *and/or* a free-spirited yogi.
Welcome to Hunter's world.
Thankfully, no one has to choose.

Content Warning

Potential triggers include mentions of past abuse child, homophobia, on page emotional and physical abuse of an adult child by a parent, death of a parent, physical injury and blood, miscarriage, and suicidal ideation.

Additional context for the miscarriage and suicidal ideation triggers is available on the next page in the Author's Note.

Reading the Author's Note will reveal spoilers for the story.

Author's Note

Dear Reader—

The story that unfolds throughout this series is emotionally dark and heartbreaking. It's also triumphantly joyful and hopeful. And, of course, because this is romance, it will all end with an epic HEA.

I want to draw extra attention to two topics in the content warning and hopefully provide more context for anyone who may benefit from it. The suicidal ideation featured in this book is vague and is written from the point of view of a person suffering from an undiagnosed mental illness.

Joey from Lake Chapel taught us that anxiety is the shittiest shit. Hunter from South Chapel is about to reveal the horrors of Premenstrual Dysphoric Disorder (PMDD).

So Wrong lays the groundwork for a mental health crisis later in the series related to this diagnosis. Although Hunter is not in crisis in this book, she will be in the next book, so it's important to understand how some of her trauma and thought patterns will manifest as her story unfolds.

The portrayal of miscarriage in this story spans multiple chapters. You'll read about cramping, bleeding, and passing clots from a main character's POV in chapters 38-43. Please note that these chapters were written with care and from a place of lived experience. My heart goes out to anyone who has also experienced the physical, emotional, and mental pain of pregnancy loss.

If you have questions about any of the triggers mentioned in this book, feel free to reach out to me directly via email at authorabbymillsaps@gmail.com.

Sincerely,
Abby

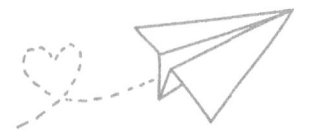

Chapter 1

Hunter

NOW

"Move over to the left. No! Jo-ey. *Your* left." I hold my phone closer to my face and squint, trying in vain to make out the details on the bodice of the deep crimson dress my best friend is modeling on the tiny screen.

It would be so much easier if I'd gone shopping with her today. But taking twenty-one credit hours means I have to be disciplined about my study time, especially so close to what's coming at the end of the week.

"You're hopeless," I tease as her image blurs again. We're both laughing so hard our screens are shaking. When she finally lines up the shot and I get a real look, I gasp.

"What do you think?" she asks, hip popped as she worries her lip. "Too much?"

The dress is a fit-and-flare style, and it's covered in tiny crystals that glimmer each time they catch the light. She looks amazing. Beautiful. She's shining from the inside out.

It makes me giddy to see her this damn happy. No one deserves it more than her.

"It's *perfect*," I practically squeal. "Kendrick's going to die when he sees you in this."

Joey cocks one brow, then uses her free hand to adjust her tits in the dress. "I'm not looking to take anyone out. You're sure it's not too much?"

"I'm more than sure," I assure her. "Plus, I could get you off on involuntary manslaughter. You can't help it that you're a knockout, Joey Crusade. That's the one."

She grins, her blue eyes sparkling. "You're good for my ego. Want to come over this weekend and help me figure out my hair and makeup?"

Sighing, I flop back on the couch and pull my sweatshirt strings tighter. The sun barely gives off enough warmth to be outside without a coat so close to winter, but I love the fresh air and peacefulness of studying on the balcony off my room. I'll happily sit out here year-round. That's what hoodies and blankets are for.

"I wish I could," I lament. "But I promised Dr. F I'd go with him to the South Chapel game on Saturday."

Lake Chapel University already wrapped up its football season, hence the reason Joey is shopping for formalwear. She's accompanying Kendrick to the end-of-season awards ceremony.

South Chapel University will play their final conference game this weekend. They won't be going to a bowl game, despite their winning record. College football playoffs don't make sense to me, but I'm not sad to see the football season winding down.

Although I'm not sure this is really the end for Greedy.

Dr. Ferguson, my stepfather, is under the impression that this is his son's last collegiate football game as starting quarterback for the South Chapel Sharks. He doesn't know yet that Greedy is considering a victory tour as a fifth-year senior.

Though Greedy is QB1 now, he didn't start his freshmen or sophomore years, so he has another year of eligibility—even though he's already taken the MCATs and has been accepted to medical school.

He's got some big decisions to make. Soon.

And some conversations to have with his dad.

"Well at least take a backup battery so I can text you," Joey proposes.

"I will. Promise."

Once we've said our goodbyes, I toss my phone across the balcony onto the soft lounge chair. It's the best way to avoid the distraction.

I *have* to get a ridiculous amount of work done this afternoon, or I'm going to have major regrets come next week.

Time to focus. I can do this.

I'm in the zone, flying through my schoolwork a few hours later when a hand lands on my shoulder, startling me so badly I fly three feet into the air.

Whipping my head around, I home in on the hand and forearm veins I swear I still see in my dreams. Maybe not in my dreams, exactly. More like in that hazy transition between sleep and awake where anything is possible.

I always see him in those moments.

Always.

I lift a hand to my chest, willing my heart to settle.

It's beating erratically because he startled me. That's the only reason.

Shrugging off his touch, I sit straighter, pop out my earbuds, and level him with a glare. "What do you want, Greedy?"

His face falls in response. *Good.*

Before he can open his mouth to answer, I double down. "Why are you here? You can't just let yourself into my room."

"We share a balcony, Tem. Plus I knocked a dozen times," he huffs, glaring right back at me.

"Don't call me that," I hiss for what might be the thousandth time since I returned to North Carolina.

Moving back into my stepfather's house six months ago was not my first choice.

Or my second. Or third...

But after my dad cut me off at the insistence of the stepmother I've never met—she's only three years older than me and currently pregnant with their second child—my options were limited, and I decided my multi-year "gap year" in Europe was over.

Greedy rolls out his neck, making the tendons there spasm like they always do when he's agitated.

I interlace my fingers in my lap to stop myself from smoothing a hand along his jawline and reminding him to unclench. *Like I always used to do.*

It's not my place. It's not my job. Greedy is nothing to me nowadays. He *has* to be nothing.

"We need to talk."

My stomach sinks. I'm sure he thinks we do.

Greedy's been trying to edge back into my life since the moment I reappeared in South Chapel, and he's relentless. I'm usually pretty good at dishing up the cold shoulder or acting unaffected, but despite my efforts, I've suffered from a few moments of weakness...

I rise to my feet and plant my hands on my hips. I go for nonchalant, regardless of how impossible it is to feel nothing in his presence with the towering heap of baggage and leftover damage between us.

I will my voice to hold steady, even as I tremble inside. "We don't have anything to talk about."

Brow furrowed, he hits me with another annoyed look, though it lacks real heat.

It's ridiculous to wish he were angry with me, but I'd love nothing more than to make him loathe the day I reappeared in his life.

Regardless of the barbs I throw at him and the cold shoulder that's become my default, Greedy never looks at me like he hates me. Like what I did to him is unforgivable.

If he only knew.

When he regards me, there's no hate. Only sadness.

Sometimes I wonder if he knows just how sad I am on the inside, too.

"We need to talk about Levi. He's home. Well," he says, rubbing at the back of his neck, "not home. He's at Lake Chapel General. He's having surgery today, and he's asking about you. He said he wants us to be there when he wakes up."

My heart stutters in my chest as Greedy's words sink in.

Flashes of hazy summer nights and swimming at the Quarry dance in my vision. Memories of sparkling blue eyes and country-boy charm infiltrate my thoughts. Snippets of days when I called him Duke, and he loved to call me Daisy.

Greedy brought us together, his best friend and his girl. For that one magical summer, the three of us were inseparable.

Levi.

He was such a good friend. To me. To Greedy. Loyal to a fault and always ready to help.

It's been a long time since I've allowed myself to think about the other boy I left behind when I fled to Europe.

"Yeah, okay," I agree. How could I not?

A little voice in my head mockingly reminds me that I don't have time for this.

I shift my weight from hip to hip, glancing down at the reading I can't put off. I have two weeks' worth of work to complete in the next ninety-six hours.

Even so, I don't have it in me to turn my back on our friend.

Levi was there, comforting me when I didn't know what to do. He sat by my bedside as I sobbed. He consoled me and calmed me as best as he could before I booked the one-way plane ticket that completely changed the trajectory of all our lives.

He let me go—*he helped me escape*—and if Greedy's standing in front of me willing to go visit him, I have to assume Levi's kept my secret safe after all this time.

I owe him so much.

So if he needs a friend right now, I can do that. It's honestly the *least* I can do.

Greedy clears his throat, interrupting my not-so-pleasant stroll down memory lane. "I'll drive. When do you want to leave?"

I meet his eyes, and another fragment of my heart crumbles to dust.

I miss him. In my heart of hearts, in my deepest, most private moments, I miss him. So fucking much. Sometimes I can't even look at him for more than a breath without feeling as though I'll drown in my sorrow.

Swallowing past the emotion clogging my throat, I give one last hopeless glance at my homework.

"I can be ready in an hour."

"Bring your work with you." Greedy nods at the pile of textbooks and errant pads of graph paper I've been worrying over. "We'll have to wait for him to be assigned a room, and I'm sure he'll be out of it for a while."

Relief washes over me. Why didn't I think of that? Studying will keep me from focusing on Greedy. I hope.

Rather than letting him see the way my tension eases at his suggestion, I slip into my default setting with him, popping my hip and pursing my lips. "Thanks for that, Captain Obvious. Now get out of here so I can get ready."

His nostrils flare, like they always have, at my bratty attitude. Based on the way Greedy looks at me nowadays—hard-set brow, mouth fixed in a scowl—I get the sense that he'd be better at calming me in Brat Mode than he used to be.

But I'm not his to handle anymore.

Just like he's not mine to worry about.

He stares at me for another breath, so I tip my chin and hold my head higher. It's a familiar place, this standoff we've found ourselves locked in over and over for months.

"See you downstairs," he finally relents with a sigh.

As he turns to leave, as he walks away, I have to envision there are cement blocks encasing my bare feet. It's the only way I can keep myself from running after him.

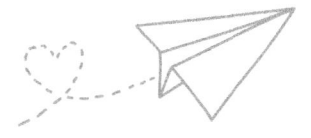

Chapter 2

Hunter

THEN

"Let's take it from 'rock steady.'" Tossing my water bottle to the side, I hustle back to the grassy practice area, then tighten my ponytail and wait for the others to meander over.

I'm met with a cacophony of less-than-enthusiastic grumbles from the other girls, but I shrug them off. As head cheerleader, it's my job to lead by example and create the Lake Chapel spirit our squad is known for.

"Line up. Come on, ladies! Let's see some hustle."

Once they're all in formation, I nod toward one of the JV girls to let her know she can start the music. It's a cheer we've been doing since middle school, but I want it to be perfect for the showcase.

By the time we finish up the fifth run-through, the May humidity has gotten the best of me and I have to wipe sweat off my brow. Then, after another swipe, this time over my upper lip, I rest my hands on my hips and focus on catching my breath.

"Grab some water, then we'll stretch," I announce to my team.

More grumbles.

I swear I'm surrounded by sourpusses.

I get it. The season ended months ago. Senioritis is oh so real, especially when the sun is shining and we're just a few weeks away from graduation.

But a big-name college sports reporter who's been following our high school's football team for years is coming into town this weekend, so the athletic department is throwing together a spring showcase.

A friendly scrimmage between Lake Chapel High School and our closest rivals, South Chapel, has devolved into a weekend-long event, complete with a pep rally, a signing, and a festival to round it all out on Sunday. All because the media is obsessed with our quarterback.

"Heads up!"

I dodge to the right as a football whirls past my head. This is not my first rodeo.

The ball bounces a few feet away, close enough to the other girls that they squeal and scream.

With a huff of annoyance, I run after it and scoop it up. Turning, I toss it underhand to the starting quarterback for Lake Chapel High School.

"Sorry about that." Decker grins mischievously, then eyes the group of girls who are now on their feet and apparently not so scared of the football after all.

Behind me, they're inching closer, tittering and whispering as they crowd my back. The energy is suddenly much more lively and bright than it was a few minutes ago. I can't imagine why.

"Thanks for doing this." Decker lifts his practice jersey up to wipe the sweat off his brow.

An audible gasp escapes from one of the girls behind me at the sight of his sweat-drenched abdomen.

"I know it's a pain to get the full squad together just for a friendly scrimmage—"

"We don't mind!" Clarissa chirps, all bubblegum sweetness and pep now that Decker Crusade is in the vicinity. Wasn't she just complaining about being hungover?

I fight back an eye roll, but Decker, clearly catching on, grins at me, eyebrows raised.

Decker and I have been pals for years. He's one of the good ones. Maybe a little too serious sometimes, but still good.

"Are you done for today?" he asks.

"I am," I confirm with a nod.

"Us, too." He jerks his head toward the parking lot. "Come on. I'll walk you to your car."

A disdainful scoff comes from behind me, making Decker's grin go impossibly wide.

I take a deep breath in, centering myself. Once I'm sure I won't burst out laughing, I turn and regard his unofficial fan club. "Why don't you lead the girls in stretching, Clarissa? It'll be good practice, seeing as how you'll be captain in a few weeks."

Without giving her time to argue, I spin and jog over to our pile of stuff and scoop up my bag. Once my water bottle is stashed inside it, I fish around for my keys.

Decker waits for me silently, then we fall in step together as we make our way to the parking lot.

"You guys looked good out there," I say, hip-checking him playfully.

He doesn't miss a step. "Thanks. Most of the seniors are planning to play at the collegiate level, so we've been lifting and conditioning together all spring. Honestly, though, I'll be glad when this whole media charade is over."

Based on the way his jaw ticks, it's pretty clear he's less than thrilled about this weekend's festivities. Even though he's the reason it's all happening in the first place.

"Have you decided about next year?" he asks, popping the football up in the air, throwing a perfect vertical spiral that he catches easily.

He's not prying, but I stiffen all the same.

He's been declared for Lake Chapel University since our junior year of high school. Everyone I know has decided where they're going.

I, on the other hand, still have no idea where I'll end up, and the deadline to decide is next week.

Cheeks puffed out, I sigh. "Probably Lake Chapel."

LCU is the easy choice. It's our local college, a place I'm familiar with, and the campus is beautiful. But more than that, Lake Chapel University has a great prelaw program. I could live in the dorms if I wanted, and despite its proximity to home, it's a big school, so I'd meet a ton of new people.

Trouble is, in an effort to keep my options open, I applied to thirteen schools. I never expected to get into all of them.

Lake Chapel University would be the logical choice. But the allure of the West Coast—or even one of the Ivies I considered a long shot until the big fat welcome packets arrived in the mail—is ever-present.

If only I were braver. Bolder. More of a risk-taker.

I applied to all those schools, never imagining I'd get into half of them. They felt like pipe dreams, not possibilities.

But now I'm frozen with analysis paralysis. The deadline is looming, yet I feel no closer to a decision than I did in the fall when the first welcome packet arrived.

I wish I had a sounding board. A person who would truly listen, who would challenge me, or offer wisdom or guidance. Someone who actually gives a shit about my thoughts and feelings.

My senior year of high school, that I've spent years looking forward to, has been overshadowed by my parents' nasty divorce. I can't seem to talk to either of them without "picking a side" and upsetting the other, so I stopped seeking out their opinions entirely.

"A fellow Crusader, huh? Will you cheer?" Decker asks.

I wrinkle my nose. The very idea grates on my nerves like nails on a chalkboard.

"Probably not." If I'm sticking around Lake Chapel, I need to carve out an identity that's mine alone. I don't want to become just a facsimile of high-school Hunter. Daughter of Magnolia and Michael St. Clair. Head cheerleader. Straight-A student.

I want to be somebody new.

Who that person is, I'm not sure yet. But a little thrill shoots through me when I consider the possibilities of who I could become.

Decker slows as we reach my car, and once I've unlocked it with the clicker, he opens the driver's side door for me.

Cradling the football against one hip, he grips the top of the doorframe of my white Audi coupe with the other hand and arches a brow. "So probably Lake Chapel, but probably no cheerleading? Any other probabilities you want to share?"

He's just teasing me, but the words pack a bigger punch than I expect them to.

Stomach clenching with nerves, I cross my arms and lean against the side of my car. My back hits harder than I intended, and I wince.

With a sharp breath in, I meet Decker's kind dark brown eyes and force myself to be blatantly honest before I lose my nerve. "Do you ever feel like your whole life has already been decided for you? Before you've even had a chance to make any mistakes or figure it out on your own?"

Decker's eyes widen a fraction. He's shocked by my outburst, I'm sure.

That makes two of us.

"I just mean—" I backpedal.

"I know exactly what you mean," he says, cutting me off. The words are hushed, the confession just for me, and his expression goes soft. "I get it. More than you know. Hunter, what do you wa—"

"Yo! Crusade!"

Decker snaps up straight, his expression morphing into the self-assured mask he wears more often than not.

The moment is gone, the spell broken.

"I was hoping to catch up with you, man."

I turn to the guy calling out behind me and do a double take. Not one, but two gorgeous jocks wearing South Chapel colors make long strides across the parking lot to close the distance between us.

"Hey," Decker replies with a casual chin lift, as if we weren't just on the brink of an emotional heart-to-heart.

It may have been the realest conversation I've had in a week. It's not often I find a person who wants to talk to me about anything of substance.

"You both played well," Decker says with a nod to the boys he scrimmaged with tonight. Turning to me, he offers a quick apologetic smile.

"Hunter, do you know Greedy and Levi?"

"No," I say, pushing off my car. "I don't think we've met before. Hey, I'm Hunter St. Clair," I offer sweetly, extending my hand to the first boy to reach us.

He's got wavy blond hair and, even at first glance, it's obvious he possesses an effortless country-boy charm. His eyes are the color of well-worn denim. When he smiles, his whole face lights up, and a single dimple appears on the left side. He's got defined cheekbones and these full, plush lips. Despite the mud smeared on his cheek and the sweat trickling down the side of his jaw, he's striking. Beautiful even.

"Hunter?" He takes my offered hand in greeting, his warm, strong grip sending butterflies dancing in my belly. "Levi Moore. It's a pleasure to meet you."

Gosh, his eyes are magic. I can't help but grin right back.

"I've been playing against these two since our Little Dukes U-12 days," Decker explains. "Levi's an exceptionally talented tight end. Too bad he never wanted to be a Crusader."

Levi mutters a "hey now" and play-swings at Decker, but Crusade is quick to defend himself. The boys roughhouse for a minute, then football talk commences. I've officially lost them both.

The other guy steps forward and offers me his hand.

"I'm Greedy," he says with a cocksure smile.

Greedy. Decker introduced him that way, but...

"That's not your *real* name, is it?" I sidestep to inch closer and hold my hand out. "*Greedy* is an adjective."

"I could ask you the same thing. *Hunter* is a common noun."

He grasps my hand, and for an instant, my world is turned upside down.

I expected the sizzle from Levi.

I was absolutely unprepared for the high-voltage shock that rocks me to my core when I shake hands with Greedy.

I freeze, my cheeks warming as I study the man before me.

He's lean and lanky, similar in size to Decker, but with a soft, youthful boyishness and a sweet smile.

His eyes are the color of moss-covered wetlands: an earthy tone that isn't truly green or blue.

Angling in closer, he keeps my hand locked in his. "If you tell me yours, I'll tell you mine. Hunter's not your real name either, is it?"

I grin. Joke's on him. Hunter Annalee Charlotte St. Clair is, in fact, my real name.

"What on earth do you think *Hunter* could be short for?"

Greedy releases my hand but steps so close I can feel the heat radiating from his body.

"I don't know. Huntress? Artemis, Goddess of the Hunt?"

Even though we're no longer touching, his presence is so overwhelming my core hums in response to him.

If Levi's attention caused butterflies, then Greedy's feels like the deafening vibration of a thousand cicadas screaming in unison.

"That's not a bad guess," I admit. My tone is pure flirtation. I can't help it.

"Artemis it is," he replies without missing a beat.

"Decker."

The new voice breaks the revelry, and all four of us turn and find Kylian Walsh approaching. He's not a football player, but he's a mainstay at all the games. He's also one of Decker's best friends.

I don't bother saying hello. Kylian is callous on his best days and rude on his worst.

"Hey, Hunter," the taller boy trailing behind Kylian calls out. Nicholas Lockewood. His cheeks are red with exertion. His sweat-soaked shirt is draped around his neck, showing off the beginning stages of what looks like a neck tattoo.

His face flushes even deeper crimson when he catches me staring.

Kylian doesn't spare a glance to anyone but Decker. "It's time to go," he says, his tone clipped.

Decker turns to me and lifts a brow. "You're good?"

"I'm good," I assure him with a small nod. "See you at the bonfire."

He raps his knuckles on the roof of my car, then skirts around the bumper to follow his friends.

A charged silence blankets us as Decker walks away. I suddenly feel shy and a bit guarded standing next to my car with this pair of boys I just met.

Starving and in desperate need of a shower, I slip into the driver's seat and turn the car on. "Uh, it was nice to meet you," I tell Levi, then Greedy. I roll down the windows to help get the air circulating and buckle up. "See you around!"

Before either of them has a chance to say goodbye, I put the car in drive and navigate out of the parking lot.

· ♥ · ♥ · ♥ · ♥ · ♥ ·

I had no intention of stopping on the way home. But my car's AC is out, and the humidity is relentless tonight.

Having it fixed shouldn't be an issue. Either of my parents are more than willing to pay for it, if only to one-up each other in the arms race for my affection.

But being without a car—even for an afternoon—makes me twitchy. My dad has been in Europe since last fall. My mom takes off and stays gone for a few days at a time. If she leaves on a whim, I don't want to be stranded.

With my signal on, I turn into the QuickieMart and pull in to one of the last available parking spots. It's a popular meetup place for Lake Chapel and South Chapel students. They're open twenty-four hours a day; the lighting is good, so it feels safe; and the owner Marty lets people leave cars in the expansive dirt lot behind the building overnight. It works out well for him on the weekends especially, when people show up in droves to claim their cars as well as the donuts, breakfast burritos, and coffee he stocks each morning.

The station is teeming with people, as expected. Some I recognize, but a lot I don't. I'm not really interested in hanging out or socializing tonight. All I want is a big strawberry slushy. And maybe a Mallo Cup. I could go for some chocolate. My period must be coming sooner than I expected.

I stick a pink Lake Chapel cheer cap on my head and grab my wristlet. As soon as I rise out of the car, someone calls out to me.

"Hunter! Seriously? This has to be a good omen."

My ponytail swishes as I spin and zero in on the guys standing at a gas pump.

Levi and Greedy.

What are the chances?

"Hey." I approach the rusty white pickup they're standing beside cautiously.

Greedy gives me a cocksure smile. "Did you follow us here?"

I pull a face. "Cute," I deadpan. "I'm pretty sure I left the field before you guys."

Not just pretty sure. I'm certain of it. I have no idea how they got here before me, unless they took the back roads and went about double the speed limit.

While Greedy is leaning over the hood of the truck with his phone in one hand like he's scrolling, Levi's standing next to the gas pump, muttering under his breath as he fiddles with the gas cap.

"What's wrong?" I ask, tipping my head to one side. I take a couple of steps closer.

The easy-going and carefree vibe I got from both guys at the field is gone. Now, there's a tension roiling through them. Greedy's pinched expression screams annoyance. Levi's rigid jaw makes him look downright agitated.

The truck is in even worse shape than I thought now that I'm inspecting it up close. It's rusty and at least twenty years old, with worn tires and a dent in the back fender.

"Had a little mix-up," Greedy offers with the wave of his hand.

Levi bristles and shoots a glare in his friend's direction. "By 'mix-up,' he means he pumped diesel into the gas tank."

Oh. Shit.

"I'm assuming your truck doesn't take diesel?" I ask Levi with a grimace.

He releases a pained groan and rubs at the back of his neck. "It's my dad's truck."

As I take a step closer, the worry rolls off him in waves. I want to hug him. Console him. Help him somehow.

"Bro, we'll figure out how to fix it. He'll never know. Maybe if we drive it to an auto shop—"

"You can't start the engine!" I shout.

At the same time, Levi doubles down on his concerns. "I'm so fucking screwed. He's going to kill me. *Literally* kill me." His voice trembles with fear, his light blue eyes frantic when he meets my gaze.

"Hey," I soothe, rounding the hood—and Greedy—to step closer to Levi.

Swallowing audibly, he regards me, his gorgeous face screwed up in a look of sheer panic.

I reach for his arm on instinct. I'm desperate to make this better. "Don't stress," I say. "I'll help."

He dips his chin and focuses on my hand where it rests on his forearm. Then he lets out a heavy breath. "I can't afford to take this truck into a shop." He looks to the vehicle, then back at me, squeezing his hand into a fist and then stretching it out again, causing the tendons in his forearm to flex beneath my touch.

"Leev."

I startle at the sound of Greedy's voice so close. He's behind me, and I can feel the heat of him at my back.

When he speaks again, his breath tickles the little hairs on my neck. "I'm the one who goofed. I'll pay for it."

I prop my hands on my hips and tip my head, taking Levi in. Then I turn back to look at Greedy.

"Neither of you knows anything about cars, do you?"

Their blank expressions confirm my suspicions.

"You really are lucky I showed up. If you start the engine, the diesel will make its way into the fuel line and combustion chamber. We've got to drain the diesel, rinse the gas tank with regular gas, drain it again, then fill it back up."

"Holy. Shit. How do you know that?" Greedy chuckles, his brows arched to his hairline like he's impressed.

Lips pressed together, I consider how I want to respond. Do I brush it off like it's common knowledge for an eighteen-year-old cheerleader to know the ins and outs of car maintenance? Or do I tell these virtual strangers the deeply personal reason I read car manuals and cookbooks and every brochure or flyer my dad came across for years?

One more glimpse of Levi's still forlorn, desperate expression gives me my answer.

I can trust them. I like them. They need help, and I can be that person right now.

"When I was little, I had a speech impediment." I hold my breath, waiting for one of them to interject or make a douchey comment.

Neither says a word, their focuses intently set on me.

I sigh, relieved they aren't, in fact, asshats, and go on. "My mom hated it. She put me in pageants, tried to force me to answer questions and perform on stage, thinking that would help."

I shudder at the memories. I still have nightmares about scented body glitter roll-ons and downing Pixy Stix for "extra sparkle" before being ushered onto a stage.

"That tracks. I could see you as one of those little pageant princesses," Greedy quips, one elbow propped up on the hood of the truck and one leg crossed over the other.

I hit him with an unamused glare. "It didn't work."

I leave it at that. They don't need to know that it had the opposite effect, and that I became so fearful of speaking in public I refused to talk at all for half of third grade. This wasn't supposed to be a personal trauma dump. I have a point to make.

"So once my mom gave up that ridiculous notion and my life no longer revolved around rehearsal and pageants, I spent a lot more time with my dad. He traveled for work during the week, but the weekend was our time. He loved tinkering with old cars, so I'd help. Or we'd make a complicated dessert from a Julia Child cookbook. I would read the instructions from the manuals and the recipes aloud, and he'd do the work."

My dad was always so patient and encouraging; genuinely warm and empathetic. It's mind-boggling that he and my mom ever got along at all. Those are some of my very best childhood memories, working on cars and cooking with my dad. And along the way, I picked up a slew of useful skills.

Levi nods, blowing out a long breath. "Okay. Good. This is good." There's a levity to him now that wasn't there before. "You think you can fix this?"

"Think?" I ask with a smirk. "I *know* I can fix this." I readjust my hat and pull my ponytail through the back, ready to get down to business. "Come on. We need supplies."

I lead the boys over to my car, pop the trunk, and grab my cheer bag.

It takes us nearly an hour, but eventually, I manually siphon out the diesel with the resistance bands I use for stretching. Then I do it again with the regular gasoline we pumped into the tank to rinse out the remaining diesel. Greedy pays for all the fuel, as well as the containers we buy inside the station to siphon it all into.

As I get started, he offers to hold my phone and wristlet for me, then not so subtly asks if he can put his number in and text him mine. For future car emergencies, he claims.

He buys me an extra-large strawberry slushy when we're all done, which I slurp down the second we pay at the register.

"Thirsty?" he teases.

I was thirsty when I pulled in an hour ago. Now I'm parched to the point of dry mouth. I'm also desperate to wash away the bad taste in my mouth. I didn't suck down any fuel while siphoning—thank god—but I can practically taste the stench. I can't wait to get home and shower.

"Ravenous." I arch my brows at him playfully and take a long pull on the red plastic straw.

His attention drifts to my mouth, and his eyes darken. Then that playful grin flattens into a scowl. His focus is hard, set, and so heated it feels like a living, breathing energy between us.

Mesmerized, I slowly drag the straw out of my mouth and lick the tip as I release it.

Greedy's eyes shoot up to meet mine, his mouth slack as he watches me work the straw. I lick my lips, the bright summertime sweetness of strawberries casting away the lingering scent of fuel.

In my periphery, a man enters the QuickieMart, headed straight for us. Greedy shifts closer and shelters my body between his and the rows of candy near the checkout. His body is so close, and yet he inches even closer and grasps my hip with one hand.

He doesn't shift back after the man passes. Nor does he move his hand.

Why is that so hot?

I peer up at him through my lashes, fighting back a grin.

"Thirsty, Greedy?"

He groans. "You're killing me here, Artemis."

I snort. It's the most unladylike sound imaginable. My mother would be appalled, but I'm so amused, I hardly have it in me to be embarrassed. "That's a truly awful nickname. Please don't call me that."

Chin dipped, he edges a little closer. "What should I call you, then?"

I bite into my bottom lip and tip my head back. I can feel the warmth of his hand through my thin tank top. He holds me with just enough pressure to convey a fondness and obvious interest. "You can just call me Hunter," I suggest.

One brow cocked, he scoffs. "No way. Levi calls you Hunter. Decker Crusade and his buddies call you Hunter. I'm sure all your friends call you Hunter."

"And?" I press. We've known each other for all of two hours. It's not like he's asked me out or made any real effort to get to know me. For him to presume—

"We're going to be a lot more than friends, you and I."

He doesn't give me a chance to refute that claim before he tips his head and takes a step back, headed for the door. "See ya around, Temi."

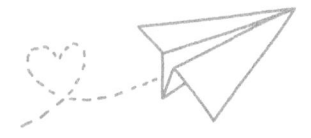

Chapter 3
Hunter

NOW

Textbook balanced on my thighs, I take notes on the section I just read, hoping I can decipher my chicken scratch later.

The setup is frustrating. The chairs in the recovery room are uncomfortable. The air is dry and filled with that sterile hospital smell. Various monitors beep. A nurse has been in and out at least a dozen times over the last hour.

Levi hasn't woken up yet, but according to Greedy, he underwent an extensive surgery, and he may be out for a while longer.

The information we have doesn't extend much further than that. Greedy knows little about Levi's current prognosis, and it's clear he's frustrated with the lack of information: both from Levi and from the nurses and staff who keep putting off his questions. He mentioned something about a "dead leg," but that means nothing to me.

I've just gotten my book and notebook balanced perfectly when Greedy strides back into the room.

"Here." He thrusts out a textured Styrofoam cup in offering.

Head bowed over my work, I continue scribbling notes.

"It's coffee," he adds when I don't acknowledge him.

I sigh and shake my head. "I'm good. Thanks anyway."

He scoffs. Loudly. "Just take the damn coffee, Hunter. It could be hours before he wakes up. This'll give you a boost so you can get your schoolwork done."

Greedy knows I'm taking twenty-one credit hours this semester. He knows I'm desperate to graduate in less than four years so I can play catch-up and get control of my life again.

But he has no idea about the internal clock that's ticking or what I'm up against over the next few days.

Just like he has no idea that I haven't touched a drop of dark roast in over two years.

"I don't drink coffee anymore," I tell him quietly. I keep my gaze focused on the notebook in front of me despite the way his eyes bore into the side of my head.

He sits to my right, but he leaves a seat between us.

"You love coffee," he argues, though his tone is low, dejected.

"Loved," I correct. "I loved coffee." I swallow past the emotion suddenly taking up residence in my throat. "The acidity and caffeine don't agree with me these days."

He says nothing, because there's nothing else to say.

We've quickly reached the same impasse we've found ourselves hitting for months.

Greedy desperately clinging to memories of the girl I used to be, reminding me over and over of a person I haven't been for a long time, doing all he can to resuscitate her.

Me wishing like hell he would give up already. Partly because it would be easier to just forget. But also because deep down, I miss that girl, too.

My phone buzzes then, vibrating in the seat between us.

His eyes flit to the screen before I have a chance to grab it.

Heat rushes to my face as I scan the message preview that appears on the screen.

It could have been from Joey, or my mom. Someone from my study group. But no…

> **The One and Only:** I miss you, Mahina

And then, because he has absolutely no chill:

> **The One and Only:** Call me before it gets too dark. You are strong, my love. We may be separated by oceans, but you're never alone.

"Tem—"

I jump to my feet, mentally scrambling for a distraction before Greedy can comment. "I'm going to stretch my legs and grab a coffee. Shit. No. Tea! I meant tea." I scurry for the door. The heat in his eyes and the anger emanating from him are too intense for me to deal with.

Not today. Not this week. Not right now. Not ever again.

But before I can get more than two steps away, another voice calls out.

A deeper, grittier voice.

"Daisy?"

I stop in my tracks and turn on my heel, breath catching as Levi cracks his eyes open.

"You're really here?" His speech is husky, labored.

My heart aches as I look at him lying in that bed, helpless and hurting.

"I'm here." I approach the bed from one side as Greedy stands and steps up to the other.

"I didn't think—I didn't know if—"

I cut him off before his post-anesthesia haze reveals too much.

"Are you in pain? Want me to call the nurse?"

He yawns, then winces. "Yeah. Ibuprofen would be good. And water."

Greedy is already pushing the call button on his behalf.

"Rest, brother. We're not going anywhere. We'll be here when you wake up again."

Levi's eyes are closed and his face is slack before Greedy even finishes speaking.

Chapter 4

Greedy

NOW

Hunter's not around when Levi comes to again.

I've pulled a chair closer to his bed, watching as he sleeps.

The grimace he pulls every few breaths, even while he's still out, makes it obvious he's in more pain than he admitted when the nurse came to administer meds. He took the OTC pain reliever, insisting he didn't need the narcotics.

"You should take the meds they offered," I tell him when he finally opens his eyes.

His reason for not taking them is bullshit. He's nothing like his dad, and even if he did slip, I wouldn't let him falter.

"Greedy. Hey, man." Another grimace as he tries to sit up.

"Here." I rest a hand on his arm to stop him, then I adjust the bed so he's in a more upright position.

With a grunt, he shifts, trying to get comfortable.

"Seriously, Leev. Let me call the nurse back in. You need something stronger."

"No." It's barely more than a whisper, but his tone is resolute.

"You've always been a stubborn ass, you know that?"

He says nothing, so I press on.

"What do you think is gonna happen if you take the pain meds you clearly need?"

He stares at me blankly, his eyes hazy and his face drawn, but he doesn't respond.

Dammit. My chest aches for him. "Seriously, Levi. There's nothing wrong with accepting help."

Lowering his chin, he focuses on his lap, mindlessly tracing the IV still running in his arm.

"Okay, no pain meds." I'm not giving up. But I can give him a reprieve for now. "How about you tell me how this happened?"

His silence persists. He doesn't look up, and I swear he sinks a little farther into the mattress.

He's always been stubborn and bullheaded.

But so have I.

"Seriously, man, if you're not going to talk to me, then why the hell did you ask us to be here? You think I'd choose to spend the day here, being ignored by Hunter?"

That finally gets his attention.

His blue eyes blaze with indignation as he looks up and pins me with a glare.

Another grimace.

Another sigh.

And then, gaze averted again, he finally cracks. "I didn't know who else to call." The words are barely more than a whisper, but there's no masking the tremble in his voice. "It happened so fast. I was asleep in my bed in California two nights ago, man. And now... *Fuck*. And now I'm here."

I respect the weight of the situation. But I can't help him if he doesn't open up and really talk to me.

Shifting closer to the bed, I duck my head, trying to catch his attention. "What happened?"

He closes his eyes, head lolling to the side. He's quiet for so long I wonder if he hasn't drifted back to sleep. I've resigned myself to sitting back and waiting again when he speaks.

"Three weeks ago, I took a hard hit. It was a fair play. The tackle was clean. But I took an ill-placed helmet to the quad."

"Did you sit out the rest of the game?"

The room is silent aside from his pained breathing and the beeps of the monitors.

I know the answer. I found the footage online. He didn't sit out for the rest of the game. He didn't even sit out for the next *play*.

Legs spread wide, I lean forward and rest my elbows on my knees. I'm supposed to report to the weight room in less than an hour, but I refuse to leave Levi's side now that we're actually making progress.

"Why didn't you sit out? Why didn't you tell your coaches you were injured?"

"The adrenaline masked the severity of the injury at first," he admits. "After the game, I iced it, and I took it easy the next day. I figured it was a contusion."

"What did the training team say when they looked at it?" I press.

He grits his teeth and turns away almost imperceptibly, which is all the answer I need.

Stomach twisting, I rough a hand down my face. Making no attempt to mask my condescension, I ask, "You didn't tell your coaches *or* trainers?"

That does it. *Finally.*

Levi detonates. He sits up straight and thrashes in a way that has to fucking hurt, given that he's only been out of surgery for a few hours.

"You have no idea what it's like! Fuck, man. To have a full ride athletic scholarship. To have your entire future—your entire fucking life—tied up in the ability to perform."

He huffs, clearly in pain, and sucks in a deep breath. Then another.

"I don't have a rich daddy or med school to fall back on, *Garrett.*"

I let the insult land. He needs the outlet. If railing at someone will make him feel better, I'll gladly take the brunt of his anger.

"So it was about the money?"

"It's about my fucking *life*, Greedy!" He's breathless and grimacing, but he doesn't stop. "My future. My whole fucking life."

"Oh."

In unison, we turn our heads and zero in on the doorway.

Hunter's there, Styrofoam cup in hand. Face pinched, she rushes to Levi's other side, sets her tea down, and immediately fusses over his pillow and the angle of his head.

"You're awake. What can I do for you? What do you need?"

He gives a soft smile, his demeanor instantly morphing from fury to relief.

Hunter leans closer, brushing a few stray hairs off his forehead. The simple move sends a jolt of jealousy through me. She touches him so easily. Speaks to him with such kindness. A kindness I haven't been on the receiving end of in years.

"Can I get you something to drink? Water? Tea?"

Levi rests against the pillow she just fluffed for him, shaking his head back and forth gingerly. "It's so good to see you, Daisy."

She stills, her shoulders lowering and her expression softening. "It's really good to see you, too." The smile she offers him is brilliant and sincere. The sight of it is like a punch to the solar plexus.

Levi left for college two days after I headed to football camp. Hunter had disappeared just a few days before.

The full ride athletic scholarship to California Coastal Tech was life-changing for him.

His dad was an alcoholic and a pill popper who had a fatal heart attack before he turned fifty.

His mom let Levi's dad beat on him when he was a kid. I can't say I have much respect for a parent who doesn't stand up for their own child. I couldn't count how many nights Levi ended up at my house, fresh bruises blossoming on his body that he brushed off as nothing.

I spent most of the summer before college living with him. We'd realized months earlier that his dad would leave us the hell alone if he knew it was two against one.

Ultimately, I was glad Levi had gotten out of this place. Even if he had to leave when I needed him most.

When Levi left for college, he was gone for good. He didn't come home for holidays. He stayed in California each summer. Over the years, we've exchanged the occasional text, but our relationship has never been the same.

Part of that is because of what happened.

Part of that is my fault.

Something broke inside me when Hunter left.

I didn't have it in me to make the effort.

But he changed, too.

Envy taking over, I cross my arms over my chest. "If you two are done making heart eyes at each other, Levi was just about to tell me how he ended up back in North Carolina, needing emergency surgery."

Hunter plants one hand on her hip and hits me with the scowl I've become so goddamn familiar with these last few months.

Good. I'd rather she glare at me with disdain than look at him so lovingly.

"Football injury. It was worse than I realized." He shrugs, schooling his expression. "I went to the ER earlier this week because my leg kept going numb and the swelling was getting worse. At first, they suspected myositis ossificans."

"Myo-ossif-what?" Hunter asks.

"Calcification of the muscle after injury or overuse," I explain, pushing away the hurt, because *fuck*, this shit is serious. "Bone starts growing in the soft tissue because the muscle didn't properly heal."

"Ouch." Hunter frets, frowning down at Levi.

"Yeah," he confirms, affecting a bullshit nonchalant tone. "Ouch." Turning to me, he adds, "X-rays weren't conclusive, so they ordered an MRI. There was calcification for sure. But they also mentioned compartment syndrome."

"Fuck, man." I instinctively assess his wrapped and immobilized thigh, searching for signs of swelling I can't see. If blood flow is affected by the leg for too long, he could lose all feeling and function of his leg. "I can't believe you endured a cross-country plane ride like that."

"Didn't have much of a choice," he offers.

"Why are you here, Levi?" Hunter asks gently, grasping his hand.

I hold my breath. Now we're finally getting somewhere.

"If you needed emergency surgery, why wouldn't you stay at the hospital in California and—"

"It didn't make sense to stay in California." Levi bows his head. "I lost my scholarship. I can't afford to pay for this surgery as it is. And I'm gonna need help getting around and rehabbing this leg if I ever want to walk or run again."

Hunter softly gasps. "It's that bad? From a football injury?"

Frustrated, I can't help but interject. "It's that bad from a secret football injury that he neglected to have treated."

My accusation doesn't affect the sympathy rolling off Hunter. "Oh Levi, I'm so, so sorry." Her bottom lip wobbles as she surveys our friend. A second later, she's throwing her arms around his neck.

The envy is back. I roll out my shoulders, trying and failing to tamp down on the bitterness engulfing me as I watch her hold him, wrapping him up in what I assume is a warm, comforting embrace. What I wouldn't give to be the one in her arms. It's not until she releases him and steps back that I realize I've been holding my breath.

"You won't be able to play football again, will you?"

He meets her gaze but says nothing. He doesn't have to.

Her eyes widen as a silent understanding passes between them.

I do a double take when a single tear spills over my friend's lashes.

Fuck.

My chest constricts at the thought. I'm still pissed, but I fucking feel for him. I hate that he didn't prioritize himself or seek medical help when he needed it. But at least he's here now.

I don't know the depth of his pain or the complexity of his struggles. But I won't let him go through any of it alone.

"We're here for you, Levi," I vow, nodding to Hunter, then back to my best friend.

Hunter nods along in agreement, her face solemn.

"Whatever you need, however we can help," I say. "We're here for you."

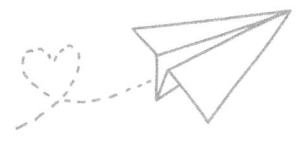

Chapter 5

Hunter

NOW

"You're sure you don't want me to drop you at home?"

"No." I shake my head.

Greedy is heading to campus for a few hours, and though we rode together, there's no way I'm leaving the hospital now.

He gives me a quick nod, then flicks his gaze to Levi. "I'm going in for film review and a quick lift. I'll have my phone on me. Text or call if you need *anything*."

Levi blows out a breath, then slowly nods. "Thanks. I will."

"I'll be back to pick you up in a few hours, Tem."

He pulls the door closed behind him before I have a chance to argue.

Instinctively, I lean in, desperate to comfort my friend.

"I'm so sorry, Levi." I wrap my arms around his bicep in a half hug, my heart aching for him. "This sucks."

He smells different nowadays. Even under the mask of the sterile hospital stench, the change is noticeable. The scent of drug store body spray and fresh cut grass have been replaced with subtle notes of cedar and something almost fruity, like peaches.

It's one more reminder of how much time has passed since we saw each other last.

"You don't want to be here, do you?" I give his bicep a final squeeze, then sit up and really take him in.

"In North Carolina, thousands of miles away from home, laying in a hospital bed? No. I don't want to be here."

Yeah. Okay. Dumb observation.

He reaches for my hand. "But waking up and being greeted by the prettiest girl in North Carolina?"

I snicker.

His face lights just a little for the first time since he woke up. "That part wasn't so bad."

We sit like that for a few minutes, nothing but the sounds of the IV drip and the subtle buzz of the overhead florescent lights filling the silence.

With anyone else, it might be awkward.

Not with Levi.

"Tell me about the girl... or guy," I hedge. "Who did you leave behind?"

Levi bristles. "Who said I left anyone behind?"

I interlace our fingers. His hands are warm and dry—tanned from life on the West Coast, with thick veins bulging prominently against the skin.

"Heartache knows heartache, babe." Ducking closer, I give him a sad smile. "I can see it in your eyes. You left more than college football back in California."

With a squeeze, he releases my hand. Then he closes his eyes, effectively shutting me out. After a few beats, his breathing slows.

It's late afternoon now, and I'm sure he's exhausted. I can't blame him for wanting to sleep, even if he's doing it to avoid my questions.

"His name's Trey," he finally says, startling me.

"Is he—"

"*Was.*" Levi swallows thickly. "He *was* my boyfriend. We'd only been official for about a month. He's the punter on our team. A fifth-year senior. He stuck around so he could complete a spring internship with this architectural firm in San Diego."

"And when you say *was*?" I press. Because the fresh anguish etched into every line on his face goes beyond the physical pain of surgery.

"He didn't want me to come here. Told me point-blank that if I left California, he and I were through."

Seriously? Who gives a person they care about that kind of ultimatum?

"What did he expect you to do?" I demand, bereft on my friend's behalf.

An alarm connected to Levi's IV starts beeping, meaning a nurse or tech will be in shortly.

"He wanted me to have the surgery in California. Recover out there. Trey knows about my mom... her church. I think he was trying to protect me."

Levi grits his teeth and shakes his head. He heaves out a breath like he's ready to continue, but when the nurse sweeps into the room, he clamps his mouth shut.

After she's asked about his pain, she checks his blood pressure and comments that it's higher than she'd like to see.

I'm sure it is, considering we were just talking about his bigot of a mother.

Mrs. Moore is a real piece of work. And that's saying something, considering my own mother isn't winning any awards in the parental department. Levi's mom is very involved with her church. She does their books and leads the youth group and the choir.

I have no problem with people who love Jesus.

I do have a problem with two-faced hypocrites who don't practice what they preach.

She never even tried to protect Levi from his dad. If Mr. Moore were still alive, she'd probably still be making excuses for him, or pretending like he wasn't a mean, habitual drunk who was notorious for falling asleep at the bar after being served too much whiskey.

The list of people I dislike in this world is short, but Patricia Moore has earned a permanent spot near the top.

When the nurse finally leaves the room, Levi, head hung, continues.

"I couldn't stay in California. I couldn't put that kind of burden on him. I'm going to need a ton of support while I recover and help getting to physical therapy and follow-up appointments. I didn't even have a car out there."

"But you had him."

With a sigh, he fixes those denim blue eyes I know so well on me. He doesn't have to say it out loud. The contrition on his face makes it clear he's not sure he made the right choice. My throat clogs at the sight. I feel for him. Second-guessing is one of my specialties.

"I had him," he admits. "But how long do you think that would last? How long until he got tired of driving me to every appointment and taking care of me? I wasn't about to ask him to upend his life to be my full-time caregiver."

"If he was willing, though—"

He groans and buries his face in his hands. "He *thought* he was willing. He didn't know what he was signing up for. How could he take me to daily PT and doctor's appointments between school, practice, and his internship?"

He sits up straighter, his expression hard and determined.

"I refuse to be anybody's burden, Daisy. Full stop."

"I'm so sorry," I offer again, heart sinking.

"I don't want your pity," he retorts, his tone dripping with disgust.

"I get that," I whisper, taking his hand once again. "But I care about you, Levi. I hate to see you hurting."

The heavy burden of heartache blankets the room as we sit quietly, both lost in thought.

Life isn't fair. No one is guaranteed a happily ever after. But there's solace in knowing that there's a person in this world who sees me and knows me. Levi knows my darkest moments and witnessed my lowest lows, and despite it all, he stuck by me.

I'll do the same for him. Always.

With a sniff, he buries his face in his hands, but he's not fast enough to hide the single tear rolling down his cheek. I reach out and swipe it away with my thumb, cupping his jaw and hoping he can feel the comfort I'm offering.

"You're okay. I'm here. Greedy and I are both here for you."

He sniffles again, then speaks without looking up. "I was happy, Hunter. I already miss that version of myself."

"You can still be that person."

This time, he eyes me cynically and peels my hand off his face. "I can't. Not here."

I press my lips together, desperate to argue. Before I can formulate a response, he speaks again.

"My mom already set me up on a date next week," he bemoans, his voice cracking. "Next fucking week. I won't even be able to walk without crutches by then."

My stomach twists at the thought of Mrs. Moore sinking her claws into Levi all over again. Back in high school, he was always concerned about upsetting his parents. He walked a fine line of obedience, one that was drawn with the charcoal of fear. "Why would she do that?"

He gives me a knowing look.

"Easy. If she can't *pray away the gay*, maybe she can set me up with a nice girl who's eager and willing to get married and have babies."

We share a pointed look. Levi is bisexual. He tried to come out to his mom in high school, before he and I even met. But the way he tells it, she shoved him right back into the proverbial closet. Then she regularly started leaving conversion camp brochures in his room.

His shoulders sag, and he deflates before my eyes. "She also has a meeting scheduled at the bank."

Confused, I frown, but I remain quiet while I consider why the hell she'd do something like that.

"She wants me to take out a small business loan. Invest in a local branch of Chapel Hill Insurance. She already talked to a man from church who's supposedly agreed to be my mentor while I go through the training program."

"That's bullshit." I sit ramrod straight, clenching my fists in my lap. "She can't just force you into a life she designs for you."

Levi meets my eyes and offers a defeated smile.

"She can if I'm dependent on her to care for me, take me to all my appointments, and keep me on her health insurance to cover all this." He waves his hand dismissively around the hospital room.

"No." I shake my head, adamant. "No fucking way. I'll talk to Greedy. We can help, Duke. We'll figure something out."

I'm so angry on his behalf, so frustrated and determined to come up with a solution that doesn't involve Mrs. Moore orchestrating Levi's life, that I almost miss the way his smile softens.

"I'm glad you two are getting along," he offers.

I snap my mouth shut.

It's easy to forget that I haven't actually seen and I've barely spoken to Levi in over three years. It was hard at first—ignoring his messages, avoiding his calls.

It was best for all of us if I cut ties and kept my distance.

But now that he's here... Gosh. I missed him. I missed him so damn much.

We've always clicked, the two of us, and I've always felt safe when I'm with him. He gets me on a level so few other people do. He sees me for who I am and knows my darkest secrets, and he still loves me.

He's here under the worst circumstances. But the situation doesn't have to be hopeless. I won't take this second chance with him for granted.

"It's been... rough." I pause there, waiting until Levi meets my eyes before continuing. "I came back to town in August. I've been living at Dr. Ferguson's house since. I've tried to keep my distance, but..."

I'm not ready to divulge the extreme lengths I've gone to keep my stepbrother at arm's length over the last several months.

Just like I'm not ready to admit to all the times I've slipped up. All the times I've let the connection between us spark back to life, given him hope that we could be more.

And I'm really not ready to confess what happens on the darkest nights, when there's no moon in the sky or hope left in my personal well.

"He doesn't know," I whisper. I choke back a sob at the thought of the secret I've held tight to for three years. "I don't *ever* want him to know."

Levi furrows his brow and clenches his jaw, studying me.

After a few breaths, he blinks. "He won't find out from me."

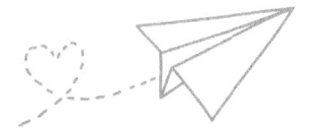

Chapter 6

Hunter

THEN

"Hey! I'm home!"

I hang up my cheer bag in the mudroom, then head to the kitchen and refill my water bottle at the sink. Even after polishing off my entire slushy, I'm still so thirsty.

The slushy Greedy bought for me.

I've got a full night of internet sleuthing ahead of me. The guys mentioned they'd be at the bonfire this weekend—part of the pregame events for the senior showcase game. I'm more than a little eager to learn all I can about them before I see them again.

Before things go any further.

Giddiness bubbles up at the thought. Internally, I squeal as I replay that moment in the QuickieMart when Greedy stepped in close and watched me drink my slushy like he wanted to devour *me*.

And then there was his promise.

"*We're going to be so much more than friends.*"

"Oh, good! You're here."

My mom rushes into the kitchen, pulling me from thoughts of Greedy, securing an earring in place one-handed while she carries two pairs of high heels in the other hand.

"Which shoes?"

"Hi to you, too," I murmur, coming closer to inspect her outfit and the footwear choices.

My mother is the definition of beautiful. Her chin-length golden blond hair is cut into a blunt bob. Her green eyes are lined dark, and though she's in her early forties, her skin is flawless and wrinkle-free.

She's religious about med spa appointments and maintenance. Until the divorce, the two of us used to spend an entire day at the salon together once a month.

"Hunter," she snaps. "Help me."

I force myself to focus on her, assessing her outfit and the shoes she's thrusting at me. Strappy black Louboutins or edgier Jimmy Choos.

"How old is he?"

She scowls for a beat, considering.

With another sip of water, I wait her out. I'm not judging her. She's been on dozens of dates over the last year. This is nothing new. Even if the divorce has yet to be finalized. It shouldn't be long now. Hopefully by this summer, it'll all be done so we can all start to heal and move on.

Or I can. My mother has obviously already started moving on.

"He's a little older, but not by much. He's a *doctor*," she gushes. "Widower. One son, maybe around your age? Or maybe a little older. I don't remember."

If he's older, the choice is easy. "Wear the Louboutins."

"Yes. You're so right. What would I do without you?"

With a sincere smile, she sits at the table and slips her feet into the heels. Once they're in place, she strides into the foyer and gives herself another once-over in the full-length mirror near the door.

I pad to the fridge and assess my options for dinner since it's clear I'm on my own tonight.

There's not much by way of leftovers, and the fruit and vegetable drawers have been cleared out for a few days. I guess I'm going grocery shopping this weekend.

I pull a block of white cheddar from the dairy drawer and snag the carton of eggs. From the weight of it, I'm pretty confident there will be enough for an omelet.

I've just popped the top, revealing four eggs nestled in their cardboard nooks, when my mom calls out to me.

"Hunter, can you come out here before I go?"

Abandoning the ingredients on the counter, I head to the front of the house and find my mom still standing in front of the mirror, applying a final coat of lip gloss.

"Here." She holds out her phone. "Take my picture, please."

I work hard to keep my expression even as I accept her unlocked device. If she's feeling herself tonight, why not document it?

She poses, and I snap several shots.

When I'm finished, she reviews and deletes them all, then makes me do it again.

"Let's take a selfie," she declares when one of my pictures finally meets her editorial standards.

She makes me hold out the phone but adjusts my arm to her liking to get the best angle.

"There," she demands once the shot is lined up how she wants it.

"Oh my gosh," she gushes once I've taken several and she's scrolling through the pictures. "I'm going to post this on Facebook. People will think we're sisters."

I hold back an eye roll. She's fully done up while I'm fresh from cheer practice and still smell like gas from the QuickieMart. We're not exactly comparing peaches to peaches here.

"Have fun tonight," I call over my shoulder as I turn back to the kitchen.

Without a response, she steps into the garage, and a moment later, the overhead door opens.

I exhale a slow, calming breath.

It's been a long day. Thankfully, it's almost over.

I make quick work of prepping the eggs and grating cheese. Then I get out the omelet pan and let it heat on the stovetop.

The whiff of natural gas that hits me as the flame ignites reminds me once again of my encounter with Greedy and Levi. It also reminds me that I'm in desperate need of a shower.

I'm looking forward to a quiet night in. I'll eat. Shower. Watch a bit of TV. Then I'll probably reread one of my favorite Sarah Dessen books and turn in early. I don't mind being alone.

I sigh again, letting the quiet of the empty house engulf me as I watch a pat of butter start to melt in the pan.

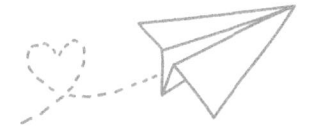

Chapter 7

Hunter

NOW

"Everyone's going to think we planned this," Dr. F teases, nodding to our matching tops.

When we realized we were wearing matching number 2 jerseys, he offered to change, but I insisted that it's fine. Greedy will be glad his dad could make it to this game. He'll be even more thrilled to see him in his jersey. I want him to have this memory, to be aware of his dad's sweet gesture.

Dr. F is sporting dark jeans and a long-sleeve tech shirt under the aquamarine jersey. I'm not sure I've ever seen him look so casual, but he wears it well.

I assume he's here because he's under the assumption that this is his son's last collegiate football game. It's not my place to tell him that may not be the case.

"All right, kiddo. What'll it be? Popcorn and M&M's, obviously." He gives me a pointed look.

That's been my favorite combo for as long as I can remember—and he's come home to find me making a meal of that combo on more than one occasion. We haven't seen a whole lot of each other in the five months I've been living in his home, but when we do, he does his best to engage with me. He's not home often—being chief physician at Lake Chapel General takes up most of his time—but I appreciate the effort he's put into getting to know me.

"Anything else? What do you want to drink?"

"I'll take a water. Want me to get it? I don't want you to miss kickoff."

With a wave of his hand, he insists he's got it. Then he disappears beneath the stands.

South Chapel has had a great season, and the majority of the guys on the offensive line are only juniors. They could go even farther next year.

As I wait for the game to start, I fight the pull I feel toward the end zone.

I spotted number 2 on that end earlier. I know without looking he's still down there.

To distract myself from thoughts of him, I pull out my phone and text Joey. She's getting ready for the big fundraising gala where Kendrick will receive the Lake Chapel University player of the year award. She's been sending me pics and updates all afternoon.

I send Levi a quick text, too, checking in. He'll be in the hospital for another few days, but he claims he's doing well. After a few messages back and forth, I promise to visit him tomorrow.

Occasionally, I let my eyes drift to the field. It's impossible not to, no matter how hard I try.

At least there's safety in the bleachers. I'm camouflaged by a sea of aquamarine and white. I can sit back and enjoy the anticipation of the game. I can also discreetly watch Greedy in his element, with no chance he'll catch me staring.

I love football. I grew up on the sport. I started cheering in second grade and continued all through high school.

Our school, like a lot of the districts in the area, doesn't offer competitive cheer. Even so, it's a rigorous, demanding sport. Cheer taught me tenacity and focus. It also helped me develop an exterior armor I can call upon quickly.

I can tune out anyone, smile through anything. I have the ability to slip into a role and drown out all the background noise when I need to.

That particular skill set has come in handy while co-existing in close proximity to Greedy for the last several months.

Dr. F makes it back just in time for the coin toss. South Chapel U wins, then defers.

They're playing an undefeated team from Tennessee. It's highly unlikely the South Chapel Sharks will come out on top. Still, we watch intently every time Greedy and the offense take the field. But we both sort of zone out when it's the defense's turn.

After a particularly long drive from the other team—it's almost halftime, and the South Chapel defense has been on the field for nearly seven football minutes—Dr. F stashes his phone away and turns to me.

"I appreciate you being here, Hunter. I know it means a lot to Garrett, too."

I roll my lips and bite my tongue. Only when I know I can affect a cheerful tone do I speak. "Happy to support him today." Sitting up straighter, I keep my gaze fixed on the South Chapel bench.

As if he can sense me staring, Greedy turns around. We're close enough to the field that I catch the motion, but we're far enough away that I can't make out his expression.

It doesn't matter. I can feel him from here. He doesn't even have to look at me for my body to light up in response to his. It's like muscle memory, but instead of a skill or exercise, my body is attuned to react to him.

Flovely.

Fucking. Lovely.

"Have you made it to many games this season?" Dr. F asks.

I blow out an exasperated breath. He's just making small talk, but each question feels like an interrogation. For months, every question he asks me feels like a little pinprick poking and prodding around the truth of my connection to my stepbrother.

If he only knew...

Dr. F and my mom believe Greedy and I met at their engagement dinner three summers ago, and that's the way I want to keep it.

"This is my third game this season," I tell him. "My best friend's, uh—" I catch myself and decide to rephrase. I'm not interested in getting into polyamory with Dr. F. "I attended a lot of Lake Chapel games this fall with my best friend Joey, so I've only seen SCU play a few times."

Dr. F glances at the scoreboard, then looks back at me. "Joey's well, I take it?"

I smile and nod, like I've trained myself to do.

Dr. F continues. "I was surprised you ended up at LCU, kiddo. I know that was your original plan, but I always assumed—"

"They have a great prelaw program," I say, cutting him off. "And their admissions director was gracious enough to work with me." That, or they know who my stepfather is, and they're hoping he'll eventually open his wallet for LCU the way he has for SCU over the years.

I honestly didn't mean to defer for three years. It just sort of... happened.

I was so damn nervous to contact the admissions office at Lake Chapel University this year. But apparently they're seeing more and more transfer and nontraditional students, so it wasn't a big deal after all.

Dr. F grants me the grace of a subject change.

Although now we're on to an even touchier subject.

He shakes a few sunflower seeds into his palm, inspects them, then pops them into his mouth. "Have you spoken to your mother lately?"

My stomach knots instantly.

Spoken to?

No.

But we exchange the occasional texts, and I keep up with her on Instagram.

I haven't actually seen my mother in the flesh since I left Lake Chapel three summers ago.

Despite also being in Europe for most of the time I was abroad, she never made the effort to meet up. If anything, she avoided me. When I did talk to her and suggest seeing one another, her plans would conveniently allow her to just miss me. It took me an embarrassingly long time to realize that it was likely intentional.

"I haven't talked to her for a few months." Though she has been in contact more frequently. There have been texts. Voicemails. Now that she knows I'm here, she sounds eager to come back to North Carolina. I'll believe it when I see it.

"She came home for the holidays last year," Dr. F offers. "I'm hoping she'll be back this year, too."

Lips pressed together in a firm line, I side-eye him.

I can't imagine this is the happily ever after he hoped for when he married Magnolia St. Clair. I swear she's traveled more than she's been home since she married Dr. F.

More than that, I don't want her here. I loathe the idea of sharing space with her.

My mother is a narcissist. For most of my life, I didn't have the vocabulary or the understanding to comprehend that. But after years of counseling and some hefty healing on my part, I now see her for what she is.

She's poison.

She should have never been a mother.

My life is better without her. I have more peace without her. I'm a better person when she's not around.

"I'm hoping we can all spend Christmas in the mountains," Dr. F continues. "Did you like the cabin? That's where you went when that storm rolled through last month, right?"

"Yes, that's where we evacuated to for Tropical Storm Theo."

I don't mention that I had been to the cabin many times before that trip.

"Has my mom ever even been there?"

He lets out a slow breath. "Not yet."

The Fergusons' cabin is like a mini resort. Built into the side of Beech Mountain, with every luxury amenity available, it's a haven for relaxation. A shudder runs through me at the thought of my mom tainting the place.

"Just give her a chance, kiddo."

I stiffen at the request, but I keep my mouth shut.

"When she gets home, I'd like for us to have a fresh start. All of us."

He thinks he's helping. I know he thinks he's helping…

"And don't think I'm not going to give Garrett the same lecture."

That pulls a quiet scoff from me. Greedy hates my mother. Absolutely despises her.

But again, his dad knows nothing about why his son carries an epic grudge against my mom.

Rather than make promises I don't intend to keep, I smile.

I smile, and I pretend like it's fine.

Everything is fine.
Everything is fine.
Everything is fine.
My phone chimes with a notification. Regardless of how prepared I am for the alert, pain lances through me as I dismiss the reminder.

For now, everything is fine.

Later, none of it will matter anyway.

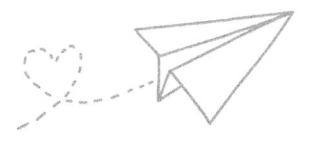

Chapter 8

Hunter

NOW

The knob turns easily.

I tiptoe into the room, careful to shut the door without a sound, and pad toward the bed.

At the foot of the mattress, I hesitate.

There's nothing pushing me forward. There's nothing holding me back. I'm not here. And yet I can't bring myself to go anywhere else.

Come tomorrow, it won't be this intense.

Come Monday, it'll be nothing but an afterthought.

But I won't make it through tonight without a tether.

And the one I've counted on during the darkest nights is on the other side of the world right now.

"Greedy?" I whisper.

I hate disturbing him, and I don't want to give him the wrong idea. I shouldn't be doing this. There are a million reasons to stay away. The biggest is because, with each moment we share space, I'm hurting him more.

I hate hurting him, but I have to hate him.

It's killing me. It's also keeping me alive.

His breath hitches, and then there's a weighted silence where he must hold his breath. I can just make out the whites of his eyes, staring intently, searching for everything I try to hide. He watches me in the dark, like he hopes he can get a read on me.

Then he exhales, clears his throat, and pulls back the blankets.

"Get in."

I release an audible exhale of my own, relief flooding my system as tears stream down my face.

An ache grows in my chest with each step closer.

I hiccup. "This doesn't mean—"

He cuts me off with a sigh. "I know, Tem. Just like last time, right?"

I answer by climbing in beside him.

He reaches for me, his warm hands gripping my hips, and guides me over his body.

I go willingly, crawling over him to the empty spot beside him. Except I don't make it to the other side.

My body gives out, my energy sapped, my longing too much to resist when he's physically this close. All that remains is a hollowness in desperate need of an anchor to the here and now.

I drape my limbs over his torso, bury my face in his chest, and silently sob.

Beneath me, he tenses, his hold on me rigid.

This isn't fair to him or to his heart. It's not fair to me. I should have never—

"Shh," he soothes, relaxing his muscles and holding me tenderly, one arm banded around my middle and the other stroking my hair. "I've got you. You're safe. You can cry. I've got you."

His words, his tranquil tone, flip a switch in my brain. For the first time in hours, I stop thinking. Stop obsessing. Lay down every shield, and let my body relax as the intrusive thoughts storm the gates of my mind.

They're always there. Month after month, I fail to keep them at bay.

But when I'm in Greedy's arms, I know they won't win.

He won't let them take me.

I cry until my sobs turn to sniffles, my tears pooling on his bare chest. As my breathing levels out, I peel myself off him and settle onto the mattress.

He doesn't speak and he doesn't move as I get comfortable.

But he's there. Right there. His warmth, his concern, his *love*.

Day after day, I commit so much energy to shutting him out. I ignore just how deeply he loves me. But the intensity of his devotion is overwhelming with my guard down like this.

It's all-consuming, but I can only accept it when I'm like this: hollow and hopeless, with no consideration for tomorrow or next week, let alone my next breath.

Once I've found a comfortable position, I will my body to relax again. When I stop moving, he inches closer, one hand smoothing up my thigh and over my hip. He cradles the small of my back, lining up our pelvises until we're pressed together in the most intimate way.

Nothing but his boxer briefs and my little sleep shorts separate us.

It's a closeness I crave in the hazy moments between sleep and consciousness. As if my body and my heart are conspiring to betray me, fully committed to taking what they want with no concern for the consequences.

Consequences.

There are always consequences.

With a sigh, I melt into his arms.

His voice is tentative when he asks, "Will you stay and let me hold you tonight?"

It's unlikely I'll sleep. I never do on nights like this.

Silently, I nod, angling forward until my forehead brushes his damp chest.

With careful movements, he wraps his arms around me and hitches one leg over mine. One hand finds its way to the back of my head, his fingers weaving into my hair and resting against my scalp.

He's everywhere. He's everything.

"Just promise you'll let me go in the morning."

He doesn't answer.

His breathing matches my own, our bodies syncing up and reacquainting themselves. The way we fit together is ingrained, permanent.

He's a part of me. He's the best of me.

Every aloof response and surly glare is designed to push him away. Does he know it hurts me every time I do it?

After what feels like an eternity, Greedy's breathing slows, and when I'm sure he's drifted off, I kiss his sternum. Then I place my palms on his chest and cuddle closer, giving myself this moment and this night to lay down my guard and remember.

Chapter 9

Greedy

NOW

It's been two days.

Two full days. Two lonely nights.

She's in there. I can sense her presence. I've also passed outside the double doors that lead from her bedroom to our shared second-story porch and glanced inside several times to confirm it.

My initial worry has morphed into annoyance.

She's done this four times since showing up in South Chapel.

Day in and day out, she pushes me away. Evasion is her default. Until one night, she comes crawling into my bed. She's spacey each time, not fully present. Or maybe she's just tired of fighting it. I know I am.

She slips under the covers and clings to me throughout the night. Drapes her lithe frame and perfect fucking curves around me. Holds on so tightly I swear she remembers every inch of me, too.

Then, when she wakes in the morning, I pretend to be asleep. It's easier than being met with the regret in her expression and the blatant rejection.

She slips out without a word.

For the next few days, she goes radio silent and makes herself scarce.

When she finally does emerge, there's no mention of that night. No explanation for her appearance beside my bed. No discussion about why she's willing to give in and let me hold her about once a month.

All I want to do is fucking hold her.

My MO is to give her space. I don't push. I've been so fucking patient, waiting for her to come back to me. We both know damn well I'll take her any way I can have her.

Levi's reappearance in South Chapel is a welcome distraction from my efforts to figure out Hunter. *Who is she now, and why won't she allow herself to be honest about her feelings most of the time?*

Levi's scheduled to be discharged in a few hours, and he's asking after her. She's either coming with me, or she's letting him down.

I knock on her bedroom door. "Tem," I call out, loud and strong.

She shuffles slowly to the door. It's the only warning I get before it swings open and my stepsister greets me with raised brows.

Fuck. She's so pretty.

With a deep inhale, I fight the urge to grab her and kiss her senseless.

Lips pursed, she crosses her arms over her chest and takes me in. Green eyes the color of glass marbles track my movements as I scratch at the back of my neck.

Her expression is cold, removed, distant. Like she can barely stand to be near me.

"What's up?"

Even as it causes another fissure in my heart, I scoff at the aloofness.

She acts as if we're merely acquaintances. As if I wasn't cradling her body against my chest while she sobbed less than forty-eight hours ago.

While the ache in my chest grows, like it has every damn day for years, she gives me nothing. Her expression is emotionless as she peers up at me.

"Levi is being discharged today. He's asking if we'll come visit him one last time."

Her face screws up in question, but her façade remains intact.

"You know how he gets about his mom. He probably won't want us visiting much once he's at her house."

For the first time since she opened the door, Hunter shows a shred of genuine emotion. Her brows knit together, and her pink lips turn down in a scowl.

"I feel so bad for him," she murmurs, shaking her head.

I do, too. Even if Levi's a stubborn fucker. He's self-righteous and so unnecessarily prideful that he gets in his own way. He'd rather suffer under his mom's roof than accept help from his friends.

Sighing, I rest one arm against the doorjamb and lean in. "I offered to let him stay here. I figured, between the two of us—"

"You and I could totally handle it," she declares. Her eyes are suddenly bright, and there's a fresh excitement in her voice.

"I offered," I say with a huff. "But he refused. We can't force him to accept help from us."

Hunter's face falls. Then she glares—at me, as if I'm the bad guy here. Typical.

I knock twice on her doorframe and turn to leave before I do something stupid.

Like kiss her senseless. Or carry her back to my room and keep her there indefinitely.

"I'm leaving in ten minutes," I say without turning around.

"I'm coming with you!" she calls after me.

Satisfied, I smirk. I'm in for an afternoon of that signature Hunter aloofness blended with the silent treatment, that's for sure. But when it comes to my girl, I'll take her any way I can get her.

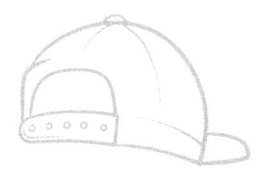

Chapter 10

Levi

NOW

"Sit up. No, not like—scoot *forward*."

My mom's tone gets shriller with each syllable, her frustration palpable.

She always did have a knack for making a scene.

It's a struggle, and fuck, does it hurt, but I shift to a spot that's seemingly acceptable for her. I bite my tongue to keep from mentioning that I'd prefer not to need my mother's help to put my goddamn pants on either.

"There," she declares proudly as she straightens. She swipes at nonexistent sweat on her brow and blows out a satisfied exhale.

I'm dressed, and I'm showered, thanks to the help of the male nurse tech who worked last night. By all definitions, I'm ready.

It's discharge day.

I'm not sure I've ever dreaded anything more.

With her hands on her hips, my mom purses her lips and assesses me. Brows knit, she stares with an intensity that makes my cheeks heat.

She's looking at me a little too closely. A little too *hopefully*.

It'd be easier if she'd look at me the way she did the summer before I moved to California. I'd take the reserved defeat over this any day. Hell, I'd even take outright disappointment.

Because now?

Her eyes gleam with potential.

She always did love a project.

That's how she views this ordeal. My unceremonious return to North Carolina. The dashing of my dreams. She sees it as a second chance. An answered prayer. An opportunity to course correct and put me on the straight and narrow—*literally*—while I'm healing and dependent on her.

She's gone as far as forcing me to commit to attending church with her each week and allowing her to help me get "reacquainted with South Chapel society." It's all part of the deal we made when I explained the details of my surgery and rehab.

I need her help. I need to be on her insurance, and I need a place to stay where I don't have to pay rent for the foreseeable future. But I can't help the dread that's been churning in my stomach all morning.

The door cracks open, and a nurse clears her throat. "I've got your discharge instructions," she announces as she enters the room.

"Oh, I'll take those," Mom insists, holding out a hand.

Nurse Heather quickly sidesteps and falls back into the pocket, using her computer station to put space between herself and my mom's prying hands.

"These are for the patient," she asserts.

Hands on her hips, my mom huffs. "Well, I'm his mother."

Unbothered by my mother's frustration, Heather clicks away at my chart without looking up. "That you are."

I try to hide the chuckle that works its way out of me behind a cough but fail.

Mom's glare hits me hard. My body is so conditioned to cede to her, it takes genuine effort to keep my head up.

I met nurse Heather my second night here and instantly knew I liked her. She didn't lecture me about staying on top of the pain or not being a hero by refusing meds. From the beginning, she's respected my choice to refuse narcotics. She's always professional, and she hasn't pushed to uncover the reasons behind my denial of the medication.

"Since I'll be my son's sole caregiver for the foreseeable future, I'll need to know the instructions," my mother presses. "Wouldn't it be easier to go over them now so we can ask questions? Tell her, Levi."

Shoulders sagging, I turn to my nurse. She's young, probably just a year or two older than me. She's been nothing but accommodating and kind during my stay.

When Heather meets my gaze, a flash of pity mars her pretty features. It doesn't take a genius to deduce what kind of person Patricia Moore is at her core.

There's no use fighting the inevitable, so I nod my consent.

Nurse Heather keeps her attention locked on the screen as she rattles off instructions.

My mom scrambles to the other side of the room, where she left her purse on a chair. Then she pulls out a lined yellow steno pad and clicks her pen.

"No weight-bearing activities for at least two weeks. Resting and attending daily PT sessions are the biggest priorities. Stay on top of the pain"—she pauses then, likely adjusting the next orders for my benefit, and side-eyes me—"by alternating acetaminophen and ibuprofen. That should do the job. There's a script being sent to the pharmacy on file, just in case—"

"No," I reject, cutting her off.

They can call it in, but I'm not filling it. I won't take it. The last thing I want is my mom hounding me about it for the next—

Fucking hell.

I have no idea how long it'll take to heal and rehab. No one does.

Because I didn't seek medical care immediately after the incident, the injury took on a life of its own. Literally. Calcified bone started to grow inside my hamstring. We won't know about the final nerve damage for weeks or maybe even months.

I'll be dependent on my mom—on the person who stood by, muttering scripture under her breath, as my old man beat on me—until I regain feeling in my thigh and rebuild my strength.

Any amount of time would be too long. But having no idea what the timeline looks like is excruciating.

I don't feel strong enough to endure what's required right now.

Gritting my teeth, I take in a cleansing breath. It does little to ease the pit of despair taking up residence in my chest.

"Take it easy for the next few weeks," Heather continues. "Your body is still recovering from surgery, and your system needs this reset. Lay low as much as possible. Your daily trips to PT will be about all the exertion your body can handle for a few weeks."

"What about Sundays?" Mom interjects. "He won't have therapy on Sundays, will he?"

Heather looks at me, her eyes full of kindness and empathy, and I nod my assent again.

"The care coordinator will call within twenty-four hours of discharge to set up the appointments. But no, PT doesn't typically see patients on the weekends."

"Thank heavens," Mom mutters. She fusses with the edge of the hospital blanket, then rests her hand on my leg.

"Shit," I curse, jolting away from her touch as pain shoots through me.

"Levi, *language*," she hisses.

Never mind that her hand is still settled on the leg with the five-inch incision.

"Mom," I grit out, peeling her hand off my thigh.

"Whoops," she mutters, her tone more absentminded than apologetic, and turns to Heather. "If that's all…"

The nurse nods.

"I can breathe easier now, knowing our church routine won't be affected by all these therapy appointments." She stashes her little notebook back in her bag.

"Levi." Heather keeps her eyes on my mother, her expression wary, as she steps around the computer and comes to stand by my bedside. "I would strongly recommend not overdoing it once you get home. Even a few hours out of the house will be exhausting, and it puts you at risk for reinjury or delayed healing, since, like I mentioned, you should avoid all weight-bearing activities."

The *reminder* at the end is directed at my mother.

"Nonsense," my mom declares with a wave of her hand, clearly unfazed by the warning. "The Lord heals, and the Lord provides. There's a wheelchair available at the church for this very need: to usher in the sick and broken and to bring them home to the Kingdom of God."

A foggy memory of the vestibule leading into my mom's church swirls in the back of my mind. Now that she mentions it, I remember the wheelchair hidden in a corner of the lobby. A rust bucket that might as well be a relic. It was ancient when I was a kid. I can't imagine what shape it's in now.

Just like I can't imagine having her wheel me into a place that outright condemns the very nature of who I am.

"Mom, I don't think it's a good idea—"

"Hush, sweetie. You need rest. You heard the nice nurse," she patronizes.

I snap my mouth shut. There's no point wasting my energy arguing a lost cause.

I'm better served saving my strength so I can heal as quickly as possible and get the hell out of here.

I'm at my mother's mercy from now until who fucking knows when.

I can already smell the stale air and the unmistakable scent of old hymnals that rest in the holders on the back of each pew. I can practically feel the stiff chemically treated red fabric cushioning of each bench under the pads of my fingertips.

A wave of nausea washes over me as the memories infiltrate my senses.

Mom fussing over my outfit, all while frowning and muttering under her breath.

Pinching my tricep to keep me alert and sitting at attention throughout the service.

Squeezing my kneecap firmly when the pastor spoke about homosexuality—and the sanctity of *biblical marriage*—of poison and sin, of the path to heaven.

One memory after another thrashes against the walls of my mind.

Then suddenly, the memories aren't the only things rioting inside me.

"I'm going to be sick." Heaving, I bolt upright, which causes a wave of pain to roll through me, and grab for the mauve container I've been stashing my phone in all week.

Fucking hell.

My eyes burn, and so does my throat, as I choke back the bile rising within me. My incision throbs an erratic rhythm as my pulse quickens. My stomach twists and contracts, and I cough and gag, but mercifully, nothing comes up.

When I'm sure I'm not going to be sick, I right myself and shove the pink puke bin with enough force that it rebounds off the tray table and clatters to the floor.

A surprised squeak snags my attention. When I look up, Hunter and Greedy are standing in the doorway.

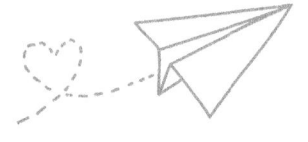

Chapter 11

Hunter

NOW

"Hey, man. How's it going?" Greedy strolls into the room casually, like we didn't just overhear Levi's mom going off on a religious tangent, spewing warped sentiments about how the Lord heals or provides or some other nonsense she molds to fit her perceptions.

I'm a southern girl through and through. North Carolina born and bred. I know better than to push back on a person's religious beliefs and love of Jesus. Not only would it be futile, but it'd be downright rude.

That doesn't stop my hackles from raising as I side-eye Mrs. Moore and slink around Greedy.

I'm by Levi's side a second later.

He's pale and covered in a sheen of sweat.

"Hey," I say, my voice low.

His eyes meet mine, and yet he's a thousand miles away.

I know that look. I know the feeling that inspires that look, or rather the lack of feeling. That thousand-mile stare is typically accompanied by a hopeless hollowness I know all too well.

I ache to comfort him. To console him. To assure him that I really see him.

My heart splinters a little at the anguish rolling off him as his guard goes up and a steely mask shifts into place.

"Duke," I murmur, instinctively reaching for his hand.

"Who are you?" his mother demands as I squeeze his fingers in a silent show of support.

I can feel her focus on our joined hands just as potently as I can feel Greedy's glare from behind me.

For a breath, we're all silent. Levi blinks, a slow, drawn-out motion. His lashes flutter, and then his eyes close completely. Though he's quiet and calm, a single tear forms at the corner of one eye and streaks down his cheek.

He releases my hand, like he's in a rush to bat the tear away.

I refuse to let him go.

On the other side of the room, Mrs. Moore tsks. "It's nice to see you, Garrett, but now's not a great time. What do you say you come over to the house on Sunday morning? You could help me get Levi loaded in the car for church. You could even attend with us."

Greedy replies to Mrs. Moore, his voice a low rumble, but I'm not focused on them. Not anymore. All my attention is fixed on Levi as he tries to pull his hand away again.

I grip his fingers tighter.

He's hurting. And not just physically.

It kills me to see him cry.

I'll be damned if the woman inspiring the anguish etched into every line on his face is the person he has to solely rely on.

Anger bubbles up inside me at the thought. We can't let him go home to a house he hates, with a woman who doesn't see him or accept him or give a shit about his well-being.

An idea sparks to life inside me, igniting a hopeful flame. Levi is minutes from being released, so I don't have time to really think it through. Even so, I'm going for it.

Based on the look Greedy and I shared in the hallway, we're on the same page.

Well, maybe not the same page, exactly.

But he won't mind.

Too much.

Bending low, I bring my lips to Levi's ear, positioning myself to hide the wet trail on his cheek from the others in the room.

"Did you actually puke before we walked in?"

He said he thought he was going to be sick. We heard that much. He may have even gagged. The puke bin on the floor appears to be unused, but I have to be sure.

He shakes his head once, the movement causing his jaw to brush my lips.

"Then follow my lead."

I kiss his cheek, erasing the evidence of his despair.

Then I wind my arms around his neck, dip my head lower, and press my lips into his.

Chapter 12

Levi

NOW

Soft, plush lips glide against mine as a fruity sweetness overwhelms my senses.

I freeze, too stunned to move.

Hunter scrapes her fingers against the back of my skull and murmurs "kiss me back" against my mouth.

I open for her. Without thought. Without a clue about what the hell she's playing at.

When the tip of her tongue brushes mine, an unexpected jolt of arousal ignites in my veins and warms me from the inside out.

"Levi Daniel Moore!"

The sound of my full name in my mother's disapproving tone blasts over me like a bucket of ice water.

Hunter pulls away and gives me an encouraging smile. "We've got this," she whispers, standing straight and smoothing her hands over her skirt.

She turns to face my mother, effectively blocking me from her view in the process.

"Oh! Hello," Hunter chirps. As if she just noticed my mom's presence. "You must be Mrs. Moore. I'm Hunter St. Clair."

I can't help but check out her backside: her perfect posture, and the glossy blond hair cascading in loose waves down her back. She's wearing a denim miniskirt short enough to show off the tan skin of her upper thighs.

Across the room, a throat clears. *Greedy.*

He's propped against the far wall, arms crossed and a scowl plastered on his face. When our eyes connect, he raises one brow in question.

With a shrug, I shake my head.

Hell if I know what Hunter's playing at either.

"Hunter, you said?" My mom steps closer and peers past Hunter to focus on me. "As in—"

"Greedy's stepsister," Hunter supplies, taking another step forward and placing herself directly in my mother's path.

Hunter never met my parents. I wouldn't allow it. I kept her as far away from my house as I could. But if Greedy mentioned her to my mom before we all went off to college—

"And Levi's girlfriend," she adds, extending one hand. "It's *so* nice to finally meet you."

The room is silent for a beat. Another.

And then chaos erupts.

"Tem—" Greedy growls, taking a step toward her, hands balled at his sides.

She cuts him off with a sharp "don't."

"Levi? What is the meaning of this?" my mom shrieks, her tone frantic as she looks from Hunter to me and back again.

What is the meaning of this?

Hunter said to play along.

"Well, uh." I scratch at my jaw and dip my chin. "I've been meaning to talk to you—"

Nurse Heather clears her throat, saving me from lying through my teeth.

"I'm done here," she states. "As soon as I log out of your chart, Levi, you're officially discharged. Just to confirm, you'll be going home with…"

"Us," Hunter declares. She tilts her head slightly as she glances at Greedy, but I can't read her expression since she still has her back to me.

He nods, but I don't miss the wary resignation in his eyes.

"Us," she repeats. "Levi is coming home with us."

Chapter 13

Greedy

NOW

"Fuck," Levi hisses through his teeth as my Denali hits another bump in the road.

"Careful," Hunter scolds.

Jaw locked tight, I glance at her in the rearview mirror. Her brow is furrowed, and her attention is focused solely on the man beside her in the back seat.

Her "*boyfriend,*" apparently.

I work my molars back and forth and clutch the steering wheel tighter. I have half a mind to tell them both off. This is absurd. We should have at the very least talked about this ahead of time, come up with some sort of plan.

I keep my mouth shut, though, because realistically, this is the best way forward. No amount of preamble or discussion would've changed the outcome.

Hunter and I both heard enough of what Mrs. Moore was going on about inside that hospital room. She was chomping at the bit to get Levi back to her house—back under her control.

Since his daddy's dead, he's no longer at risk of physical harm inside the Moore household, but the amount of emotional trauma and mind-fuckery his mother is capable of is unmatched.

She was so eager to get him out of the hospital and back into her church. She talked about Levi as if he were a project, not a son in need of love and care.

I won't condemn him to being dependent on her. He's better off with us. I know that. I get it. But Hunter could have clued me in to her brilliant idea.

At the very least, we could have come up with a plan that didn't involve her kissing him.

Fuck.

I press down on the gas with more force at the reminder, but then I have to brake harder than usual to get over in time for the South Chapel exit.

"Greedy," Hunter scolds again as the truck slows a little too abruptly.

"Dammit, Tem," I snap back. "It's not like I was expecting to transport a person who was just released from the hospital. We should have brought pillows. A few blankets. If you had given me a heads-up about what you were planning to do—"

"I didn't plan it," she asserts.

I look at her through the mirror again. Hunter has always worn her heart on her sleeve. I don't doubt she's telling the truth. The sincerity in her eyes confirms that when she meets my gaze.

Levi grunts as he sits up straighter. "You didn't plan that?" he asks Hunter. Then, to me, he adds, "It's all good, man. I know you're doing the best you can."

With a deep breath in, I let his genuine appreciation ease the anger bubbling up inside me and make a point to take the next turn slower than I normally would.

Hunter lets out a frustrated sigh. "Before we came into your room, we heard your mom going on about getting you home. About getting you to church. She was going to just wheel you into Sunday service in a few days when you can't even put weight on your leg?" A little shudder racks through her. "We couldn't just leave you with her, Duke."

I hum my agreement.

I may not like her methods, but I sure do like hearing the sound of "we" on Hunter's lips.

Like we're in this together. Like we're a team.

"Besides, this solves more than one problem." Hunter flips her hair over her shoulder. "You have a place to stay. Greedy and I can get you to and from rehab and doctor's appointments." She peers at me through the rearview mirror, her expression questioning.

I nod but tip my chin in warning. "I still have practice—"

"I know," she insists. "I'll do most of the chauffeuring. He's my fake boyfriend, after all." She grins at Levi playfully. "Plus, now your mom can't set you up. She can't force you to go on a date with someone when you're already dating me."

I turn into the driveway a little faster than necessary, bumping over the lip at the end and eliciting an *oomph* from my back seat passengers.

This whole fake dating idea is already grating on my nerves.

I didn't fight it in the hospital, because it made sense, and I want Levi with us. It really is the best option for his recovery.

I didn't expect either of them to keep up appearances after we left the hospital, though.

"We're home." Thank fuck. I park the car, hop out of the driver's seat, and round the hood so I can help Levi out of the vehicle. "Let's get you inside and situated."

My mom was a musician. Classically trained on cello, piano, and vocals. She spent two years performing with the national tour of *RENT* before she settled down with my dad. An entire room in our house is dedicated to her music, even now.

It's located across from my bedroom. As a boy, I'd wake to sounds of her softly playing piano on nights when she couldn't sleep, and I'd fall asleep to lullabies about gentrification and Maya Angelou.

She was inimitable, my mom. Loud and loving, sincere and silly. A myriad of contradictions. I've met very few people as spirited or joyful as Nora Ferguson.

The massive elevator that was installed to bring her instruments up and down hasn't been used in years, but my dad's always been good about keeping it serviced. It'll come in handy today.

Hunter takes the lead into the house. I follow, supporting Levi as best as I can as he slowly makes his way inside on crutches. When we pass my dad's study, I realize I haven't even mentioned this to him yet.

I don't expect it to be an issue, seeing as how he's the one who welcomed Hunter back without question when she reappeared out of thin air.

But I still need to give him a courtesy heads-up.

"In the middle room?" Hunter asks without turning.

By *"middle room,"* she means the bedroom that separates her room from mine.

It makes sense to put him in the guest room between us. The bed's already made, and the bathroom should be well-stocked. Even so, I can't help but feel like this is one more thing standing in the way of me making any true progress where Hunter is concerned.

How will Levi's presence affect her? Will I still find her at the foot of my bed once a month? Or will she retreat into her shell, or worse, use Levi as a shield?

They're already standing outside the door, waiting for my confirmation.

"Yeah, that'll work," I finally reply, skirting around them to push the door open.

I help Levi ease onto the bed, then regard him. "This is okay?" I ask, flitting my eyes around the room as he blows out a long breath.

Hunter has already disappeared into the bathroom. Drawers and cabinets open and close, one after another, echoing through the quiet space, as Levi and I regard each other.

Levi swallows thickly, his Adam's apple bobbing. "Yeah, G. This is more than okay. You sure you don't mind me being here?"

The sincerity in his tone surprises me. I pestered him all week to come stay with me, but he rejected the offer over and over again. That is, until Hunter took the reins and didn't give any of us a choice.

"No wrong moves," I remind him, keeping my expression neutral. "I'm glad you're here."

He averts his eyes, looking toward the bathroom to where Hunter disappeared. I take that as my cue.

"I've got to be on campus soon. I'll be home after dinner," I tell him, being sure to speak loud enough that Hunter hears me, too.

Without a backward glance, I show myself out, pulling the door closed behind me.

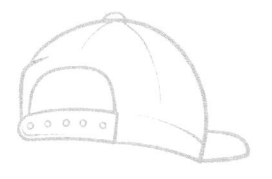

Chapter 14

Levi

NOW

Greedy leaves the room, and I'm left alone for the first time today.

My nerves are shot. My leg is throbbing. My arms hurt from my wrists to my shoulders—muscle atrophy, I'm sure, plus some soreness from the use of the crutches.

It all hurts.

But being here? At Greedy's house? Among friends, without having to depend on my mother? It's a balm I didn't know I needed.

This is how I'll heal.

This is how I'll survive what I thought would be the most stressful, insufferable months of my life.

Here, I don't have to hide.

Here, I can be myself. I don't have to put concerted effort and energy into playing a part.

I'm so fucking grateful to be here, and it's all thanks to the pretty girl flitting around the bathroom.

"He's gone," I call out to Hunter with a low chuckle.

She appears in the doorway, scans the room, and then visibly relaxes her shoulders.

"So you and Greedy are roomies, huh?"

Her attention snaps to me. The grimace on her face makes it clear I've hit a nerve.

Instead of clapping back with that bratty sass I secretly love, Hunter deflates, and her face falls. Shoulders slumped, she makes her way over to the bed and plops down on the mattress beside me.

"I didn't expect it to be like this," she confesses quietly, turning to meet my gaze. "This is just a stopover for me."

I nod but remain silent. There has to be more. It's up to her if she wants to share it.

She picks at the pink polish on her thumbnail for a few breaths before she continues.

"Last summer, my dad gave me an ultimatum. He said if I didn't start using my college fund by this year, I'd lose it. I didn't even know that was a thing, but I guess it has something to do with taxes."

She shrugs, defeated.

"His new wife was ready to try and roll it over into a college savings plan for their new rugrats."

"Your dad got remarried?" I ask, shifting to ease the ache in my leg.

Hunter nods. "To a woman he met in France. They have two little kids. A boy and a girl."

"And you didn't want to stay abroad for school?"

Green eyes the color of sea glass lock with mine, shining with emotion.

"I never expected to be gone that long, Duke."

Nodding, I bite back all the questions populating in my mind. There are so many details I'm desperate to know.

When she left North Carolina, I didn't think that we were saying goodbye forever. I never expected to not hear from her again. I thought she needed time; space.

It hurt when she never reached out. When she never tried to reconnect once she was settled.

It took a while, but eventually, I came to accept that I was collateral damage.

I got left behind, but I wasn't the most significant person left here wondering about her. I missed her like crazy, but there was another person out there, missing her even more. The guilt and shame I felt for picking sides and not being there for Greedy forced me to cut ties with him, too.

Nothing went as planned after that summer. And yet, here we are all, under the same roof once again.

"After that conversation with my dad, I called Dr. Ferguson to ask for his advice. He was still paying my credit card bill each month. I honestly didn't know who else to ask."

"Where's your mom?"

Hunter snorts and shakes her head. "Not sure. I could check Instagram and figure it out, though."

My heart sinks at the defeat in her tone and her expression. "Your mom doesn't live here?"

"I haven't seen my mom since the engagement dinner at the country club."

My brain is working overtime to piece together the information. "You didn't go to the wedding?"

Hunter averts her gaze and picks at the comforter beneath us.

Frowning, I regard her for a heartbeat. "Weren't they going to Europe for a honeymoon?"

This time, she shrugs. "That was the plan. I tried to meet up with her a few times when I was in London. Then once when I was in Italy. After that, I gave up."

"Daisy..." I take her hand and give it a squeeze, but I drop it quickly when I notice she isn't even looking at me.

Instead, she talks to the comforter, tracing a little bit of stitching with her finger.

"Dr. Ferguson encouraged me to come home. He made a lot of valid points about getting my undergrad studies out of the way. I don't want to be the oldest student in my law program, ya know? He offered to pay my tuition, which I did not want him to do, but he said it was ultimately my choice. I think he hoped it would entice my mom to come home, too."

"Did it work?" I ask.

Hunter snorts. "It hasn't yet." With a sigh, she pulls her feet up under her. "He offered to put in a good word at SCU and suggested I move in here. Then he replaced my car. I know it's selfish..." Her voice cracks on the last word. "It was just nice to have a parent care. I don't plan to stick around here long, but I figured this was my best shot at a fresh start."

She clears her throat and straightens, signaling that her story is complete.

Except it's not. I can't even begin to imagine her and Greedy sharing space, sharing a home, and pretending like they're stepsiblings. Or worse, pretending they're casual acquaintances.

"So you and G live together and act like you weren't madly in love once upon a time?"

Her answering scowl sends a shiver from my skull to my tailbone.

"Don't," she snaps. Then, softer, "Please don't go there. It was a long time ago—"

I scoff. "It was three years ago, Daisy. You can't really expect me to believe—"

"I expect you to believe that I'm doing my best," she says, cutting me off. "That I'm trying to figure this out. That I'm desperate to get a place of my own, to put more distance between Greedy and me. I'm taking twenty-one credit hours, playing catch-up the best I can, and this is all I can manage at the moment."

Eyes closed, she blows out a breath and shakes her head. When she looks at me again, she's more determined than before.

"I'm not trying to hurt him any more than I already have. Most days, we're so busy we don't even see each other. I can go a full week without running into him. Hell, I've spent more time with him visiting you this past week than I have in the months since I came back. This is a stopover for me. I'll be out of his way soon enough."

"Do I even need to ask how Greedy feels about all of this?"

Hunter's mouth tilts up in the saddest smile I've ever seen her muster. "The kindest thing I can do for him is keep my distance and get out of here as soon as possible. Like I said, I'm working on it."

The mood is somber and heavy as I contemplate her words. The dejection in her voice makes my chest ache. I hate that she thinks her presence is the problem.

"I feel like I should have been made aware of this situation before I agreed to take the room between you two," I joke in an attempt to lighten the mood.

She catches on quickly, pursing her lips and narrowing her eyes as she stands and stretches her arms overhead.

Her shirt rises up a few inches, showing off an expanse of smooth skin just below her navel.

She tugs at the hem of her shirt and meets my gaze. With a devilish smirk, she asks, "Want me to call your mom and ask her to come pick you up, then?"

"Ah, come on!" Laughing, I hold out my arms. "I'm just teasing you, Daisy. Come here."

She makes her way back to the bed and bends to meet me.

I wrap her up in a hug and hold on extra tight. "Thank you," I whisper into her hair. "You and I both know the gravity of what you did today. You have to know what you saved me from. I appreciate you so damn much, Hunter."

She melts in my arms and lets me take her weight for a few seconds, then gives me a final squeeze and releases. "Will you be okay up here for a while?"

I nod against her shoulder. "I'm going to take a nap. Greedy mentioned he'd bring me some clothes later. What else could a guy need?"

She backs away, smiling. "I've got to study. Text me if you need anything."

I return the expression. Honestly, I can't imagine her doing or giving me anything more than she already has.

Chapter 15

Greedy

NOW

I made it back from campus just as the sun was starting to set. I was anxious to get home—to check on Levi and to make sure Hunter was okay, too. The need to be with them—to keep an eye on them—had nothing to do with the pang of jealousy that twists in my core every time I recall Hunter bending down and kissing Levi this afternoon. That would be ridiculous.

All three of our rooms open to a shared second-floor balcony, and that's where I find the pair after dinner.

"Nice night." I shut the door leading from my bedroom, then amble toward the sectional couch where they're set up. A set of crutches is propped up near the French doors to Levi's room, explaining how he got out here without my help.

It appears that Hunter hasn't left his side since we got home.

Except now she's getting twitchy. She clearly doesn't want to be out here. Every few seconds, she adjusts her textbook in her lap and squints at the pages because of the soft lighting of the balcony.

She's restless, and she can't focus. She needs a break, and I'd bet she doesn't even know it.

Levi isn't helping.

He's scrolling on his phone, lounging with his leg up. He's too distracted to realize she's also distracted, desperately trying to get reading done or study for an upcoming exam.

"Tem," I call out, plopping onto an overstuffed chair and arranging the pillows.

She snaps up straight and hits me with an agitated look.

For once, I'm not the cause of her frustration. Or at least not the only cause.

"I'm in for the night. If you want to head inside to study, I've got this," I tell her, tipping my chin toward Levi.

He looks up, finally aware of my presence.

"Hey, man," he greets. Then he turns to Hunter. "Daisy, you've got to see this," he insists, holding his phone out to her.

She slams her textbook shut and quickly hops to her feet.

"I've got to study," she tells Levi, wearing an apologetic frown. Then she fixes her attention on me. "Text me if you need help getting him back inside or ready for bed."

"I'm right here," Levi huffs.

Hunter's expression softens. "I know. And I'm glad you are." She bends down and wraps him in a hug, squeezing him tight.

"Okay, okay," he insists with a laugh as Hunter finally releases him. "Why do you always smell so good?"

A smile tugs at the corners of her mouth. "A lady never tells," she teases. "Although now that we're dating, maybe I'll have to share some of my secrets." She bends down once more and smacks a kiss to Levi's cheek, then turns to leave.

"Good night, boys." With that, she saunters to her room, hips swaying, and closes the door behind her, punctuating her exit with a soft *click* of the lock.

"Fucking hell," Levi says on a sigh. He slumps back, resting his head against the back of the couch, his gaze fixed on the ceiling of the balcony. "What a day."

Elbows on my knees, I grunt my agreement. "It's good to have you back, Leev. I missed you, man."

We lost touch, and not from lack of trying on my end. Once he took off for California, Levi sort of slow faded from my life.

It hurt, but mourning our friendship took a back seat to my efforts to piece together the details of Hunter's disappearance and her refusal to return my calls and texts.

"Look, G, I'm sorry we lost touch. And I'm sorry I haven't been home much—"

"Don't," I insist, dropping my head and letting out a breath. "You were my best friend. Still are, if I'm being honest. I know you're here under less-than-ideal circumstances, but I'm grateful we get a fresh start."

Levi presses his lips together like he wants to say more, but eventually, he nods.

"A fresh start," he murmurs, cracking the knuckles of each finger on his left hand, then the two that still crack on his right. It's a habit as familiar to me as any of my own.

His daddy smashed his right hand under the heel of his work boot when we were in tenth grade, and that hand never did heal properly. He played through the last few games of that season with his hand broken in multiple places.

Figures he didn't heed any sort of caution or rest when he got injured in California. Levi's been playing through pain his whole life.

"Are you going to graduate this year?" he asks, bringing my thoughts back to the present.

We have so much catching up to do. Now seems like as good a time as any to start.

"I could," I answer honestly, sitting back in my chair. "But I don't think I will."

He tilts his head and watches me, brows pulled low in consideration.

Levi is a great listener. Talking to him is as easy as breathing, and the connection between us has always been effortless. Even now, after years of silence and physical distance, I feel it as strongly as I did back then. I could tell him anything. I want to tell him everything.

"I have another year of eligibility, and I'd like to keep playing." I say it softly, because it's a truth I'm just starting to come to terms with myself.

I love football. I'm nowhere near ready to be done. And with the team we've been building, and so much of the depth chart consisting of sophomores and juniors, I'm jonesing to see what it'll look like next year. How far we could take it.

"Plus, I'm not ready to move on. Leave here and head to med school."

Understatement of the fucking year.

"Hunter showed up without warning a few months ago." I swallow past the lump in my throat that's been lodged there since the moment she returned. "Moved back in. Started taking classes."

"At South Chapel?"

"LCU," I amend with a scoff.

She could have received a full ride to South Chapel University. My dad sits on the board of the science and medicine college.

But Hunter does what she wants. Always has. Much as I hate to admit it, she probably always will.

"And she's doing okay?"

His question catches me off guard.

I sit up straighter, regarding the man before me.

I lost him the same week I lost Hunter. I always wondered if the two of them stayed in touch.

It wouldn't have surprised me. But his question confirms he doesn't really know the new Hunter either.

The three of us were inseparable that summer after high school.

I didn't know who I was when they both up and disappeared.

I always wondered if the loss was hard for them, too.

Or if I was the only one left feeling like my heart had been torn out, since I was the one who was left behind.

"I don't really know," I finally reply.

Some days—most days—Hunter is bubbly and vivacious, full of attitude and that sass I used to love.

But then there are the dark days. The silent moments. The nights when she slips into my bed unannounced and pleads for me to hold her. Or even moments like the one I walked into today, while she sat out here tied up in knots, so anxious she could barely sit still.

It breaks my fucking heart to see her like that. But I can't say I'm not grateful for the moments when she lets me in.

If that's the only way I can have her, I'll take it.

"She seems good. And she looks *great*," Levi muses, glancing at the double doors that lead to her bedroom.

Hackles raised, I lean forward. "About that." I clear my throat and wait for him to look at me. "I understand why she did what she did today. But you two *pretending* to date? That could cause issues. Be careful, Leev."

He bristles. "Careful how?"

"Don't catch real feelings for Hunter," I warn him. Then, before he can interject, I add, "She's mine."

His deep blue irises widen in surprise, then quickly narrow in what I assume to be challenge.

"Does she know that?" he asks, lifting his chin in defiance.

I don't blame the guy.

If Hunter grabbed my face and kissed me like she did to him earlier, I'd be smitten, too. That may be jumping to conclusions. I have no reason to suspect there's anything brewing between my best friend and my girl. But while we're here, while he's in my house, I'm laying down some ground rules.

"She's mine," I repeat, my voice thick and solemn this time. "And she knows it. She might not be ready to admit it, but she fucking knows it."

His glare holds more of a challenge than I expected.

Softer, I add, "It was only ever her, Leev."

He searches my face, like he doesn't get it. Like he's looking for the deeper meaning. But I'm not being purposely evasive. I have no shame. If he doesn't understand, then I'll come right out and fucking say it.

"She's the only woman I've ever been with. The only woman I ever *intend* to be with," I add, my damn heart clenching like it does every time I think about her. "It was only ever her."

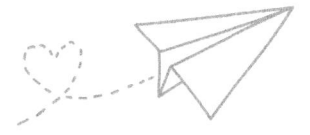

Chapter 16

Hunter

THEN

The first bonfire, the one put on by the school and the city council, wrapped around ten. It was held in the grassy meadow outside the high school stadium, and the flames were managed by the Lake Chapel fire department. The mayor was there. Decker Crusade's dad even made an appearance.

Once it was over and most of the town had gone home, we headed to our second location. Bonfire number two is where the real fun is.

"Do you want a drink?" Greedy asks, not so subtly brushing his arm against mine with each step we take. We drove to the North Marina together, along with Levi. Once we parked, we trekked through the woods along a single-track dirt road for fifteen minutes before reaching the clearing.

Lips pressed together, I consider as we take in the scene. The bonfire is set up in the middle, with a handful of vehicles nearby. Music is bumping, and the crowd is humming with anticipation.

Rumor has it we're playing capture the flag.

I'm highly competitive by nature, so I want to win, and I'm not keen on running through the woods inebriated.

I shake my head. "No thanks."

Greedy catches my hand for a heartbeat when we come to a stop near the fire.

With a flirtatious smile, I add, "I need to keep my wits about me so I can beat you at whatever comes next."

With a laugh, he places one hand on the small of my back. The heat seeping through my shirt only increases the excitement coursing through me. I step in close so that our hips are touching.

The tension between us grows as thick as the humid night air.

"Right. You might not want to drink, but I do," Levi announces, startling me.

I was so wrapped up in Greedy I forgot Levi was even there.

With a dip of his chin, Levi skirts around us. "Be right back."

Greedy stays put by my side, his hand still at my back.

"You're not drinking?" I ask.

He shakes his head, his expression suddenly serious. "I drove you here. I had no plans to drink tonight."

A shiver rolls through me. I love a guy who takes responsibility like that.

"Are you cold?" He shucks off his letter jacket without waiting for a response. Then he holds it out in offering.

I bite my lip playfully and shake my head. "A little, but there's no way you're getting me in a South Chapel jacket."

He hits me with that cocksure smolder, lowering his head until he's so close I can breathe in his distinctive vanilla and leather scent. "I wouldn't be so sure about that, Artemis."

The whole Artemis and Temi bit was silly at first, but now when he uses either version of the nickname he's bestowed on me?

I shiver again. This time, it's not from the cold.

"Fine," he drawls, his expression still full of heat. "I get it. I'm not getting you in it. Not tonight, at least."

Half the people here are from Lake Chapel High. There's no way I can be seen wearing South Chapel *anything*. Just standing hip to hip with the quarterback from South Chapel could ignite a firestorm of rumors.

The irony of the situation is that in a few weeks, it won't matter. Graduation is imminent, and my friend group has been drifting apart all spring. So many of them are going out of state, and those of us staying close to home are desperate to create new identities for ourselves. Maybe that's why I feel so confident standing by Greedy's side. That, or I just really, really like being close to him.

"Okay, listen up!" Decker Crusade is standing on a plastic folding table that wobbles precariously beneath him. He must have dragged it out into the woods for drinking games.

"Now that the dog and pony show is over," he says, referring to the first bonfire, "the real fun can begin. We're playing Sticks. It's basically capture the flag with multiple flags. Or, in this case, glow sticks."

A murmur of excitement rises among the group so palpable it sends goose bumps skittering down my arms.

"The teams are Lake Chapel versus South Chapel. The boundaries are the highway and the lake."

Eagerness buzzes through the crowd. Voices rise, and guys slap one another on the back, getting fired up. The forest stretches for a couple of miles between here and either of those natural boundaries. This is going to be intense.

Decker continues. "Lake Chapel will place ten blue sticks in the woods for South Chapel to find. Then South Chapel will hide ten pink sticks for Lake Chapel to find. If you get tagged at any point, you're out. Glow sticks have to be visible. The team to collect all ten first wins."

Now the glow sticks make sense. Anything else, even flags, would be too hard to identify in the woods at night.

"Each team has five minutes to strategize. Finish your drinks, be safe out there, and when you hear three blasts from the foghorn, head back here immediately. We're not losing anyone in the woods tonight."

A few people around us laugh. Per usual, Decker Crusade has thought of everything. Those of us who know him well don't mind playing by his rules. The guy brings a sense of confident control to every situation.

Finished with his instructions, he hops off the table and lands lithely on both feet. His friend Kendrick stands by his side and holds a hand out to him.

Decker takes what he's offering, and then, in unison, they crack the glow sticks, casting a neon glow of hot pink and vibrant blue.

"Ferguson," Kendrick calls into the crowd.

Greedy steps up without hesitation, and he and Kendrick clap each other on the back in a friendly bro hug. Then he accepts the handful of glow sticks and tips his chin at Decker.

Once Greedy has passed the glow sticks out to his teammates, he navigates through the crowd and returns to my side, empty-handed.

Levi appears a moment later, chugging a fruity-smelling drink from a red cup.

Greedy stretches an arm across his chest like he's warming up. I take that as my cue.

"Good luck, guys," I tell them with a small wave.

I make it all of two steps before Greedy captures my hand.

"Whoa, whoa, whoa. Where do you think you're going?"

I glance down at our joined hands, then drag my gaze up. When I zero in on his stern expression, I frown apologetically. "You heard Decker. Lake Chapel versus South Chapel." I shrug. "See you after we beat you."

Levi snickers at my flippant sass, so I shoot him a saucy wink. I love making him laugh.

"No way, Temi," Greedy whispers, gently pulling me back to his side. "You're with us tonight."

With two fingers under my chin, he tips my face up to meet his gaze. When he looks into my eyes, I swear my brain chemistry changes. Every cell in my body is on high alert, tingly and eager for him to come even closer.

"Says who?" I challenge for the hell of it. I'm absolutely not opposed to switching teams, not when I'm under his spell like this, but I don't want to come across as too eager.

Greedy dips close and brushes his nose along my jaw until his mouth is at my ear.

Another shiver runs through me, and my heart takes off at a sprint.

"Says me," he whispers.

He's so close I'm engulfed in the scent of leather and vanilla. His breath ghosts over the sensitive skin of my neck, making my knees weak. In this moment, I want nothing more than for him to kiss me.

I tip my head back and lock eyes with him, licking my lips in anticipation. I'm not shy about making the first move.

But then his hand finds my nape and his lips are at my ear once again. "And based on how fast your pulse is thrumming right now." He guides his other hand down my neck until two fingers rest on the pulse point of my throat. "Says you, too."

I inhale a shuddering breath. Then I look back at Levi.

The instant I zero in on him, he averts his gaze and throws back the rest of his drink. I absolutely caught him watching.

Licking my lips, I regard Greedy once more. "If Decker or any of my friends catch us, they'll have questions."

That cocksure grin I'm learning to love paints over his expression once more. "I guess we better make sure they don't catch us, then."

Once the game officially begins, I'm giddy with excitement. Adrenaline and anticipation fuel me, and Greedy and Levi seem just as eager as I feel.

The three of us make an amazing team. Levi and Greedy are fast, and I'm quiet and stealthy. Thirty minutes in, we've already collected four blue glow sticks.

A fifth comes into view, only it isn't totally visible. It's buried in a pile of sticks and leaves.

While the guys hang back, I sneak forward to grab it, scanning my surroundings to be sure I won't be tagged in the process.

I fumble to take possession of it because it's been worked into the ground well, which is absolutely against the rules.

Those stinkers.

My breathing escalates as I sprint back to where the guys are hiding behind a tree. Thankfully, nobody spots me or taps me out as I make my way into hiding again.

With a hand splayed to my chest, I suck in lungfuls of air, steadying my breathing, and hand the glow stick to Levi. He's got our whole stash in his back pocket.

Greedy pulls me into a hug, and as I loop my arms around his neck, Levi wanders off, pretending to scout the area. It's unlikely there are more sticks so close, so I assume he's giving us a moment.

"I love watching you run," Greedy whispers in my ear, his warm hands pressing into my back as I will my heartrate to settle.

"Oh yeah? And why's that?" I ask, breathless, but not just from exertion.

He tugs me closer so we're touching from knee to chest. For the past half hour, it's been nothing but subtle grazes and little touches. It's like each time we're within arm's reach, we can't help but gravitate into each other's orbit.

The way he grazes my back with his fingertips sends sparks skittering through me, while being wrapped up in his arms fills me with a warmth I've never experienced.

In this moment, what I want more than anything in the world is for him to kiss me.

"I love watching you run," he repeats, his tone low, "because I get to fantasize about what it would be like to catch you."

My breath hitches in my chest. Rather than the sweet murmuring I expected, his confession is full of heat. My pulse races and my blood ignites. I lick my lips and tighten my hold on him. I'm practically standing on tiptoes, silently begging him to put me out of my misery and kiss me already.

"And what would you do if you caught me?" My tone is sweet, but I scrape my nails against the short hairs at his nape. There's no masking my eagerness as I inch closer to his mouth.

He hums, then ghosts his lips along my jaw. "I'd hold on tight and keep you forever."

I swear my heart leaves my chest and floats into the atmosphere in response to those simple words.

I'm grinning so wide my cheeks ache when he finally asks, "Temi, can I kiss you?"

"Yes."

I barely get the word out before our lips meet, our bodies press together, and my world tilts on its axis.

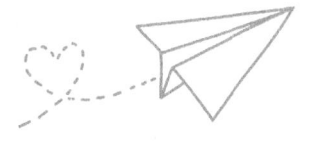

Chapter 17

Hunter

THEN

"I think I'm gonna be sick," Levi moans.

He's crouched down beside me and gripping the side of the boat like his life depends on it.

Greedy huffs. "Don't you dare puke on this boat."

I roll my lips and hold back a laugh. Although now that I'm looking closer, Levi really doesn't look well.

I'll never get tired of listening to these two bicker like an old married couple. The boat in question belongs to a man Greedy's dad plays golf with. Or maybe it was someone from work? Either way, it's a really expensive vessel, and it offers us the perfect hiding spot to film the prank that's about to go down.

I've been leading a double life all week, it seems.

I was privy to the details of the prank Lake Chapel played on South Chapel High before it went down.

The seniors from Lake Chapel set dozens of timers to go off simultaneously and hid them throughout the school. The cheap magnetic kitchen timers were stuck everywhere: under the bleachers, in the teacher's lounge, even under the serving trays in the cafeteria.

It took the student body hours to locate them. And then, near the end of the day, a brand-new set of timers went off.

The reaction videos are hilarious.

I don't know how the heck Decker and his friends pulled that one off.

Although I have a sneaking suspicion his friend Kylian, who's always got his head buried in at least two devices, had something to do with it.

Now it's South Chapel's turn for retaliation. And I'm in on this one, too.

The prank is simple enough, but it required a good amount of planning.

At least half the seniors at Lake Chapel are in for a rude awakening this afternoon when they arrive at the North Marina. Every car in the parking lot is covered in Post-it notes.

Bright aquamarine Post-it notes.

It took hours to cover them all, but we had a sizable team. The rest of the crew is gone, but we remained to film Decker's reaction, because he has the nicest car in the lot.

"Here they come," Greedy whispers, his mossy-green eyes sparkling with excitement.

We crouch lower, hiding behind the sides of the docked boat.

Levi lets out a little moan. I really hope he doesn't puke. It would not be fun to be stuck on this boat, smelling like vomit.

As the sound of the engine gets louder, I peek over the side, confirming that the big SUV that's pulling up belongs to Kendrick Taylor.

It slows and turns in, then navigates through the parking lot. I'm already imagining the look on Decker's face when he steps out and sees his beloved G-Wagon covered in sticky notes.

I fight back a snort and slap a hand over my own mouth to keep quiet.

"Temi," Greedy growls in warning.

I definitely don't want to give this away. But also... I have the worst poker face in the world.

"Temi?" Levi repeats. He's resting on his knees now, with his face buried in his hands.

I put one hand on his back in hopes of soothing him.

He peers up at Greedy, his skin peaked. "You call her that all the time. What does Temi even mean?"

"Don't worry about it," Greedy bites out. "It's an inside joke between Hunter and me."

"Explain it to me," Levi says with a pathetic groan. "Maybe that'll keep my mind off puking."

Greedy locks eyes with me and shakes his head. *No.*

He said it before: the name is special because he's the only one who knows the meaning behind it.

"Fine," Levi huffs when neither of us gives in.

"If you get to give her a nickname, then I want to give her a nickname, too."

Greedy scowls and reaches around my back to shove our friend. "You don't just get to give her a nickname."

Good thing Levi's already sitting on his knees. Otherwise, he'd topple over.

I'm pretty sure Levi knows the deal. Greedy and I aren't officially official, but we're definitely on our way there.

"Why not?" Levi teases, suddenly sounding a little less pitiful.

A tickling sensation on my leg pulls a startled yelp from me, and I bat at the spot on instinct.

Levi pulls his hand away, bringing a string from the frayed edges of my jean shorts with him. "I'm going to call you Daisy, because these jean shorts are a certifiable hazard."

A cackle escapes me before I can throw my other hand over my mouth.

Once I've pulled myself together, I lower my hand and whisper, "You can call me Daisy, but only if I can call you Duke."

"Perfect." Levi grins, looking a little less pale. "Daisy and Duke. Duke and Daisy. Together, we're double D."

"Do *not* call us that," I warn him.

"Will you two can it before you give us away?" Greedy hisses.

We watch over the edge of the boat with bated breath as Decker and his friends pile out of the car.

Greedy positions his phone, then hits Record. I can barely contain my laughter as Decker Crusade marches to his car, his posture so rigid his movements are jerky.

He glares at it for several seconds, then very tentatively peels one single Post-it note off the bumper.

His friend Locke curses loud enough for us to hear, and then all four guys get to work pulling the sticky squares from Decker's G-Wagon in earnest.

It took more than an hour to cover his car.

It's going to take them *at least* that long to remove them all. And that's if they don't notice the ones in the wheel wells.

I'm still fighting back my laughter when the boy with the glasses looks our way. Greedy curses and lowers his phone. I go utterly silent as Kylian stares in our direction for a breath, and then another.

We're all as silent as can be, swaying with the motion of the docked speedboat. Within minutes, I'm restless and suddenly realizing that we'll have to sit out here until they board their own boat and head to the Crusade isle.

We've been silent and watching for several minutes when Levi lets out a soft snore.

After all that, the motion of the boat lulled him to sleep. I guess listening to him snore is better than bearing witness to him losing his lunch.

With a giggle, I carefully turn his backward baseball cap forward to shield his eyes from the sun.

"Hey," Greedy says, the word whisper-quiet.

When I turn to give him my full attention, I'm met with a lustful, hopeful stare.

"Hey yourself," I tease.

His gaze finds mine, our connection instantly charging the energy between us like it always seems to do.

"Be my girl," he says.

Brows raised, I give him a once-over, not bothering to tell him I already am his girl. That I've wanted nothing but to be his girl since the moment he kissed me in the woods last weekend.

I bite down on my lower lip and nod.

"Yes?" he asks, ducking his head and moving closer.

"Yes."

"Good." He kisses me on the lips quickly. "I want you to come with us to my cabin next weekend for a graduation trip."

Delight soars through my veins, making me lightheaded. "I'd love that. Who will be there?"

"Levi's coming. A few other guys from the team, plus their significant others. It's a small group, and the trip will be chill." He grasps my hand and squeezes. "It's a good-size place, but there are only so many bedrooms. Do you want me to see if one of the other girls wants to share with you, or..."

He's so thoughtful and so sincere, but he can't hide the hopefulness in his tone.

"I want to be with you," I quickly confirm, grinning.

He matches my smile, then reaches over, takes my hand, and kisses the top of my knuckles.

I close my eyes and commit this moment to memory. The sun warms my upturned face, and the lake gently lulls me into a hypnotic state of happiness and tranquility.

I've never been quite as happy as I am in this moment.

Next weekend and every day after, I want to be Greedy's girl.

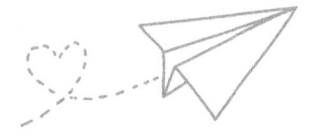

Chapter 18

Hunter

THEN

The cover of my hot pink moleskin notebook is soft and well worn against my hands as I flip through the pages until I find the one I need. I've been journaling and doodling in this same style of notebook since I was a kid.

For years, I've dreamed of being a lawyer. But the hopeless romantic in me still loves to write poetry and song lyrics. Most mornings, I jot down the details of my dreams, and throughout each day, when inspiration strikes, I scribble ideas on the pages, so I almost always have a notebook with me in some capacity.

I wrinkle my nose when I find the page I need. As the salutatorian of our graduating class, I was asked to read a poem at the ceremony.

Annoyingly, I didn't even get to choose. But I've done my due diligence and memorized it, nonetheless. I guess I can contain multitudes, too.

Predictably, Kylian Walsh is valedictorian. Rumor has it, though, that he is refusing to give a speech, so Decker is stepping up to take his place. No one thought to offer the second in the class an opportunity to give a speech, I guess. That, or they wanted the pomp and circumstance that comes with the Crusade name.

The school secretary emailed a link to my assigned piece weeks ago, and I've had it memorized since. But I'm shut in my room tonight and feeling wound up after my latest run-in with my mom, so it's as good a time as any to refresh my memory.

I should be used to her mood swings by now. The highs and lows that dictate her entire existence. It doesn't help that she's downed at least two bottles of wine so far this weekend. She never allows herself to get totally inebriated, but she maintains enough of a buzz to channel the melodrama. And to get away with doing and saying things that are downright mean.

She's been worse since my dad left. That, or maybe my dad protected me more than I realized when she went on a bender.

I miss my dad. He used to travel a lot for work, so we're used to staying in touch via email and text. His business trips always ended though. He'd come home, and everything in my world would right itself.

It took me several months to realize that he wasn't coming back. That no one is coming to restore peace in this house. I'm on my own, and no amount of frustration or self-pity is going to change the reality of my situation.

I just have to make it through the next few days, then the rest of this summer.

Once I'm on my own on my own terms? Watch out, world.

For now, I'll bide my time, holed up in my bedroom and avoiding any sort of confrontation with my mom. She's downstairs now, working on bottle number three and bemoaning her status as a woman old enough to have a high school graduate.

I've been under the impression that this stage in life is one parents are proud of, yet she's in a true state of disbelief and maybe even a little disgust.

I had every intention of tagging along with Greedy tonight while he makes a grocery store run before our trip to the cabin.

Graduation is tomorrow. For the next few days, every senior in town will be attending one epic pool party or beach party after another. On Friday, we'll head to Greedy's cabin up past Beech Mountain.

When I told her my original plans for tonight, she accused me of abandoning her. It's the night before my high school graduation, yet she made it about her. She has no interest in spending time with me, but she doesn't want me to leave the house and have fun without her.

It wasn't worth the fight. If I appease her now, it will make it easier to get out of the house for the graduation parties this week, and heading to the cabin this weekend is my top priority. She hasn't come up to check on me or mentioned dinner.

My stomach growls on cue at the reminder that I haven't eaten since before graduation practice this afternoon.

My phone vibrates where it's charging near my nightstand. Heart leaping, I jump up and rush to retrieve it, grinning before I even see who it is.

> **Greedy:** special delivery for the prettiest girl in North Carolina

Butterflies flutter in my belly like they do every time I hear from him. He's so damn sweet.

> **Greedy:** come to the window

Startled by his request, I spin around and rush to the large picture window. My hands tremble a little as I push the frame up. If he's here, my mom might see him.

I have to squint to make out more than just his silhouette where he's standing on the sidewalk below my room, so I pop out the screen and lean out to get a better view.

"What are you doing here?" I ask in a loud whisper.

"Just wanted to see my girlfriend," he tells me, his face lit up with a smile. "We got everything all set for this weekend." With his hands shoved into his pockets, he steps a few feet closer to the window. When he's as close as he can get, he tips his chin. "Do you feel okay?" he asks, his voice full of genuine concern.

My heart sinks with disappointment once again. We had tentative plans to meet up later, but that's clearly not going to happen. I already texted him an excuse, saying I just wanted to stay in tonight.

"I'm fine," I insist. "My mom wanted me to lay low tonight since it's such a busy week." I shrug like it's no big deal. As if it's typical for eighteen-year-olds to do whatever their parents tell them to.

"I could come up and keep you company," he offers, taking two steps back like he's going to head for the front door.

"*No*," I say too quickly and a little too loudly.

The last thing I want is for him to have to interact with her or be tarnished by her in any way. Greedy is special to me. He's mine, and I'm his. Getting him tangled up in my mom's melodramatic bullshit tonight jeopardizes that.

He stops and comes back, his face set in a concerned frown.

"I'm sort of stuck in my room, trying to avoid my mom," I admit.

The sigh he lets out is one of defeat. "How long have you been up there?"

I check the time on my phone. "Most of the night." My stomach responds as well, growling loudly.

So loud, in fact, that Greedy hears it from the lawn two stories down.

"Did you eat dinner, Tem?"

I don't bother lying. I wasn't hungry earlier, but clearly, I am now.

"No." I give my head a slight shake. "I haven't eaten." I've been waiting for my mom to go to bed, though I don't bring that up. Again, the last thing I want to get into with him is my mother and her issues.

"Hunter," he scolds, whipping out his phone. "I'm ordering food for you."

Before I can push back and tell him not to bother, he holds up one hand.

"Don't tell me not to. Not on this." He glances up from the screen and offers me a soft smile. "I hate that you're stuck at home tonight, but if that's easiest, I get it."

He's quiet for a few moments, and all the while, my heart pounds out a rhythm just for him. Each time we're together, he shows me more of his genuine kindness. Greedy makes me feel like I'm easy to love. Because of that, I think I might be falling in love with him.

"Done," he tells me, stashing his phone away. "I left instructions to leave the food on your porch and to not ring the bell or knock. You can sneak down and get it when you're ready."

My stomach twists in gratitude, but also with a pang of anxiety at the prospect of trying to sneak food past my mom. Although given the rate she was going when I shut myself away, she'll be passed out sooner rather than later.

"Thank you," I tell him, my throat clogging with emotion as I hang out my window a bit more and smile down.

"Wait, stay right there." He spins on his heel and hustles back to his truck. He opens the back door and rifles through a plastic bag, from the sound of it.

He doesn't have to worry about me taking off. The exceptional view of his backside in those jeans keeps me firmly in place, hanging half out the window.

Greedy mentioned there's a hot tub at the cabin, and I'm more than ready to get a peek of him in something other than jeans.

A rush of excitement rolls through me again. Graduation is so close I can taste it. I can't wait to go to the cabin this weekend. I can't wait to finally be free.

Greedy jogs back with something white in his hand and tips his chin up. "Open the window all the way and stand back."

I do as he says. We've only known each other for weeks, but he's shown me over and over again that he's worthy of my implicit trust.

A moment later, the white object soars through my window and lands softly on my bed.

A paper airplane.

As I pick it up off my comforter, my smile widens. Because the dark indentations in the paper hint at a note he scratched onto it for me.

I unfold the middle section carefully, just enough to reveal the words.

His handwriting is small and neat, despite how quickly he jotted down the words while leaning halfway inside his truck.

> *I can't wait to be with you this weekend.*
> *And I really can't wait to be together next year.*

With the paper clutched to my chest, I let my own excitement for the future wash over me.

I decided yesterday that I'm officially going to Lake Chapel University.

Greedy lit up when I told him. We don't have to consider whether we want to try long distance. Our relationship is so new, yet it feels so right. With him at SCU and me at LCU, we can let it continue to progress without forcing anything.

He's been committed to South Chapel for a while, so we'll be thirty minutes from each other for the next four years.

I head back to the window while carefully refolding the treasure so I can keep it.

"You promise you're okay?" he asks again, his expression still full of concern.

"I'm more than okay," I tell him.

A rough night with my mom is nothing new, but this kind of positive turn is. Greedy's appearance and his genuine care have made it exponentially better.

"Okay. Text or call me before you go to bed."

"I will," I promise.

With another sweet smile, he turns and heads for his truck again.

"Hey," I call out, keeping my voice low.

He spins, then he freezes where he stands, looking so damn beautiful in the moonlight.

"I'm really excited about next year, too."

Grinning, he sticks his hands into his pockets and walks backward to his truck.

He doesn't take his eyes off me until he has to get in the cab and finally drive away.

As his taillights disappear, I hold the little paper airplane to my chest again.

This weekend will be amazing, no doubt.

But next year is going to be the start of something brand new. Something so much better.

I can't wait to do it with Greedy by my side.

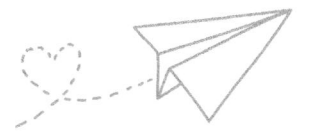

Chapter 19

Hunter

NOW

"Week three, done and dusted." Levi brushes his hands together as he strides toward me.

And stride, he does. He graduated to a walking boot this week. There's a literal spring in his step now that he's ditched the crutches.

I drink him in as he approaches.

He's dressed in athletic shorts and an oversized cutout T-shirt that shows off every ripple of muscle along his arms, upper back, and obliques.

He's covered in a sheen of sweat built up during his PT session. He's pushing himself, that's for sure.

"You look good, Duke." I mark my place in my American history textbook, then snap it shut and stash it in my bag. "Ready to go?"

I've been driving Levi to and from physical therapy Monday through Thursday for the last three weeks. Greedy covers Fridays, since he doesn't have class and the South Chapel Sharks football team has officially transitioned to their offseason training schedule.

The routine works well. Levi and I sip our morning beverages—tea or matcha for me, creamer with a splash of coffee for him. Sometimes we chat on our way to the sports rehab facility, but mostly, we ride in comfortable silence.

I get a guaranteed two hours of studying done while he goes through his exercises and meets with the trainers assisting with his rehabilitation. On the days he has an evaluation or an extra sports massage scheduled, it's closer to three hours.

Dr. Ferguson hooked him up. The rehab center is across the parking lot from the hospital. It's a state-of-the-art facility, with every bell and whistle imaginable. Levi is receiving top-tier care. I haven't asked, but knowing Greedy's dad the way I do, it's likely Levi won't pay a cent for the physical therapy and extra services he's receiving.

By the time I reach him, he's collected his belongings, too.

Side by side, we head for the exit, but as we get close, he ups his pace so he can hold the door for me.

Always the southern gentleman.

Before I have a chance to walk through the open door, someone calls out across the entryway.

"Levi Moore!"

A man in his late fifties or early sixties comes to stop before us. He's stout, with a trimmed beard and mustache that are mostly white. One arm is wrapped in a sling, but he extends the other out to Levi.

Levi shoots me an apologetic half smile, then steps forward and shakes the man's hand.

"It's great to see you, son," the man offers warmly.

Levi's posture is stiff, but his tone is polite when he responds. "It's nice to see you, too, Pastor Tomlin."

I instinctively step forward, positioning myself at my friend's side.

His sudden change in demeanor and the formality with which he addressed this man put me on edge.

I place my palm on the small of his back, hoping to imbue a little comfort. Instead, he jolts at the contact.

Before I can remove my hand, he relaxes a fraction and gives me a small smile, so I leave it in place. I just want him to know I'm here.

"Your mother told me about your accident," the pastor says, nodding toward the walking boot on Levi's foot.

Accident?

I drop my arm to my side and open my mouth to correct him, but Levi catches my hand in his and squeezes. Either it's not worth correcting, or the pastor isn't one to take correction.

Okay, then.

"Are you, uh, are you here for rehab?" Levi asks, his voice laced with discomfort.

"Shoulder replacement," the pastor confirms, chuckling.

He's yet to introduce himself or even acknowledge my presence. Instead, he's kept his full attention fixed on Levi, as if I'm invisible.

"May says I use my hands too much when I'm preaching." The laugh that escapes him is self-deprecating, but it fades quickly, and his faux-jovial expression transforms into one much more stern. "Speaking of... your mother says you've been home for almost a month now, son. We can expect you to join us this Sunday, I assume?" He scans Levi from head to toe and gives his boot a pointed look. "It appears you're getting around just fine now—"

"*Oh...*" I can't help but interject. Being blatantly ignored will do that to a girl. "This Sunday?"

For the first time, the man looks down at me. His eyes make a sweeping assessment. To his credit, he doesn't leer like some men do, but his gaze snags on our joined hands, and he lifts a brow, unimpressed.

Rather than speak directly to the good pastor, I tip my chin up to Levi and level him with the sweetest smile I can muster. "You promised you'd be my DD this weekend, Duke."

Levi's eyes widen in surprise, but he plays along. "Uh, yeah. Sorry, Pastor T. I'm busy this Sunday."

"Next week, then," the man insists, straightening and puffing out his chest.

His tone brooks no argument.

Personally? I'm not a fan.

The idea of this man, or anyone, for that matter, trying to control or manipulate someone I care about makes my hackles rise. I suffered through years of manipulation shrouded in the guise of love. I don't tolerate that shit anymore. Not for myself, or for my friends.

"Oh, shucks," I say, going for earnest, and run the fingertips of my free hand across Levi's chest.

He's so warm and solid under my touch. And I swear he shudders, just slightly, when my nails scrape his pecs.

"I signed you up to DD next weekend, too, babe."

Levi squeezes my hand in warning.

Too far?

It's probably too far.

I bite back a grin and school my expression.

"Young lady. Perhaps it's not my place," the Pastor starts, as if that justifies what'll come out of his mouth next, "but what sort of *extracurriculars* are you involved in that require a regular designated driver on Sunday mornings?"

I offer my most saccharine smile. "Smut brunch, sir. It's a spicy romance book club. Bottomless mimosas and romance novels are necessities." I giggle. "They're a match made in *heaven*." I place extra emphasis on the last word.

Levi coughs uncontrollably, his shoulders shaking with the force of it.

Yep. Definitely too far.

But I'm not one to back down from a challenge, so I double down.

"Levi here, my *boyfriend*," I emphasize, "loves supporting smut brunch. Isn't that right, Dukey?"

As soon as I say it out loud, I hear it.

But the damage has already been done.

I fight to keep from cringing and bat my lashes at him instead.

Dukey it is.

"Yeah, Daisycakes," Levi confirms, still gasping for air after his coughing fit. "It's cute when you get together with your friends. I'm happy to be your DD." He drops my hand but wraps his arm around my shoulder.

The pastor eyes us warily. Probably working on a retort.

I've already come this far, and I don't give a shit what anyone thinks about me—not anymore—so I triple down, this time going for shock factor.

"Dukey." I giggle.

My giggle evolves into a snort, because I'm apparently twelve.

I do my best to recall whether the dog poop kind of "dookie" is spelled with a *y* or an *ie*, then give up and go in for the kill.

"It's not just *cute*. It's *educational*. You know you love it when I get drunk at brunch, then come home ready to jump your bones so we can try all the kinky things I've been reading about."

Now it's the good pastor's turn to cough uncontrollably. Wincing, he grasps his upper arm, probably in a bit of pain if he just had a shoulder replacement. Oops.

Levi squeezes my hand tighter and takes a step toward the exit, pulling me with him. As he does, I can't help but drive the point home.

"Plus, it's *so* much better now that we're living together. We don't even have to use FaceTime to fornicate. I can have my way with you whenever I want," I muse, trailing one nail along Levi's clean-shaven jaw as I bat my lashes at him.

"Simmer down, Daisy. You've made your point," Levi murmurs, guiding me through the door by the elbow. "And please don't ever say *fornicate* to me again."

"Good to see you again, Pastor Tomlin," he calls over his shoulder. "Take care."

Always the southern gentleman.

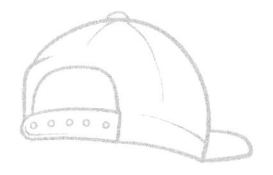

Chapter 20

Levi

NOW

I skim the instructions on the back of the pasta box, reading them again to make sure I didn't miss anything. I took a nap this afternoon specifically so I'd have the stamina to make dinner tonight. I'm not the best chef, but I've mastered a few of the basics.

Plus, I want to prove to myself that I'm making progress. That I can handle this. Thanks to my fancy new walking boot, I'm more than ready to start pulling my weight around here.

For weeks, Hunter and Greedy have been doing too much for me. It's time I show my appreciation.

I dump the pasta into the boiling water and set the timer. Then I check the veggies roasting in the oven. I hum mindlessly as I work, then abruptly stop when I remember I'm not the only one in the kitchen.

Typically, I'd listen to music or watch sports highlights on my phone while doing something like this, but I don't want to disturb Hunter.

She's set up at the kitchen island, hair piled on top of her head and magically held together with a pen. I want to tease her about her weird habit of sticking pens in her hair, but this isn't the time.

When she's concentrating like this, it's best to leave her alone.

She's completely focused on the textbook on the island, tracking the words on the page with a finger while she takes notes.

She's so serious, almost mechanical, in the way she processes information.

Exams are this week, so it makes sense that she's stressed.

If only I could take away some of that tension and convince her not to worry so much about school. She's an excellent student, but she puts too much pressure on herself.

Taking twenty-one credits in a semester is crazy.

Humming again, I stir the pasta on the stove to ensure it doesn't glue together.

Hunter sighs behind me.

"You're working too hard, Daisy," I tease.

She looks up, blinking, as if she's only now realizing that I'm there.

Her answering scowl tells me I've interrupted. Again.

The little twinge of pain in my chest that blossoms each time she gives me a look like that is impossible to ignore. I'm not trying to be a nuisance, but she studies nonstop. Sometimes she holes up in her room all day long, and I only see her in passing in the hall when she's heading to class or coming home.

"You need to lighten up. The Hunter I knew was always up for a little fun."

She sighs and slumps over her textbook. "I don't have time for fun right now."

"Bullshit," I tell her, giving the pasta another quick stir. "The girl I used to know always had time for fun. She *was* the fun."

Before she can argue, I hobble over and peer down at her notebook. This walking boot is a major upgrade, but I'm still getting used to the new cadence of my stride. I'll wear the boot for two or three more weeks, and then I'll transition to walking again. I'm trying my hardest not to let my muscles atrophy while I recover.

All I do these days is go to rehab, work out with Greedy, and rest. Though I guess that's exactly what the doctor ordered.

With a glance over my shoulder, I check the time on the clock over the stove.

"Come on." I pull my phone from my pocket, pick a playlist, and hold out my hand. "Dance with me."

The song that floats on the air around us is a country song that was popular when we were in high school. It was one I listened to a lot that first year of college, when I was missing my friends and still trying to find my place out in California.

She tilts her head up and blows at a strand of blond hair that's escaped her writing-utensil-supported hairdo.

"It's finals week. I have to study."

I reach out slowly, giving her a chance to pull away.

Her eyes track my movement, but she doesn't pull back or try to stop me.

She remains still as I sweep the loose hair away from her forehead and tuck it behind her ear. A surge of pride fills my chest every time she lets me in like this.

"You can spare five minutes for a study break," I murmur.

She glances over my shoulder, then squints at me mischievously. "According to the timer, we've actually got six minutes."

Delight washes over me. "Six minutes? Sounds like the perfect amount of time for a dance with my girl."

Gaze softening, she closes her notebook and finally takes my outstretched hand.

She eases off the barstool and comes willingly when I guide her to the middle of the kitchen. With one hand on her low back, I steady myself. I'm not exactly light on my feet these days, but I'll fake it till I make it if it lightens her load or helps her loosen up.

Head tipped back, she cocks one brow. "Your girl, huh?"

"Yeah. If you're allowed to call me *Dukey* in public and go into detail about your favorite kinks with my mom's pastor, then I'm allowed to call you my girl."

She brings one hand to her chest, her mouth agape in mock outrage. "I did *not* reveal any of my favorite kinks to Pastor Tomlin."

"Semantics," I tell her.

Hunter shrugs, then offers me the first genuine smile she's cracked in more than an hour.

There she is.

It feels damn good to be the one to make her smile like that.

"You *did* make up a fake book club to get me out of church, though. Even if you took it about ten times further than necessary, I appreciate the hell out of you having my back."

Hunter quirks both brows at me this time. "It's cute you think smut brunch isn't a real thing."

"Wait." I scoff. "I thought you made that up."

"Smut brunch is a very real thing," she insists, her expression completely serious. "But you don't need to worry about being my DD. It's virtual."

"Virtual? What the hell does that mean?"

She grins. "We meet over Zoom. We make breakfast, pour ourselves a drink or six, then hang out online on Sunday mornings," she says, her green eyes alight. "We have members all over. Rachel is in Michigan. Angela's in Jersey. And Kym is in Louisiana. I even got Decker Crusade's new PR rep, Megan, to join us a few weeks ago. We may have scared her off with some of our somnophilia masked-men recs last time, but—"

I burst out laughing. "I don't understand half of the words that just came out of your mouth."

She smiles sweetly. "The only words you need to remember are these two: *Smut* and *brunch*."

"Smut brunch," I repeat. "And 'smut' means…?"

Hunter snorts again, her pretty face screwing up as the very unladylike sound escapes her. She's clearly okay being herself around me. Her real self. And I like that a hell of a lot.

"*Smut* is synonymous with spicy romance books."

I open my mouth, ready to ask her to define *spicy*, but before I can, she clarifies.

"Spicy meaning books with a lot of sex. My smut brunch friends and I read it all. Dark romance. Small-town romance. Sports romance. The options are endless," she chirps, her whole face lit up. "We'll read just about any subgenre, as long as it ends in an HEA. That's the number one rule of smut brunch. Happily ever after or bust. We won't even consider it as our book of the week if it doesn't have an HEA."

"So it's like Fight Club?"

"*Exactly*. Only hornier."

I nod, but then falter. "Wait… did you say book of the *week*?"

"Yep."

"So you read, like, four or five books a month?" I surmise, feeling a little more confident in my swaying.

"Oh, Dukey. Bless your heart."

Dukey isn't going to be a thing. But before I can nip that in the bud, she continues.

"I read four or five romance books a *week*," she declares, her chest puffing proudly and pressing against mine.

I squeeze her hand and pull it to my chest. "With what time?"

She shrugs. "I make the time. I always have my Kindle with me, and I listen to a lot of audiobooks."

With a shake of my head, I give her a teasing look. "You're crazy."

"I prefer to think of it as delightfully delusional," she says, smiling. But then her expression slips and her tone turns more serious. "And saying someone is crazy or insane is ableist. Mental health isn't a joke."

My stomach sinks, and I nearly trip over my walking boot, which is an impressive feat since I'm barely moving as it is.

"I—" I clear my throat. "I wasn't trying to insult you—"

"I know. No biggie. I used to say things like that, too. Know better and do better, ya know?" She pulls away and does a little spin move, and even when the song changes on my playlist, we keep dancing.

"Okay. So don't call anyone crazy or insane. All books must have a happy ending," I recite.

"Happily ever after," she clarifies. "And not all books. Just romance books. It's a genre requirement."

"And every Sunday you're busy—"

"And horny!" she singsongs.

"Because of smut brunch."

Her response is a wide grin.

"You're a fascinating creature, Hunter St. Clair."

With a tip of her chin, she hums. "I'll take that as a compliment."

"It was intended to be."

We're both quiet then, letting the music fill the space as we dance in the open kitchen. Although I guess we're not really dancing. It's more like swaying, with Hunter occasionally spinning around me while I stand in place.

Even when she leaves my personal space, I can't look away from her.

She's growing bolder as she moves. Loosening up. Letting her hair down—literally, because the pen she stuck through her bun is doing a piss-poor job of holding it together.

She twirls toward the fridge, then back to me again, making my heart rate pick up a little. She was a cheerleader in high school, but I didn't know her until the end of her senior year. The way she moves her body is mesmerizing. I could watch her all damn day.

"You've got the moves, Daisy."

Grinning, she places her palms on my chest. "Don't I know it. I worked at a nightclub in London for almost a year."

London.

That's where she went at the end of that summer. She doesn't talk much about her time in Europe, and I haven't dared to press the issue.

She doesn't talk about the in-between: Where she went. Where I helped her go.

But when her words register, my hands tighten into fists at my sides. It takes conscious effort to flex them and release the tension that's suddenly taken over. "You worked at a nightclub as a dancer?"

It's not exactly my business, but I still don't like it.

She shakes her head, lips pursed as she sways her hips. "I was a hostess, but I may have picked up a few moves from the girls in entertainment."

With a wicked smirk, she shows off one of those moves now, running both hands over my pecs and down my abdomen as she slinks down low, lower, *damn.*

All lucid thoughts leave my brain as I take her in. She's so low she's practically on her knees before me.

She sweeps her hands over my legs as she rises again. When she caresses my jean-clad thighs, my heart stutters. For weeks, I've had no sensation in my upper left leg, but there's no denying I can feel her touch. It's fucking incredible.

When she stands to her full height, I pull her into my arms. She comes willingly, easily. Then we're slow dancing once more. Her body molds against mine as she plays with the overgrown hair at my nape. Her heart is hammering in her chest from dancing, tapping out a rhythm that calls to mine.

Warmth spreads through me as we sway. Every time her skin brushes mine, a shock of electricity runs through me.

That's Hunter.

She's enigmatic. Electric.

Like this, so full of life, she's even more beautiful. I love knowing I can bring out this side of her.

But I hate that this isn't her default setting. She really is working too hard. I've gotta watch for that from now on.

In this moment, I make a promise to myself. I'll be the man who lightens her load. The person who pays attention. Notices when she needs a break. Gives her an excuse to let loose.

As the second song ends, I fully expect her to pull away.

But she doesn't. Instead, she wraps her arms around my shoulders and rests her cheek against my chest.

The energy coursing between us is as familiar as it is foreign. Suddenly, this feels like so much more than two friends dancing in the kitchen.

"You light up every room," I tell her, smoothing a hand up and down her back.

She tips her chin and locks eyes with me. The sincerity shining in hers hits me like an outside linebacker slamming into my chest.

Her tongue darts out and licks a trail across her lower lip.

Breath caught in my lungs, I track the movement and pull her even closer.

A sharp, high-pitched beep startles us both—the timer—and the spell is broken.

"Time's up," she tells me playfully, spinning out of my arms with one final twirl. "I'll go set the table."

I stare at her backside for so long the timer sounds again.

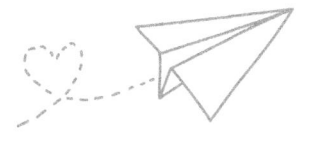

Chapter 21

Hunter

NOW

"It's not so much something you have to *understand*," Locke, Joey's boyfriend—*one* of Joey's boyfriends—philosophizes, "as it is something to accept. Material conditional in functional logic means that a false antecedent is a true statement, full stop."

I want to pull my hair out. Who knew that Logic 200 would be the most *illogical* class I would take this semester?

I'm sitting cross-legged in the middle of Joey's bed. Beside me, Joey's lying on her stomach, watching Locke with heart eyes and kicking her legs up like she doesn't have a care in the world.

Pencil in hand, I gently poke her in the bum. "Are you seriously understanding all of this?"

She yawns through a serene smile, then shrugs. "You know what they say. *Cs* get degrees. As long as I don't completely bomb this final, I'll pass the class. That's all I'm really worried about."

I bite my tongue and hold back a snide comment about her not needing to worry about much these days. Girlfriend's got it made living on a private isle in a lakeside mansion with her husband and three boyfriends.

Frustrated, I blow out a breath. Then I inhale slowly, trying to quell the bitchiness that loves to ride on the coattails of my anxiety.

I'm not mad at Joey. I'm *never* mad at Joey.

I'm just hella stressed about this exam, because it's the one class I might not ace. Logic 200 is all that stands between me and a 4.0 GPA this semester.

Locke saunters over and splays his hands on the mattress at the end of the bed. Arms spread wide, he leans forward and kisses Joey on the lips. When he pulls back, he smirks. "If I had to guess, there's at least one orgasm behind her casual demeanor. Probably two, if Kylian was involved. She was way more stressed about this test this morning."

Joey grabs a pillow from behind her and throws it at him. "Jealous, Nicky?"

He tosses the pillow back onto the bed and walks backward toward the bedroom door, both hands held out in front of him. "Nah. I'm never jealous, Hot Girl. You know I'm great at sharing. What I am is hungry. I've worked up an appetite from all this studying. I could use a snack break." He winks at Joey.

Their flirtatious banter would make me ill if it wasn't so damn adorable.

Locke hovers in the doorway, raising both arms to grip the doorframe. "Seriously, Hunter," he says. "Don't stress. You've got this. You're literally the smartest person in class. There's no way you won't pass."

I know I'll pass, but I want to nail this exam and prove to myself that I can handle twenty-one credit hours. If I maintain this pace, I can graduate in three years instead of four. But I'm not willing to sacrifice grades for speed. This semester was a test. A big test. I'm too competitive to give up now.

I offer him a weak smile. "Thanks for your help."

With a huff, I flop down on the side of the bed and read over my notes. Again.

"Maybe I need a snack break, too," Joey muses.

Deadpan, I blink over at her. "Please do *not* ditch me to go have sex with one of your boyfriends in a pantry right now."

This time I'm the one with a pillow swinging toward my head.

"No, I'm serious. You could use one, too. You're studying too hard. We both know you've got this. I don't like to see you stressed."

Easy for Miss "*C*s Get Degrees" to say. *C*s won't get me into Harvard Law.

"Ooh, I have an idea," Joey rhapsodizes. "This is your last final, right?"

"Yep, last one."

It's the only thing standing between me and winter break.

Joey rolls to her side and props her head on her hand. "Why don't we plan a girls' night? We could have a sleepover on Saturday."

Yes. A girls' night sounds fabulous.

I pull out my phone to look at my calendar, only to remember I've already committed to something this weekend, and I really want to see it through. "Raincheck. I have a friend in town, and I promised we'd do something together on Sunday morning."

Joey wrinkles her nose. "Will you think less of me if I admit that I'm jealous I'm not your only friend?"

"He's an old friend. Until now, I haven't seen him since before you and I even met," I assure her. "You're still my number one girl."

She grins at that, but her expression quickly turns to one of surprise. Then she pops up to sitting.

"Hold up. Your friend is a *he*?"

I roll my bottom lip between my teeth. "He's a *he*, yes. His name is Levi. He's a friend from high school, and he recently moved back to the area. We're, um. Well. We're dating. Sort of."

"OMG!" Joey squeals. "Way to bury the lede. Why didn't you start with the vital life update?" she demands, bouncing on the bed and making the bun on top of her head wobble. "What does he look like? I'm sure he's hot. I can't wait to meet him."

I laugh at her outburst, but a niggle of trepidation seeps in and steals the easiness of the moment.

Levi and I haven't discussed who we're telling what to. The general population believes we're dating. Is that version of the story what we want to share with our friends? What about our *best* friends?

Greedy is Levi's best friend, and he knows our arrangement is a ruse. So why am I hesitating to share that same truth with my bestie?

A sharp knock on the door garners our attention.

"Josephine," a stern voice calls from the hallway.

"Yes, dear," my bestie calls toward the door, her lips turned up in an amused smile.

"Mrs. Lansbury is asking if Hunter plans to stay for dinner."

"Why don't you come in and ask her yourself," she goads.

The handle turns, then the door swings open. Standing at the threshold is Joey's husband, Decker Crusade.

He smiles warmly at me, then sets his sights on his wife and strides into the room, all stern and uptight. Joey calls it his "Big Decker Energy," but considering I've known this guy since elementary school and he's married to my closest girlfriend, I refuse to even think the words "big anything energy" where he's concerned.

He walks to the side of the bed closest to Joey. "I tried texting you twice," he murmurs.

Brows pulled low, Joey twists at the waist, searching the surface of the mattress. "Shit on a crumbly cracker…" She smooths her hands over her duvet to check for lumps. "I don't even know where my phone is."

Decker purses his lips in amusement. "Want me to text Kylian and ask him to track it?"

"No, no," she insists, clearly unbothered and unsurprised by the notion that her guys can track her phone. "It's around here somewhere. I might have left it in Kendrick's room earlier."

Turning to me, she circles back to Decker's original question. "Do you want to stay for dinner?"

I shake my head. "No, thanks. I promised the guys I'd eat with them tonight."

"The guys?" Joey asks.

Oh. I guess I left out the part where Levi and I are also cohabitating.

"Greedy and the friend I was telling you about," I answer casually.

The unimpressed look she shoots me tells me I have a lot of explaining to do about my new "boyfriend" and our arrangement when the two of us are alone again.

It hits me then, that Decker knows Levi. Heck, Decker's the one who introduced me to Greedy and Levi.

"Oh, Decker. You know who I'm talking about. Levi Moore is back in town."

"You don't say?" Decker arches a brow like he's genuinely pleased to hear it. "Levi's a great guy. Is he home for the holidays?"

"Not exactly," I hedge.

I tread lightly as I attempt to explain his unceremonious return to South Chapel. "He's home indefinitely. Because of a football injury."

"I'm sorry to hear that," Decker offers, rubbing at the back of his neck. "Give him my number if you see him. I'd love to catch up."

"Oh, she'll be seeing him, all right," Joey teases. "Hunter and Levi are *dating*."

Her husband's brows raise again, but this time in question. "You're *dating* Levi Moore?"

"Mm-hmm." Lips pursed, I lower my focus to my Logic notes and act concerned with a smudge on the paper.

"Huh. Okay, then. Where's he staying?" Decker asks. "With his mom in South Chapel?"

Gaze still averted, I shuffle through my papers, but after several beats of silence, the discomfort settling over me is enough to force me to look up. Naturally, Decker and Joey are both staring at me.

Flovely.

There's no getting out of this one without telling a bald-faced lie. I might as well give them some semblance of the truth.

"Levi is actually staying with us. With Greedy and me."

Decker's brows descend into a scowl. He crosses his arms over his chest as he considers me.

"You're living in South Chapel, at the Ferguson residence, with Greedy and Levi Moore, the latter of whom you're currently dating?"

"Mm-hmm," I confirm, focusing on my notes once again to avoid his look of scrutiny.

At the rate I'm going, I'll have unconsciously memorized everything on the page before my Logic exam. Not a bad strategy, all things considered.

Joey's watching me, too. Her stare is so intense I worry she'll singe my hair with the way she's zeroed in on the side of my skull.

I don't dare look over and meet her eyes. I also ignore Decker's impatient stance.

"Right. Okay," he finally declares. "So you're intentionally being aloof and evasive. Got it."

His natural intensity wanes a little as he sits on the edge of the bed and opens one arm to Joey.

SO WRONG

Without hesitation, she scoots over and snuggles against his chest, then sighs contently.

"I was going to make dessert," he tells her softly. "Any requests?"

Humming, she rests her head on his shoulder. In return, he brushes a stray hair off her forehead. It's a sweet moment: intimate and assured in the way people dream of experiencing with a partner.

But then Joey has to go and ruin it.

In a tone that is pure innuendo, she says, "You know what I like."

His onyx eyes widen for a heartbeat, but then he clenches his jaw and scowls.

Shaking his head, he shoots me an apologetic look.

"I don't think Hunter needs or wants to be let in on those specific details between me and my wife."

"It's fine," I insist with a wave of my hand. "She's been like this all afternoon."

I make a mental note to text her later for deets. Girlfriend must have gotten dicked down good to still be this mellow.

Joey's grin widens, and Decker bends low to kiss her on the forehead.

"I'll make you double chocolate chip brownies," he confirms, proving that he does, in fact, know what she likes, then stands and strides back toward the bedroom door.

"No nuts this time!" she yells after him.

He chuckles from out in the hall but doesn't confirm or deny his intentions.

"I swear he tries to put his nuts in everything," she tells me, her expression one of annoyance. A heartbeat later, her words must register, though, because she dissolves into a fit of giggles like she's twelve, and I follow right behind her.

It takes several minutes to pull ourselves together, but once we do, she wipes away her tears of laughter and surveys me.

"So you and this Levi guy, huh? I'm a little hurt that Decker knows him, but I don't."

"It's new," I confess with a sigh. "And complicated."

Before she can grill me, my phone vibrates. Saved by the bell. Or, in this instance, the text.

I pick it up, expecting a message from Levi or maybe a check-in from Greedy. When I see the text on the screen, I'm hit with an onslaught of mixed emotions.

> **The One and Only:** It's all coming together, Mahina. Call me as soon as you can.

Mahina.

He promised to follow me through every lifetime—through every phase of the moon.

They were beautiful sentiments. Life-affirming words when I needed them most.

But there's nothing he can do or say to change the course I'm on now.

I'm back in North Carolina for practical purposes. To get my degree, then move on with my life, once and for all. I have a plan, and I fully intend to see it through.

"Earth to Hunter," Joey singsongs.

Heart lodged in my throat, I look up at my best friend, only now realizing I've been staring at my phone, thinking about the man who brought me back to life on the edges of Lake Como.

"I don't think I've *ever* seen that look on your face. Was that your new boyfriend messaging you?"

"Something like that," I tell her, stashing my phone and ducking my head, hoping to hide the way my cheeks are heating.

I take my time settling again, closing my textbook while I compose myself. Then I change the subject. It's clear we won't be getting any more studying done tonight.

"What are your plans for the holidays?"

"We're still finalizing details," Joey says, "but we plan to go to the cabin on Beech Mountain and spend Christmas there."

She has this dreamy look in her eye when she talks about the cabin. I can't blame her. It's a gorgeous place, and it's where she and Decker said "I do."

"Then Decker wants to go on a honeymoon," she adds, though her eyes have suddenly filled with hesitation.

"And you *don't* want to go on a honeymoon?" I challenge. "Because I gotta tell you, going on a sex vacation with four hot men who are more than happy to be at your beck and call doesn't sound like a bad way to spend winter break."

"I know," she grumbles, digging the heels of her hands into her eyes. "It's not that I don't want to go. I just have such a hard time wrapping my head around the idea of a vacation."

Head tilted, I survey her, working to understand her thought process. When she drops her hands from her face, her eyes are swimming with a vulnerability she rarely lets anyone see.

"I've never even been on a plane," she admits. "And the nicest hotel I've ever stayed in was the one I had to share with Decker at the away game in Georgia at the start of the season."

"Joey." Tilting forward, I wrap her up in a hug. "You deserve nice things. You deserve the *best* things," I assure her. "If Decker and the guys want to take you on some fancy-schmancy vacation, let them."

She sighs, returning my hug and sinking her weight into me.

"You're right. I need to get over myself," she admits with a long breath out. "But I promise we won't be gone the whole time. I definitely want to see you over winter break."

My heart aches in a good way. This woman is the best kind of friend. I want her to enjoy her time off with her men, but I can't deny that I'd love to spend some time with her, too. "Of course."

"What are your plans?" she asks.

I squint, working to visualize my calendar without pulling my phone out. I can't look at that text message again. Not now.

Exams are this week. Next week will be low key while I rest and recover. I don't have a clue what the end of the month will bring.

"I'm not sure," I admit. Hopefully Levi's mom doesn't use the holidays as an excuse to pressure him to stay with her or to go along with any of her ridiculous plans. "Maybe we'll head up to Dr. Ferguson's cabin, too."

It would be a nice reprieve from the day-to-day routine. And getting Levi out of town might be a good idea. I make a mental note to talk to Greedy later.

"I need gift ideas for Sam," Joey muses. "And Jeannie, I guess."

That last part is said much less enthusiastically. Her uncle's secretary at the salvage yard means well, but she's a lot.

"Do you think you'll see any family over the holidays?"

Lips pressed together, I consider my options.

I haven't actually been home for the holidays in three years. I have no interest in visiting with my dad's side or partaking in any celebrations with his new family in France. My mom's still MIA, thank goodness, and she doesn't have any living relatives in the area. I assume it'll just be me, Greedy, Dr. Ferguson, and now Levi.

Joey, likely reading my mind, squeezes my hand, assuring me. "You have me. And my guys. We're your family now, too."

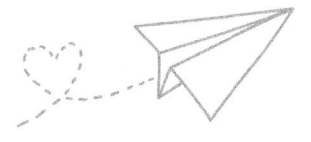

Chapter 22

Hunter

THEN

Greedy enters a code into the keypad, then pushes the oversized front door open. With a grin, he snags my hand and tugs me inside. "Come on. I want to give you a grand tour before everybody else arrives."

The drive through the mountains was breathtaking. Back home, we're surrounded by lakes and water, and yet we're just a few hours away from a magnificent snow-capped mountain range.

Hints of leather and evergreen tease my senses as I turn in a slow circle in the grand foyer, taking in the gorgeous details around me.

When I think cabin, I imagine a small, shabby structure. This place? It's massive, and although the exterior is charmingly rustic, the inside is a marvel of sleek, modern design.

Huge windows make up an entire wall along the back of the house, creating the illusion that we're actually suspended among the trees.

Despite the crisp lines of the entryway and kitchen, the living room is furnished with a number of comfy couches and oversized armchairs. The scene makes me want to cuddle up and watch a movie. Or better yet, hunker down and get lost in a book.

"I got most of the frozen stuff," Levi announces as he carries in the first load from the car. "If you want to get this put away, I'll go back for the rest of it." He moves through the cabin like he knows exactly where he's going.

The three of us drove up together, Greedy behind the wheel and me riding shotgun.

Levi sat in the back but insisted on controlling the radio.

He has a real affinity for country music, and he claimed it was a must for a drive through the mountains. Greedy begrudgingly agreed, but only after I chimed in and admitted that I like listening to country sometimes, too.

The roads were winding and nearly abandoned, only adding to the charm of the clear, sunny afternoon.

"This place is amazing. How often do you come here?" I ask, running my fingertips along the sleek brown and cream marble island in the kitchen.

Greedy looks up from where he's unloading the bags Levi brought in. "A couple times a year. Any time my dad is off for more than a day or two at a time, he wants to come up this way and go fishing. We also spend most holidays up here."

He quickly stashes the freezer items and circles the bar. When he's close, he moves low and nudges my nose with his.

"I'm so happy you're here this weekend."

Grinning, I wrap my arms around his neck and push up onto my toes. "There's nowhere else I want to be."

I press my lips against his, but the front door slams before we can take things further.

That's okay. We have all weekend together.

We have all summer ahead of us, too.

"Come on," Greedy coaxes, taking my hand. "Let me show you around."

He guides me through the main level and gives me a quick tour of the bedrooms and the game room in the basement, which features a massive pool table.

"The hot tub's off that deck," he tells me, pointing to the porch from the lower level.

We head up one set of stairs, where he points out more bedrooms, then down another. At the end of one hall, we're met with a staircase that's narrower than the last.

With a squeeze of my hand, he takes the first step, and I follow.

He looks back a few times, grinning. "Are you ready?" he asks.

"For what?" I can't help but match his smile. My heart has tripped over itself more than once on this tour. Every time he looks at me with that twinkle of excitement, it gets hard to breathe.

Still lit up like it's Christmas morning, he shows me into the primary bedroom. It's cozy and intimate, with low slanted ceilings that tell me we're probably on the very top floor.

I step into the room and release his hand while I scan each furnishing. I'm still taking it all in when Greedy comes to stand behind me.

He wraps his arms around my waist, then rests his chin on my shoulder. "King-size bed," he murmurs, tipping his chin to another door. "Plus a massive bathroom with a really great soaking tub."

That sounds like heaven.

"There's a private balcony off that door," he says, pointing to a little Juliet balcony. He unwinds his arms from around me and takes my hand again. "But this is what I really wanted to show you."

He leads me past the bathroom and the bed before coming to a stop in front of a door I didn't even realize was there.

It blends in, as if it's just another piece of the wood-paneled wall.

He turns and zeroes in on me, still wearing that grin, as he pushes against the panel, transforming it into something like a lever. He pulls it down, and suddenly the door-size panel swings in on itself.

Greedy holds my hand tight and watches me as he guides me into the hidden room. When I look around and take it all in, I gasp.

The space is almost the same size as the primary bedroom. But instead of featuring art or blank walls, almost every inch of space is covered in built-in bookshelves and filled with books.

My heart beats an erratic rhythm as I take it all in.

Forget the soaking tub and the massive bathroom. *This* is my personal version of heaven.

There's a chaise lounge in the middle of the room, and a little coffee table and a drink cart at one end. Near the window, two more upholstered seats are arranged.

I can only imagine how beautiful the light looks when it's shining through first thing in the morning.

"This is amazing," I whisper, heart lodged in my throat. "What is this place?"

"This is the library. My mom loved to read," he replies, scanning the space, as if re-familiarizing himself with it. "This room was her hideaway. It's filled with her favorites, along with plenty she bought and never had the chance to read." He gives me a soft smile then. "She died when I was seven."

I wander to the closest shelf and trace the ridges of the spines at shoulder height. The room is slightly stuffy in that old book library sort of way. I love it.

"Thank you for sharing it with me," I say to Greedy, who's standing in the middle of the space, watching me.

His answering smile makes the butterflies flutter deep in my belly. "You're still okay staying in here for the weekend? Just you and me?"

Anticipation swirling inside me, I bite down on my lower lip and nod. We talked about this. Going to the cabin, sharing a room.

I want to be here. I want to be with him.

Greedy pulls me into a hug and kisses the top of my head. "I'm so happy you were able to come with us this weekend." Taking half a step back, he tips my chin back to kiss me on the lips.

It's an unhurried, tender kiss. Even when I try to nip at his lip and take it further, he holds back.

"We have the next three days together, Tem. We don't have to rush. It's just you and me."

Him and me.

I can't wait to spend every minute we have here with him.

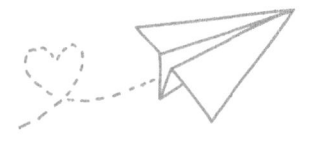

Chapter 23

Hunter

THEN

"Who needs a refill?" Levi rises from his camp chair and stretches his arms overhead.

There's nine of us here now.

Three of the guys graduated with Levi and Greedy and played football at South Chapel, too. They each brought someone, so in total it's four couples, plus Levi. There's Russell and Riley, Bruce and Dorothea, then Luca and Sully. Until tonight, I'd never met any of them, but they've all been friendly and really chill.

The sun set about an hour ago, and the temperature dropped quickly. The campfire blazing beside the picnic table where most everyone is seated helps combat the cold, but we're all bundled up in hoodies and blankets to fend off the cold mountain air anyway.

SO WRONG

I've lost count of how many games of Stop the Bus we've played at this point. Luca and his boyfriend Sully are super competitive. They've insisted we play "single elimination tournament style," and are taking the game way more seriously than the rest of us.

"I'll take another beer." Russell holds his red plastic cup high.

"I'm good." With a smile at Levi, I sigh and rest my head on Greedy's shoulder.

The warmth of him seeps into me as I survey the group stationed around the table. I didn't know what to expect when Greedy invited me, but I'm far more relaxed than I anticipated I'd be surrounded by strangers.

"Do you mind if I have a drink?" Greedy kisses the top of my head as he grasps a belt loop on my jeans and guides me so close my back is pressed firmly against his chest.

"Go for it."

With a chin tip in Levi's direction, he says, "Bring me one of those fruity seltzers, Leev. Strawberry or peach, if we have it."

Levi smirks but doesn't make any other comment as he takes off toward the cooler.

"You actually like hard seltzer?" I tease.

He sweeps my hair to one shoulder, then tenderly kisses the exposed skin on the other side. "It's okay," he says, his warm breath skating over my skin. "I just don't want to taste like beer when I finally get you alone and kiss you properly."

A shiver rolls through me at the promise of a proper kiss. The sensation turns into a full-body shudder when I consider all the improper things I'd like to do with him tonight.

Levi returns and passes out drinks, then a fresh hand is dealt around the table.

I'm doing my best to focus on my cards, but Greedy makes it damn near impossible when he slips his free hand creeping under my oversized sweatshirt and grazes my ribcage with his fingertips.

Every time he shifts beside me and touches me somewhere new, it sends warmth through my spine. So much so, my cheeks are flushed by the second round.

Greedy smirks, his eyes dancing with mirth.

Levi side-eyes us both a few times, his curious gaze making it clear that he's on to our little game.

I'm so flustered I can't remember which is the discard pile when it's my turn. Fumbling, I pick up a card, only to immediately regret it.

Levi's turn is next. With a wicked smirk, he says, "Stop the bus."

I groan. My highest card is an eight of diamonds. Dammit. I shouldn't have made that last swap.

"What's a matter, Tem?" Greedy teases. "Not happy with your hand?" He squeezes my bare hip with his hand for emphasis.

Rather than sass back about how his hands are the ones causing the problem here, I wait for everyone to show their cards, then lay mine on the table. Nose scrunched, I say, "I clearly made a wrong move."

"There are no wrong moves," Greedy replies, rising to his feet and taking my hand.

"I'm already out," I say, letting Greedy guide me away from the group. "Obviously, I made a wrong move somewhere."

On the opposite side of the fire, he sits in a camping chair, then pulls me into his lap. "But if you were still playing cards, I couldn't do this."

He ghosts his lips along the shell of my ear and loops his arms around my midsection, pulling me back so I'm resting against his chest.

"If you were still playing, they wouldn't still be distracted." He juts his chin toward the group. They're not paying us a lick of attention as the game continues. "I wouldn't be able to do this without someone noticing."

One warm hand caresses my stomach, then pauses at the waistband of my jeans.

My breath hitches, and a warmth that has nothing to do with the bonfire dancing before us spreads through my belly. Greedy toys with the button of my jeans, and in response, I arch back, seeking more contact.

"Life has a rhythm," he whispers. "Everything happens for a reason, even if we don't know what the reason is right away."

Deftly, he undoes the button. Then he slowly slides the zipper down, clearing his throat to cover up the sound. Not that it could be heard over the crackling of the fire, even if his friends weren't all still engrossed in the game.

When he brushes over my panties, I whimper.

"No wrong moves," he tells me, his tone steady and sure, as he slips that hand beneath my panties and cups my pussy.

"No wrong moves," I repeat breathily.

Holding me tight, Greedy teases and explores, caressing two fingers through my sex.

"I love this," he rasps, brushing one finger through the strip of hair along my pubic bone. "I can't wait to see how pretty you are down there."

Heat erupts inside me, and my face flushes hot. The sensation is quickly followed by a full-body blush. I'm warm from the tips of my toes to the crown of my head, but the heat between my legs is blazing and intense.

I squirm in Greedy's lap, my thighs desperate to clamp shut around his hand.

I want more. *Need* more.

"Open for me, Tem," he whispers.

With a deep breath in, then back out, I do my best to relax. Only the ache is worse when I spread my thighs and give him more access. New sparks ignite inside me at every touch. He's lighting kindling, building an all-consuming fire as he toys with me.

"Your panties are damp. Are you getting wet for me, baby?"

Fuck. "*Greedy*," I practically beg.

"Shh," he soothes, rubbing the pad of one finger over my clit. "I don't want them to hear you. I'd have to stop. You don't want that, do you?"

I shake my head frantically against his shoulder. An instant later, he pulls away, abandoning my clit. The loss of contact is so acute I shudder in defeat, but a moment later, he probes my entrance, instantly relighting the need burning deep inside me.

He takes his time, teasing and playing with my lips. It's as exploratory as it is erotic. He's testing every ounce of patience I possess.

When he finally pushes in, I exhale.

"Fuck. You're so warm, baby. So fucking tight."

My inner walls involuntarily flutter.

Greedy moans in my ear. "Fuck, baby. Do that again. Squeeze around my finger and let me feel you."

I give a tentative clench, and moisture trickles from my entrance. His words and the feel of him have me so ramped up, I'm half convinced I'm floating right now.

"Do it again."

With a groan, I obey. This time he thrusts up as I do it. He must hit some sort of internal nerve, because my whole body jolts in his lap, and a surge of moisture coats his hand.

"Good girl. Just like that," he encourages. "Good fucking girl."

Of its own accord, my pussy clamps around his hand. It's so tight it aches. It's the good kind of ache—a sensation that blossoms and grows with each stroke of his fingers against my inner walls.

"Imagine that's my cock inside you," he growls in my ear.

The moan that escapes me is so loud that the second it's out of my mouth, we both freeze.

We're getting carried away. Way, way, away.

I've never done anything intimate like this in public before. As desperate as I am to share everything with Greedy, I'd prefer to do it without an audience.

For a long moment, we sit silently, silently surveying our friends across the way. Thankfully, no one has even looked our way.

"Baby, we have to stop," Greedy grits out into my hair. "If you moan like that again, I'm going to come in my pants."

I giggle, then I nearly snort, too.

"You think that's funny?" he goads, slowly pulling out of me and tickling my stomach with his other hand.

I turn back, set on teasing him in return, but before I can, he captures my mouth in a searing, toe-curling kiss.

He makes quick work of buttoning my pants. Then his lips find my ear again. "You're going to moan just like that tonight," he promises. "But next time, my cock will be inside you."

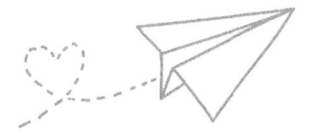

Chapter 24

Hunter

THEN

The room is darker than I expected. When we came up here earlier, it was filled with an ethereal aura, caused by the way the setting sun highlighted the warm wood. Now, the pitch-black night sky is dotted with stars, and the moon is the only source of light.

We fumble toward the bed, a mess of desire, all frantic touches and desperate kisses.

I'm a mess of nerves, too, as I'm divested of my sweatshirt and I step out of my jeans.

Greedy lowers me onto the mattress, then straightens and undresses. I watch each move, lost in the way the moon highlights every ripple of muscle.

His body is lean and hard in some places, but not in an intimidating way.

"You're sure, baby?" he asks from the foot of the bed, stroking his erection through his boxer briefs.

In answer, I sit and tear off my T-shirt. Next, I discard my bra, revealing my breasts. "I'm sure. I want you."

He joins me on the bed, his gaze flitting from my face to my chest and back again. His eyes shine with desire and reverence; hunger and lust.

"You already have me." He kisses me sweetly as I lean back and take his weight. "We don't have to have sex tonight. We have our whole lives to do this." With a sheepish smile, he brushes my hair away from my face, then cups my jaw.

Greedy looks at me like I'm worth being cherished. Like I'm a prize he can't believe he's won. His palpable desire makes me all the more sure that I want this—that I want him—and that there'll never be a more perfect moment than now.

"I want to have sex with you," I tell him, clear as day.

He grins, then his smile falters slightly. "I've never had sex with anyone before," he admits.

My eyebrows shoot up into my hairline. It shouldn't be that surprising, but with the way he was running his mouth and working those fingers earlier tonight, I thought for sure...

"Do *you* want this?" I ask, my heart pounding against my chest. He's asked for my consent multiple times; I should be extending the same consideration.

He drops his forehead to mine and closes his eyes. "With every fucking thing that I am."

Lacing my fingers into the hair at the back of his head, I kiss his lips assuredly. "I haven't had sex before either," I admit. "I'm not totally inexperienced," I rush to clarify. "There won't be any blood or anything. I just mean—"

He cuts me off with a searing kiss. "No wrong moves, Temi. You're my first and my last. I never knew what I was waiting for, but now I know it was you."

Sinking into his kiss, I revel in the way his lips glide over my mouth, my jaw, my neck, and my shoulders. I want him. I want this. I want to feel my entire body light up like a firework because of the connection we're about to share.

Greedy works his way down my body, kissing my collarbone and the space between my breasts.

I pop up on my elbows again, admiring him. "I've heard..." I swallow back my nerves and force myself to get the words out. "I've heard if the girl orgasms first, everything feels better."

Greedy freezes, his lips pressed against the top of my breast, right over my heart, then shifts back to look me in the eye. When his mossy-green irises find mine in the dark, they're smoldering.

"Baby, there was never any question about whether I was going to make you come first. It's only a matter of how." He dips his head and licks a line between my breasts, then pulls up again. "And how many times."

I gasp at the sensation, at the surety of his declaration, as a full-body shiver works its way through me.

Greedy pushes up into a plank position, biting his lip and studying me reverently. "These are such good tits."

I stifle a laugh, but then moan when warmth and wetness surround one nipple.

He doesn't just offer a playful nibble. He laps at my breast, alternating flicks of his tongue and long pulls with his whole mouth. He plays with my other breast, then eventually switches to lavish that one with the same kind of attention.

By the time he's starting in on my second breast, my hips are bucking beneath him, seeking friction.

"Fuck, baby. You love this, don't you?"

I whimper in response, focused completely on how every nip and kiss of my sensitive nipples creates a wave of undulating pleasure to the deepest pools in my core.

"Greedy," I plead, tugging at his hair.

Panting, he rests his head on my chest, his forehead on my sternum. "I know, baby. I know. I'm going to do that again, but this time, I'll do it on your clit, okay?"

I'm nodding. Panting. Shoving him down between my thighs without restraint. I want him. I *need* him. He's struck a chord deep in my soul. He's ignited a spark so visceral and heady I'm not sure I'll ever get my fill.

His first lick is tentative. He starts low, lapping around my entrance.

Then he curls his tongue and licks me from opening to clit. When he reaches my clitoris, not only does he kiss me there, but he gently spreads my thighs wider.

The light of the moon highlights his features as he gazes at my core. My whole body flushes as he really takes me in.

"You're beautiful, Hunter. I can't wait to see how you look when you're coming for me, baby."

With that, he dives in, devouring me as promised. He licks through my folds, holding my inner thighs open so wide they burn. He runs his nose through the trimmed strip of pubic hair, inhaling deeply, then suckles my clit.

He's everywhere, lapping at my lips, fucking me with his tongue, driving me higher and higher.

"Greedy," I pant, holding his head to my center and practically fucking his face. "I think I'm going to come."

He doubles down, sucking on my clit and grinding his face into my pussy until I topple over the edge. Waves of pleasure roll through me as my insides sing and my nerve endings dance in delight. My body is flying, soaring, cresting the wave and then somehow gliding even higher.

When it all becomes too much, I whimper and pull back.

Grinning, Greedy sits up and wipes an excessive amount of moisture off his face with the back of his hand. "If I don't have you right now, I might die."

I snort in response, and I don't even care if he hears it this time. I'm that comfortable with him. Then I pull him on top of me and kiss him deeply.

I can taste myself when I lick into his mouth, my arousal a tangy, heady flavor mixed with our saliva.

We're both breathless when Greedy pushes down his boxers and his cock springs free.

My hips lift on instinct, my body desperate to give and receive more pleasure, my soul aching to connect with his.

"I brought condoms," he tells me with a kiss to the tip of my nose.

"I'm on birth control," I offer, my heart stuttering as I tell him this next part. "I want to feel you bare."

His eyes widen and his breath catches. "You're sure?"

Nodding, I grasp his biceps. "I've never wanted anything more."

"I'll go slow. Tell me if it's too much, or if you want to stop, okay?"

"Greedy." I cup his face in my hands, urging him to look at me, desperate to tell him I've never experienced this feeling with anyone before. That I think I might love him. Instead, I say, "I trust you."

He guides his cock through my folds, using my arousal to lubricate his shaft. "You're so wet for me, baby," he praises.

I tilt my hips up, overcome by an almost animalistic need for him. "I want you."

"You have me." With that promise, he pushes in, inch by delicious inch, slowly but steadily filling my pussy.

"Holy shit," he groans, bracing himself with his palms splayed on the mattress on either side of me as we both adjust to the sensations.

I feel full—so deliciously full—but it doesn't hurt, nor does it feel like too much.

If anything, I want more.

I need him to move. I need him to fuck me.

I clench around his cock just like I did his fingers when we were sitting by the fire.

"Hunter." The groan that escapes him is guttural. "Baby, don't," he warns. "If you do that, this isn't going to last more than ten seconds."

Naturally, I do it again.

Grasping my face, he kisses me senseless. "I swear to god, woman."

We're both laughing when he finally pulls away, but his expression sobers when he gazes at the junction where our bodies are joined.

When he looks back up at me, his eyes shine with emotion. "This is the most spectacular moment of my life," he murmurs, the words hushed and reverent. "I don't want to rush it. I don't ever want to forget our first time."

He kisses me again, deeply, passionately, and then finally, mercifully, he begins to move.

He fucks me. I ride him. We make love, and we spoon. We both orgasm so hard and so frequently I'm afraid we'll dehydrate at this rate.

We spend hours moving together, connected in the most intimate way two people can be. Finding a rhythm and founding a love that I know, in my heart of hearts, will last a lifetime.

When we're both finally spent, we take a quick, steamy shower together, then we cuddle under the blankets and fall asleep in each other's arms.

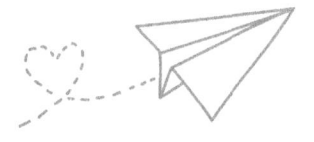

Chapter 25

Hunter

THEN

"Hey."

I gasp, startled by Greedy's presence in the doorway.

"What are you doing in here? Are you okay?" he whispers, his eyes filled with concern.

He's dressed in a pair of dark boxer briefs that sit low on his hips and nothing else, his body strong, hard, and lean. My clit tingles in a Pavlovian-like response as I take him in. It's impossible not to relish the memory of how it felt when his body hovered over me and he slid into me for the first time hours ago.

"I'm perfect," I assure him, sitting upright on the chaise lounge to make room.

"Why aren't you sleeping?" Yawning, he trudges into the room and joins me on the lounger.

With a low rumble of appreciation, he wraps one arm around my shoulders and rubs a hand over the soft T-shirt covering my arm. I grabbed the first thing I found when I stumbled out of bed a few hours ago—a clean shirt in the top of a dresser. The clothes we left strewn on the floor all smell like bonfire.

I rest my head on his shoulder and kiss his bicep once, then turn to meet his gaze.

"I slept for a few hours. This happens sometimes. Usually around the full moon." A yawn catches me by surprise. "I'm tired, but I'm more restless than anything. I don't like laying in bed fighting sleep. I usually just turn on my light and read."

"But you didn't want to wake me up," he surmises. He kisses my shoulder and breathes me in. "I wouldn't have minded, Tem."

"I know. I really like it in here, though." I scan the shelves, then take in the comfy furniture. I can't wait to see how this room glows when the sunrise streams in through the wall of windows.

"My mom loved this room."

Suddenly, a little pit of dread forms in my stomach. Have I overstepped or taken up space that wasn't mine to claim? Shit. I pull back slightly, tucking my legs under me to put a bit of distance between us.

"Is it okay that I'm in here?" I ask, fiddling with the hem of my T-shirt. "If it's weird for you, or if you want me to leave—"

"Hunter." Greedy gently grasps my arms and pulls me in so close I'm practically sitting on his lap. "I love that you're in here."

With his arms wrapped around my torso like this, the worry drains from me, and I sink back into his hold.

He loves that I'm here.

He wants me to be here.

In my heart of hearts, I believe him, and I know his words from earlier are true: he wants me.

Me? I want him, and I want to be his.

He yawns again, resting his cheek on the top of my head.

"You don't have to stay in here with me," I tell him as a yawn forces its way out of me, too. Eyes closed, I give myself a minute to snuggle against his chest, fully prepared for him to head back to bed and leave me to it.

He lowers his head and presses his lips to mine, inspiring goose bumps to erupt from my tailbone to the crown of my head.

"I want to be wherever you are." He releases me for a moment and slides lower on the chaise so his head is on my thighs and his feet dangle off the end. "I can sleep anywhere. Even with the lights on. You read. I'll sleep." He snags the book I have tented on the ground and lifts it overhead to hand it to me.

"Did you start this tonight?" he asks, scanning the shelves, as if to figure out where I took it from.

"I brought this with me," I admit, pulling my lip between my teeth.

He holds back his commentary but gives me a pointed look.

"I was being honest." I laugh nervously. "I'm not a great sleeper. I like to be prepared."

He yawns again. This one is so big it forces his eyes closed. He keeps them shut as he nuzzles his head in my lap and repositions himself until he's comfortable.

"We could swap out some of these books. This room is special, but the books aren't sentimental. I'll fill every one of these shelves with your favorites. This could be your library."

"Sounds perfect," I murmur dreamily, taking in the cozy space.

My library.

Created by my own perfect boyfriend.

For a little while, I stay like that, with my book on the arm of the chaise, and scrape my nails against his scalp. His breathing evens out, and just as I'm certain he's asleep, he speaks again.

"I want to tell you something."

"What is it?"

He doesn't open his eyes, and he doesn't sit up when he says, "I think I love you."

I freeze, even as my heart beats wildly in my chest. "Think?"

He's silent for a moment, then he turns his head in my lap and meets my gaze, his mossy-colored eyes swimming with confidence.

"No," he admits. "I know with every cell in my body that I love you, Hunter. I didn't want to say it earlier and make you think I was just saying it because—"

"I think I love you, too," I rush to reply.

"Think?" he asks, turning the question back on me with the quirk of a brow.

"I've never loved anyone before," I admit, running a now trembling hand through his hair. "My parents' divorce has made me realize that maybe I don't know as much about love as I thought. I always thought love meant staying, sticking around, seeing it through." With the shrug of one shoulder, I give him a soft smile. "My understanding is all jumbled up right now… but I think I love you, too."

"I'm not going anywhere," Greedy swears, leaning up until our lips come together in a tender kiss. "You think about it for as long as you need."

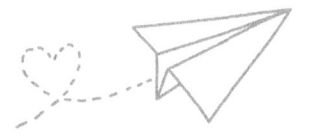

Chapter 26

Hunter

THEN

Summer soars by as lazy days and late nights blend together. Greedy and I spend as much time together as physically, humanly possible.

He stays over when my mom is out for the night. Or the weekend. We've ventured back to the cabin three times so far: once with a group of friends, and twice just the two of us.

Levi and Greedy lift weights and condition together every morning. They start early, since Levi is working for a local construction company this summer and has to be on site by seven most days.

Some nights, we've only just fallen asleep when Greedy's alarm blares and he has to drag himself out of bed to meet Levi at the gym.

I don't mind the early wake-ups. Sometimes I go back to sleep. Other times I stay up and read or watch makeup tutorials on YouTube.

Lake Chapel University sent a physical course catalog with my orientation packet. I've annotated and tabbed that sucker to death already, strategizing about how to double major in prelaw and gender studies.

In a few weeks, I'm set to stay on campus overnight for orientation. Maybe it's silly, but I'm giddy over the idea of sleeping in a dorm room.

We ventured out to the quarry today. It's off the beaten path and more popular with tourists than with locals, but Greedy swears the water's warmer than the lake. He also alluded to there being way more privacy out here than anything we'll find around Lake Chapel or South Chapel. We made great use of that privacy while we were sunbathing. And swimming.

Now I'm sun-kissed and sated as I head home for a much-needed shower.

Greedy and I met up at the QuickieMart before heading to the quarry, so when he brought me back to my car late in the afternoon, he insisted on buying me a strawberry slushy.

I'm sucking up the last dredges of icy goodness as I cruise down my street.

Our house is at the end of the cul-de-sac, and the neighborhood is filled with kids, so I always keep my speed slow. I've babysat half the kids who run wild around here, so it'll be strange to head off to college and to come home for winter break or even next summer and see how everyone has grown.

I navigate over the hump of our driveway—it's become more pronounced over the past few years as the road has settled. Once all four tires are level, I ease up and glance toward the front door.

From there, I do a double take. Then a triple take. I'd do a literal spit take if I still had slushy in my mouth.

I hit the brake so hard I lurch forward, making my seat belt catch. Then I throw the car into park and quickly unbuckle.

Shooting out of the driver's seat, I fumble to open the camera app on my phone. My hands are shaking—with surprise, with rage—as I snap a picture of the offending sign.

But before I can send a text to my mother, she calls to me from the open garage.

"Oh, good. You're finally here."

The bay doors face the neighbor's house, so from here, I can't see her. I stumble closer and crane my neck, searching for her in the darker space.

"Come help me with these," she huffs.

She's deep in the garage, hauling two oversized garbage bags my way. By the time I reach her, she's dropped one, and she's actively heaving the other into a dumpster positioned off to the side of the house that I'm just now noticing.

"Mom..."

She doesn't bother looking my way as she hefts the second bag overhand.

Exhaling loudly, she plants her hands on her hips. "I'm not as young as I once was, Hunter. You could put in a little more effort next time."

I'm still at a loss for what she's doing and why she needs help in the first place.

"Mom," I start again. Pressure has accumulated behind my eyes, but I bite down on the inside of my cheek to distract myself. "Why is there a for sale sign in our front yard?"

"Oh," she says, waving a hand. "I've been meaning to talk to you about that."

The copper taste of blood fills my mouth. Dammit. I've bitten down so hard I've broken through flesh.

"You've been *meaning to talk to me*?" I repeat, voice wobbly. "About selling the only home I've ever known?"

"Hunter," she scolds. "Tone down the theatrics, please. You're going to give yourself premature fine lines."

Clearly unconcerned with my feelings, she marches back toward the house. I have no choice but to follow.

"I'm moving in with Gary at the end of the month," she says over her shoulder, so damn casual. "You'll have a room at his place, of course. You're welcome there during your school breaks and such."

I swipe away angry tears as I follow her up the stairs. I've never even met this man, and she's moving in with him? She expects *me* to move in with him, too?

In the mudroom, there are at least a dozen more trash bags waiting to be discarded.

My stomach rolls at the thought of the contents of all of them.

My mom doesn't do clutter. It seems impossible that she could find this many unnecessary items in our house. What if she's gone through my room?

One night, when I was in third grade, I helped my dad collect the trash and take it to the road. I couldn't quite lift the bag off the ground, but I tried my best, dragging it along the driveway just enough to tear a hole in the bottom. Then, when I reached my dad and he lifted it so he could heave it into the can, the bag split, and its contents rained down between us.

Rotten food, junk mail, and dozens and dozens of papers littered the cul-de-sac. The papers were all mine. Tests with perfect scores. Artwork I had been proud of. I even fished a picture of my dad and me at the annual "Donuts with Grown-ups" fundraiser out of a murky puddle.

For his part, Dad tried to cover for my mom, insisting that she must have mixed up the piles and unintentionally thrown out my things. He knew they were important to me. He understood me in ways my mother never bothered trying.

I wandered around the cul-de-sac, agreeing, as we cleaned up the mess, trying my hardest to hold back tears.

Just like I'm doing now.

But this time, the bags aren't broken. I have no idea what's hidden inside. I can't begin to fathom what possessions—what memories—she's heaving into the dumpster so casually.

"Don't just stand there, Hunter. Help me."

On autopilot, I snatch two bags from the top of the pile.

"When were you going to tell me?" I ask mechanically, my voice devoid of emotion as I follow her out of the house.

"You haven't been home much lately."

She's got me there.

We reach the dumpster and throw in the bags. There's an audible *clunk* when they hit the bottom. I wince as the sound echoes through the half-filled receptacle.

"Where does this Gary guy live? And will I have the pleasure of meeting him before I move in?"

My mom turns from the dumpster and assesses me, her green eyes hard. "I've had just about enough of your attitude. Gary is the real deal. He wants us to be a family. He's even hired movers for us. Just have your room packed up before you go to college next month. They'll handle the rest."

"So when I leave for college, I'll be homeless."

"*Enough*, Hunter. Your room at Gary's house will be as big, if not bigger, than your bedroom here."

It takes all my willpower to hold back a scoff. As if I care even one iota about the size.

I've never been a rebellious child. It's not in my nature to be disrespectful to any adult, but especially not my parents.

I can honestly say I don't know where the words come from or how I manage the sass behind them, but in this moment, something in me snaps.

"Will your divorce from Dad be finalized before you move in with Gary?"

I hear it before I see it.

It's quick and poignant, sharp and perfectly placed.

My mother doesn't even blink as she stares at me, as if she's just as dumbfounded as I am as I raise my hand to my heated cheek and rub the stinging skin where she slapped me.

"I said *enough*."

She did. So I guess we're done.

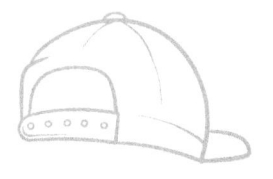

Chapter 27

Levi

NOW

God, I missed driving.

Nothing makes me feel quite as free.

The wind whips through the open windows of the cab of the truck as Hunter whoops and throws her head back in delight. I can't help but grin as we cruise down the road. Her laugh is contagious.

I've only been behind the wheel a couple of times since I got rid of the walking boot last week.

The freedom to go where I want, when I want, with whomever I please is liberating.

I didn't have a car out in California, and even if I could have driven it, I wasn't keen on driving my dad's old pickup when I got back to South Chapel.

Dr. Ferguson's got a garage full of vehicles, though, and Greedy insisted I drive his Silverado 1500 as long as I'm staying with them.

Hunter has dubbed it the Beast, and rightfully so. She has to use the footrail to get in and out, and the cab is bigger and cushier than any truck I've ever driven.

The Beast has amazing pickup, too. Every little bit I give it is returned tenfold.

The tires grip the road as I take the turns on the familiar two-lane highway.

Some of my best memories were made on these back roads with Greedy, going to and from football practice.

I steal another glance at Hunter, grinning even wider as I take her in. Just looking at her takes away any lingering pain.

She's got the passenger seat reclined and her feet tucked under her as she watches the world whizz by out the window.

She's beautiful. Effortlessly so. That's nothing new, but there's a lightness to her today that I especially love. A lightness I've *missed*. She looks truly happy for the first time since I moved in.

She had a rough go of it last week while she finished her final exams. Then she holed up in her room all weekend.

After she hadn't emerged for an entire day, I texted to make sure she was okay.

I even brought up food on Sunday night.

For reasons unknown, she made herself scarce, and I was genuinely worried about her.

She emerged on Tuesday and acted as if she hadn't completely disappeared.

According to Greedy, it happens sometimes. She'll hide away and go quiet for a few days. He didn't seem concerned, so I tried not to be either.

Maybe she needed the time to decompress after exams. I suppose that makes sense.

Even so, worry eats at me. I know what it feels like to be low. I've experienced those dips. What could she be hiding from or running from that would make her feel like she needs a reprieve from it all?

For now, I'm just hoping she'll open up about it eventually. Understand that she can tell me anything. There's nothing she could do or say that would change my perspective.

She's one of my very best friends, and she's gone to amazing lengths to make the last few months tolerable for me. Not only tolerable, but possible. Sometimes even downright enjoyable.

At the moment, I'm pretty pleased with myself. I got her out of the house today, even if we have no destination in mind. We're just out for a joy ride, but having her sitting shotgun, listening to one of our favorite country stations, fills me with a joy I'd almost forgotten exists.

Greedy always teased us. He doesn't care for country music.

I'm not sure it's Hunter's first choice either, but she knows the words to a lot of the songs.

Damn, it's hard to keep my eyes off her, and every time I glance her way, I can't help but smile.

Is there anything better than driving a big truck with a pretty girl in the passenger seat?

"You look good, Daisy," I tell her. She does, and I'm honored to be the one who gets to see her like this.

"Ya think so?" she retorts, flipping her hair over her shoulder.

"Yeah, I do."

Hunter's gorgeous. She knows it, even if she's humble about it. She's quite possibly the prettiest girl I've ever met.

Hell, she's prettier than most models and actresses after they've been airbrushed and altered by whatever they do to people out in Hollywood.

Thinking about California doesn't hurt the way it did all those weeks ago. It's strange, but I feel at home in North Carolina. After everything

I've been through with my parents, I never expected to feel this way. Hell, I never expected to return.

I love this place.

I love this state.

I love the way the wind makes the hair peeking out from under my ball cap tickle my neck.

The way the air cools in the winter but never really gets cold.

The way the sun shines down like it's shining just for us.

I especially love that I'm a car ride away from the mountains or the ocean at any given time.

North Carolina's home.

Sometimes, it still hurts when I think about what I left behind. It took a while, but eventually I realized that the ache was for what could have been, not what actually was.

Trey hasn't reached out since a few days after surgery. It's how I expected things would go down. At least I had the physical pain of recovery plus rehab to distract me.

It wasn't hard to move on, because we hadn't gotten very far.

There was an attraction between us, sure, and a level of care, but Trey and I were really just getting to know each other.

It'd be foolish to call it anything close to love. Our relationship didn't have time to simmer or fizzle. It just... was.

It was, and now it's not. And that's okay.

A new song starts on the radio, one about spinning around on a dance floor.

"Oh, I *love* this song." Hunter perks up and clasps her hands at her chest. "Can I turn it up?"

"Be my guest." I readjust my grip on the steering wheel and settle back in my seat.

She turns the volume knob until the music is so loud I can't hear my own thoughts.

I brace myself. I know what's coming next.

Hunter belts out the lyrics at the top of her lungs. It takes all my energy to fight back a grimace and keep my expression neutral.

She's an awful singer. She's pitchy and loud, but that doesn't stop her from going for every note, her voice cracking half the time.

I swear I've never seen anything more beautiful than her sitting in this truck belting out a song she loves.

She must listen to more country than I thought.

I'm easing around a bend, compressing the brake, thinking I'll have to ask her if she's still a country music fan, when a twinge of pain shoots through my right quadricep.

Fuck.

Once I'm on a straightaway, I ease off the brake and flex my ankle to stretch it out. *Dammit.* That only makes it worse.

"Shit," I mutter, gritting my teeth as that twinge transforms into a full muscle spasm. With my hands gripping the steering wheel so tight my knuckles have gone white, I breathe through the pain.

"What's wrong?" Hunter asks, angling my way and turning down the radio.

A drop of sweat rolls down the center of my back as my upper thigh continues to seize. It's a white-hot, fiery pain. Each time it crests and I think it might be over, it builds all over again.

Out of all the moments… out of everything that could go wrong…

I glance over to find Hunter watching me, wide-eyed, with her lip caught between her teeth.

I want to erase the concern etched on her face. I want to rewind and take us back to ten seconds ago when she was laughing and singing, and we didn't have a care in the world.

Instead, all I can do is grit my teeth, hold the steering wheel tighter, and fight back tears as the pain ratchets up again.

"Charlie horse," I grunt out.

SO WRONG

My right leg, my supposed *good* leg, is cramping so badly I can't even form full sentences.

We're on a straightaway now, coasting downhill.

Which is damn lucky, because there's no way I could hit the brake if I needed to.

The bend up ahead is going to be a problem. That curve will absolutely require us to slow down.

I know these roads like the back of my hand. So I have no doubt that it would be impossible to maneuver the truck around the next bend at our current speed.

My right leg hurts too fucking bad to be of any use.

My left leg is still healing and pretty numb.

There's a chance I can shift it over enough and put enough pressure on it with my hands to bring the truck to a stop.

The pain, though, might be too much to bear.

That only leaves one choice.

"Hunter," I say, keeping my tone level, "I'm gonna need you to get over here and help me stop the truck."

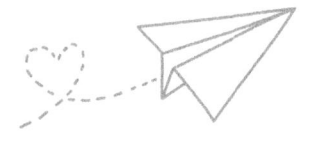

Chapter 28

Hunter

NOW

"I'm gonna need you to get over here and help me stop the truck," Levi informs me through gritted teeth.

His face is ashen and his jaw is rigid with pain, but I don't understand what the hell is happening right now.

"What's wrong?" I demand, already releasing my seat belt.

"It'll be okay," he assures me. His breathing is labored, totally contradicting his calm tone. "Just don't freak out."

"Levi Moore," I say, my heart rate ratcheting up. "Tell me what is happening *right now*."

Doesn't he know telling someone *not* to freak out is a guaranteed way to make sure they will, in fact, freak out?

"My leg's cramping," he says, grimacing in pain.

"Your injured leg?" I ask, peering over the center console to get a peek at it.

"No," he grunts. "My whole right quad is cramping. I'm afraid if I put pressure on my left leg, I'll reinjure it."

"Oh gosh. No. Please don't do that," I urge, shifting fully his way and popping up on my knees.

"I'm gonna need you to slide over here and press down on the brake for me, nice and easy."

Okay. That makes sense. I can do this. We've got this.

Gingerly, I climb over the center console while Levi keeps the truck steady. We're picking up speed as we coast downhill, and I've driven on these back roads enough to know this straightaway won't be straight much longer.

I take care to hover over Levi's body as best as I can.

"I don't want to hurt you," I mutter, wondering if I can squeeze myself between the center console and his body.

"Just sit," he grunts.

He's a big guy, and there's not enough room for us to sit side by side in the front seat, so I lower carefully.

"Fuckin' hell," he grits out when my ass brushes his thigh.

"I'm sorry," I whisper, shifting my weight so I can reach the brake from this angle.

"It's fine," he says, though his tone tells me he's anything but fine.

His whole body is wound tightly as I invade his personal space. We're so close that the notes of cedar and peaches I've come to associate with grown-up Levi curl around me and ease my fear a fraction.

I find the brake—finally—but in my haste, I compress it so hard the truck jerks, and I land squarely in Levi's lap.

"Nice and easy," he says, his lips an inch from my ear.

With a slow breath out, I compress the brake again, more gently this time.

"Yes. We've got this. You're doing great, Hunter."

How the hell is *he* the one reassuring *me*?

Levi keeps hold of the steering wheel with one hand and hits the blinker with the other, then wraps his right arm around my middle and readjusts.

As we come to a crawl and he edges the truck onto the gravel shoulder, he says, "Don't stop yet." His voice is calmer now, the timbre low. His breath is warm on my ear. He's so impossibly close. "Get us a little farther up ahead," he instructs, steering the truck where he wants it.

I ease off the brake so we continue to roll forward and focus on breathing evenly and calming my heart rate.

His chin grazes over my shoulder when he nods. "Right here."

Once we're completely stopped, I put the truck in park and close my eyes.

"Fucking hell," he groans again, resting his forehead against my back. He blows out a long exhale that warms my skin through my shirt.

Hands gripping the steering wheel, I lift up, careful not to hurt him, preparing to move back to my seat.

He stops me by tightening his hold on my torso. "Just give me a minute," he pleads, his voice shaky.

It's got to hurt to have me sitting on his leg like this. But if he's still cramping, sudden movements could make it worse, right? Shifting to his left leg isn't an option. Not only is his five-inch incision healing, but so is the muscle beneath.

Dammit. I hope whatever just happened doesn't negatively impact the progress he's—

"Shh..." he soothes.

"I didn't say anything," I snap back.

A soft chuckle rolls through his chest, shaking my body in the process. "I can hear you thinking."

"Are you okay?" I demand.

He relaxes back in his seat, his hand splayed over my stomach.

Though my heart is still pounding against my sternum, relief washes over me.

"Fuck, yeah," he says, his tone far lighter than it's been since this incident began. "The charley horse is over now. I'm so sorry I lost control like that. Are *you* okay?"

He slides his big hands over my shoulders, urging me back until I'm leaning against his chest.

I let him guide me, then tip my head to meet his gaze. "I'm okay," I promise.

With his hands still in place, he watches me, and I watch him in return, our hearts hammering in our respective chests.

I blow out a long exhale, willing my body to settle.

It's adrenaline. That has to be what I'm feeling.

"Hey," Levi says, running his hands up and down my upper arms.

I'm wearing an off-the-shoulder sweater, so the tops of my arms are bare. Each time his fingertips tickle the skin, another little shudder rolls through me.

"You're okay. We're okay now," he assures me.

It's not the situation with the truck that has me shaky, though.

It's the situation happening right now.

Sharing breath with Levi. Sitting in his lap. Soaking in the heat of his body pressed to mine, yearning to be closer.

"We're safe, we're okay, we're okay," he repeats, his blue eyes set on me in concern and his gaze honest and sincere.

I nod, but I don't trust myself to speak. Not with the way my body reacts each time I inhale his sweet and spicy scent. Or with the electricity that courses through me when his fingertips brush over my skin.

"Hunter. Tell me you're okay," he demands.

When I don't answer immediately, he scoops up my legs and cradles me in his lap.

"Leev," I protest, dropping an elbow to the console to take weight off his lap. The way he's holding me won't solve my current predicament, that's for damn sure.

"Hush," he admonishes. "You're allowed to feel whatever you need to feel, Daisy."

What I *feel* is heady attraction. A magnetic pull that grows with each shared breath. Every cell in my body is humming the same desperate pleas: *More. Closer. Now. Please.*

I nuzzle into the soft fabric of his long-sleeve T-shirt to hide my visceral reaction. It's a pretty aquamarine green, not unlike the South Chapel school color.

Breath held—*literally, because I do not need a reminder of how good he smells*—I do my best not to let his essence wash over me or fuel my libido any further.

After a few more seconds, I pull myself together and lift my head.

"I'm good now, I swear." I offer him a tight-lipped smile, hoping like hell he can't read me like an open book. Like an open, smutty, deliciously spicy book.

Levi's not looking down at me like I expected him to be. In fact, by the hard set of his jaw and the way his eyes are darting around the cab of the truck, he's doing everything in his power to *not* meet my gaze. Moments ago, he was holding me to him, but now, he's got one arm resting on the open windowsill and the other on the center console.

"Wait, are *you* okay?" I ask, my stomach sinking. I was so caught up in my own head—or maybe my own vulva—I didn't think to check in with him.

That was scary. Adrenaline must be blasting through his veins like rocket fuel.

"Levi," I press, cupping his jaw with one hand and forcing him to look at me. "Answer me. Are. You. Okay?"

"Uh, yeah," he rasps, far too quickly. Then he lowers his head to hide his face behind the brim of his hat. "I'm good, I swear."

Okay, then...

"Does your leg hurt?"

"Leg's fine," he grunts.

"Does your other leg hurt?" Maybe I'm being a bit of a mother hen, but something's clearly wrong, and he's giving me nothing to work with here.

He sighs, a long, exasperated exhale. Then he lifts his ball cap, runs one hand through his hair, and places the hat back on his head. Instead of looking at me, he sets his sights out the windshield.

We're pulled over far enough that the truck is semi-hidden from view of the road.

Not a single car has passed since we eased off the road anyway. These back roads are rarely busy.

"*Levi*," I plead. "You can talk to me. *What's wrong?*"

He lets out a self-deprecating laugh that fills the cab. "*Fucking hell.* Nothing's wrong," he huffs. His cheeks flush as he works overtime to avoid making eye contact.

Changing tack, I put a hand to his chest and ask, "What can I do to help you, then?"

He shifts back like he's trying to make space that doesn't exist. "Just get back in your seat so I can drive home."

Wait—*what?*

This sudden coldness is a shock, and I don't like his tone.

"Hunter," he warns, tipping his chin toward the passenger seat. "Just do it."

I raise one eyebrow, but I don't budge. "Seriously?"

His nostrils flare in response to my challenge.

It's cute when he's huffy.

"I've never been more serious about anything in my life," he declares.

Why the hell is he being so dramatic? Whatever the reason, he might as well have just flipped a switch in my brain.

Brat Mode activated.

Arms crossed over my chest, I lift my chin. "What if I don't want to get back over in the passenger seat?"

With a harsh breath in, he studies me through narrowed eyes. "Then we're gonna have a real situation on our hands."

I purse my lips. "Oh yeah? And what kind of situation would that be?"

He exhales, a low rumble vibrating through his chest. His entire face is beet red now—from the dimple in his cheek to the tips of both ears. "You really want to know?"

"Try me."

"Well, Daisy. There's not a polite way to explain it, so I'll just come out with it. I haven't been able to get it up since my surgery, but my cock is rock hard right now with you sitting in my lap."

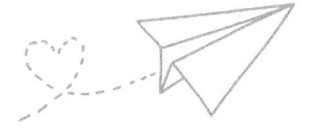

Chapter 29

Hunter

NOW

I'm frozen, my mouth wide open, staring back at him with a mix of shock and heat swirling in my belly.

"You really haven't been able to—"

"No." He works his jaw from side to side as he searches out the window once again. "They said it was a possibility. That it would be temporary, from the nerve damage. They warned me it might take a few weeks. Or even a few months. I wasn't exactly worried yet, but..."

"Hey," I soothe, cupping his jaw and guiding his face so he's forced to look at me. "I already asked once. But now I'm going to say it again. What can I do to help you?"

Levi ducks his head, his breath hitching. "You... you want to help me?"

Slowly, gently, I brush my fingertips up the length of his jean-clad thigh.

I give him plenty of time to stop me. To pull back or tell me this isn't a good idea.

With each second that passes—with each second that he lets me touch him, allows me to grow closer—my hope grows. So does my curiosity.

I'm both shocked and delighted when I discover the evidence of his rock-hard cock much sooner than I expected. Lip caught between my teeth, I meet his gaze. There isn't even a hint of embarrassment on his face now, that's for damn sure.

Good for you, Levi Moore.

The man is packing, and he knows it.

Applying the slightest bit of pressure, I run two fingers along his shaft.

In response, he throws his head back and hisses like I just deep-throated him.

"*Fuck.*"

"Is that okay?" I rush to ask. The last thing I want to do is to hurt him or to set back his recovery.

"More than okay." He captures my wrist in his hand and pulls it away. "But you need to stop. Unless—"

He cuts himself off there and blows out a pained breath.

"Unless what, Levi?"

"Unless you want things to go a hell of a lot further right here, right now."

My heart trips over itself. There's no need to stop and think about it. My decision's already been made.

Leaning into the arousal that's been churning low in my belly since the moment he pulled me against his chest, I inch my hand higher, toward the waistband of his jeans.

"Daisy," he warns.

"Duke," I snip back. "I don't want to stop," I admit, softer. "I want this to go a hell of a lot further. Right here. Right now."

"Fucking hell," he mutters, pinching his eyes shut.

Feeling bold, I squeeze his cock through his jeans. "If *you* want *me* to stop, tell me right now."

He groans in response. His dark blue eyes blaze with desire. "You want this?" he confirms, his husky tone sending shivers through me.

I bite down on my bottom lip and nod.

He dips his head and locks eyes with me. "You're sure?"

I love a man who understands and fully embraces consent. But *yes* means *yes*.

Right now, sitting on the lap of this man, my body lit up in such a visceral way, knowing he's hard for the first time in weeks because of me? I've never wanted anything more.

I brush at a loose strand of hair and tuck it behind my ear. Then I throw my arms around Levi's neck.

I want to be close to him. Even closer than this. I spin his cap so the brim is backward. Then I press our foreheads together.

"What kind of fake girlfriend would I be if I didn't help you out?"

Levi stares at me for a beat, and then another, silent, thoughtful. Finally, he pulls one of my hands free and guides it down his torso.

"Unbutton my pants, Daisy, and take what you want."

Desire clouds the air between us, filling the cab of the truck with a heady aura as I undo his belt with ease. I fumble a little to work the button of his jeans free.

He catches my wrist, steadying my shaking hand, mistaking my clumsiness for trepidation. "You're sure?" he asks again, the timbre of his voice so low the words rattle in my own chest.

I lock eyes with him, chest heaving. "Yes means yes, Duke. Don't you dare ask if I'm sure again. I want this. I want *you*."

His face transforms from genuinely concerned to devilishly cocky.

"I like you in Brat Mode, Daisycakes."

Before I can sass back, he releases my wrist, adjusts the driver's seat as far back as it'll go, and tilts his pelvis to give me better access.

"Take it out," he grunts.

I obey and instantly slip into a state of shock and awe when his cock springs free from his boxers.

I could tell he was big with that first touch, but this is beyond average-guy big. Levi is massive. His cock is long and thick, with prominent veins leading up to a fat crown that's already leaking precum.

"You want it?" His voice is heavy, laced with more of a southern twang than usual, and his eyes are hazy as he looks down at his dick.

I nod, frantic, desperate in a way that would be embarrassing with just about anyone else. I want to touch him so badly I ache.

"Prove it." His eyes are fire as he stares me down. But this isn't a contest. We aren't in a stalemate or a standoff of any kind. I am more than happy to oblige.

If he wants proof, I'll gladly provide it.

I pop the button of my own pants, then rise up on my knees. Thank god the cab of this truck is spacious enough that I don't hit my head on the ceiling and that I chose wide-legged loose-fitting pants this morning.

Without breaking eye contact, I slip two fingers under the lacy edge of my panties.

I squirm slightly when my fingers brush my clit, but I don't stop there. With a moan, I dip both fingers inside myself and skim over that perfect spot.

Before I get carried away, I pull my hand out of my pants, lock eyes with Levi once again, and hold out my glistening fingers for his inspection.

"Proof," I declare with a saucy smile.

He licks his lips.

He touches my wrist once again.

I hold my breath, waiting for him to put my fingers in his mouth. Instead, he lowers my hand. "Rub your cream into my slit."

I whimper at the command, but quickly do as he asks. Trembling with desire, I paint my arousal around his cock, taking care to rub it into the slit at the crown. Gently, I use my fingertips to pull apart the tip, widening the hole.

"Just like that," Levi encourages. He's just as transfixed as I am by the scene.

The heat in my core goes molten as I continue teasing. I'm so lost in my ministrations that I gasp when he captures my wrist again.

He lowers my hand to his shaft. "Spit on it," he demands.

I bend low and do as he says, aiming so it hits the tip where my arousal gleams.

When I lift my head, Levi uses his free hand to wipe at the string of saliva caught on my bottom lip. Then he promptly pops that thumb into his own mouth.

"I'm not going to last long." He covers my hand with his own and guides me, tugging his shaft with measured pulls.

I'm following his lead, giving tentative strokes, and he's writhing beneath me like he's already on the edge.

Panting, he tells me, "I was serious before. I haven't... been able to... feel anything... since the surgery."

He sets the pace, and once I'm comfortable with it, he releases his grip. Then he grasps the lower half of his dick. Our stacked fists find a perfect rhythm. We work in tandem, rubbing and squeezing.

"Fucking hell. You're doing so good for me, pretty girl."

A little thrill shoots through me. From the praise. At his confession. At the prospect of it all.

My own desire grows, wanton and sassy. Bold and loud.

More.

Closer.

Now.

Please.

Without slowing, I slip my free hand down my unbuttoned pants.

"Stop," Levi insists.

I freeze, heart caught in my throat.

He shakes his head and repositions my hand where he wants it on his cock. "Leave your pants on Daisy. Please." The request is tender and sweet. "There's no fucking way our first time is going to be in a truck where I'm bound to blow my load in under two minutes."

I don't bother arguing.

Instead, I spit on his dick again, then focus on spreading the moisture all over the top of his shaft.

He moves his hand lower once more, grips the base of his cock, then reestablishes the rhythm where we jerk him in tandem.

I rub.

He squeezes.

We're both breathless when his body locks up tight.

"Fucking hell, Hunter. That's it. You're doing so good for me."

His thighs tense, and he growls in warning.

I don't slow down or pull back. I want it. I want *him.*

Warm jets of cum shoot from his pulsing cock. The sticky substance coats our hands as I work him over without slowing.

He hisses and groans, offering words of praise between moments of breathless ecstasy.

So fucking good.

So fucking perfect.

You're doing so good for me.

Fucking incredible.

When his body finally stills, I slow and rest my head on his shoulder.

We're both quiet for a moment.

He holds me tenderly, keeping me close as he rubs one hand up and down my back.

I peer up and note the sheen of sweat glossing his forehead and the perspiration pebbling just below the band of his backward ball cap.

Levi guides my hand to his pants and rubs it clean. Then he shifts so he can wrap his arms around my torso, and he hugs me even tighter.

Arms looped around his neck, I lean in close and nudge him with my nose.

He springs to life then and blows out a long exhale. Sitting straighter, he hits me with one of those charming, cocksure grins.

He quickly puts his dick away, then readjusts his pants.

When he meets my gaze again, he tips his chin once, then drops his focus to my pants.

"Your turn, Daisy. Take those off and let me see that pretty little cunt."

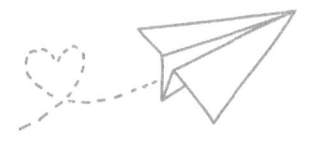

Chapter 30

Hunter

NOW

"No, no. It's fine. You don't have to return the favor," I stammer.

He reels back and gives me an incredulous look. "Your eyes are hazy, and your cheeks are flushed pink." With one thumb, he traces along my bottom lip. "What kind of fake boyfriend would I be if I didn't help you out?"

Desire licks up my spine. My linen pants are already undone, hanging open and showing off the lacy trim of my blush-pink panties.

I shimmy them down until they're at my knees and I can spread my legs wider.

Holding back a groan, I slip a hand down my stomach and watch Levi.

He's not looking back at me. His sole focus is on my fingertips as they inch lower. "Get that flimsy scrap of fabric out of my way," he orders huskily.

"They're called panties, Duke," I tease, stroking one finger over my mound and gently brushing my clit.

"I don't care what they're called. Move 'em, or I'll rip them off for you."

My heart lurches at the command. Talk about a gentleman in the streets and a freak in the sheets. Or in our case, the truck. I'm as delighted as I am intrigued.

"You want to see my pussy?" I purr.

He exhales loudly, his whole body deflating. "So fucking badly. I'm half-hard again just thinking about it."

I brush the fabric aside, revealing a small patch of hair and my clitoral hood.

Levi's eyes grow darker, his lids heavy. His chest rises and falls quickly. He's got his hands clenched into fists on his thighs, like he's holding himself back.

"Do you want to *touch* my pussy?"

"More than I've ever wanted anything in my life," he admits. "But you're going to have to teach me. Show me where to touch you and how you like to it."

He offers me his hand, palm up, two fingers lifted and ready. I bring them to my mouth, moistening them with my saliva, and then guide him so those callused pads brush my clit.

My core spasms the moment he touches me. I'm warm and wet, growing achier by the second as he locks in on what I like and starts to learn my rhythm.

He lets me use his hand, following my lead, adding a bit of pressure here or a pinch of my clit there.

"You like that, Daisy?" he croons. He keeps his attention fixed on the apex of my bare thighs, his tongue peeking out of the corner of his mouth as he concentrates.

"Yes. Fuck, yes," I preen, arching back as I chase the pleasure. I want more. I fucking need more.

"This is how you like to get off?"

I grip his hand so tightly I bet it's turning blue. I'm all twisted up, but it's still not enough. "More," I beg.

"More?" he questions, licking his lips as he meets my gaze.

More. The single word is all-encompassing. I need more pressure. I crave more grit. I love oral. I can come from G-spot stimulation, too. But I can't get myself off with just my own hand. Give me a toy... or two. Give me a man—his cock, or his tongue; doesn't matter.

Suddenly, I'm not sure I can get off, and the last thing I want to do is explain that to Levi. It's not his fault. It's not even my fault. I just know what I like, and I know what I need. My brain goes into overdrive as intrusive thoughts plague me.

"I like it rough," I admit, resting my head against his shoulder as he works me over.

"Fucking hell, Daisy. You can't say stuff like that to me," he groans. "I don't have a condom on me."

Resignedly, I exhale and sink into his lap.

With one finger on my chin, he tips my head back, gently forcing me to look at him. "You could grind on me. Would that work?"

It would, but I can't do that to him. "Your legs," I remind him, defeated. There's no way I can bear down on his incision, and with the way his other quad just gave out—

"Who said anything about a leg?" He hits me with a devilish smile, then stretches out his arm and rolls back his sleeve. He works it all the way up to his elbow, then flexes his forearm in front of his body.

Once he has his forearm positioned between his thighs, he looks to me with his brows raised expectantly.

"Well?"

Arousal slips from me, coating my inner thighs. His forearms are incredible. Tanned and covered in light blond hair. Muscled and strong. Thick and impossibly hard. I'm too far gone to look a gift horse in the mouth.

"Tell me if it hurts," I whisper, lowering myself onto him. For a moment, I graze my core against him so I can feel the ripple of tendons each time he flexes. I hover for a breath, closing my eyes and giving in to the moment.

Then I sink down completely and let him take my weight.

The flame inside me that had almost banked sparks back to life instantly. "*Oh*."

"A good *oh*?"

"A really good *oh*," I tell him. The contact is so intense I could cry. The pressure is everything I need and exactly what I was craving.

He twists his arm slightly, the muscle shifting against my clit with each flex. "Ride me," he demands, keeping his arm locked in place.

Slowly, I roll my hips, finding my pace, moaning every time my clit presses into his flexed tendons. In no time at all he's coated with my slickness from wrist to elbow.

Chin tucked, I zero in on our connection, watching as I slide up and down. It's erotic, and it feels exquisite. Every shift of my hips adds more pressure. Every flex of his forearm ratchets up my desire.

"I'm close," I pant after a few minutes of steady pressure. "I'm so close."

"Eyes on me, Daisy. I want to watch my girlfriend's face when I make her come for the first time."

Obediently, I tear my attention away from his soaking wet forearm as I grind my pussy against him and chase my release. Eye contact only ramps up the ecstasy overtaking me. My mouth falls open as the first coil of pleasure reaches maximum tautness and my body snaps.

"Fuck, yes, *yes*."

I don't look away as I grind out my orgasm.

"Thatta girl," he tells me, nodding and biting his lip as my insides sing with pleasure.

Even after my body has been wrung out and my pussy is done spasming, I don't drop his gaze. The look of pride he's wearing is almost too much. I grin back, then bury my face in his shoulder.

For several moments, he rubs my back and murmurs sweet words in my ear. My breathing is still erratic, but my racing heart has little to do with the amazing orgasm I just experienced. No, it has everything to do with the word Levi used when he referred to me. This man just called me his girlfriend.

And there was no mention of the fake part this time.

Chapter 31

Greedy

NOW

"Good evening, Mr. Ferguson. Right this way."

Though it's completely unnecessary, the concierge guides me to the table.

My father is a creature of habit. He sits at the same booth and orders the same entrée each time we come to Virtues.

It's a ridiculous name for a fine dining restaurant.

Though I don't know that any name would be fitting of a fine dining restaurant in the middle of a hospital.

It may seem like an odd location, but it probably comes in handy when it's time to entertain board members or conduct important meetings.

The space hasn't changed in years. The walls are dark blue, and as always, every table is lit by candlelight. It has an intimate feel, though that may be in part because the restaurant's mostly empty.

We're meeting up for a late dinner. Eight o'clock was the earliest I could pull off this week with the new offseason training schedule. My dad will work until the early hours of the morning like he does most nights, so it worked out okay.

"Hey, Dad."

He stands to pull me into a hug. "Hey, yourself. I'm glad we could find a time that works. Sit, please."

Once I've taken a seat, I sip my water and browse over the specials. I only look as a courtesy. We've come here enough over the years that it's entirely unnecessary.

Many a birthday and celebration dinner have been hosted at Virtues. Not that I'm complaining.

The food is excellent, and I'm grateful my dad makes time for me.

More often than not, he works upward of one hundred hours a week, but he makes an effort to eat with me as often as he can. When I was little, my mom would bring me up to the hospital for lunch in the cafeteria. After she died, my dad hired a driver whose soul mission was to get me home from practice and to the hospital a few nights a week.

My dad's an amazing man. He's a brilliant surgeon, a great leader, and an exceptional father. He's never made me feel like I'm a burden. He's not perfect, but he always puts forth the effort. I strive to be like him in so many ways.

"Where are you coming from tonight?"

"The gym. I was there lifting with some of my teammates." I leave out the part where I was also leading a team meeting with next year's returning players.

We had an outstanding season. We ranked second in the conference, coming so damn close to a bowl game we could taste it.

After a few weeks off to recoup, we're back at it with offseason workouts and film review. Our core group of guys is already hungry for next season, and I'm fucking here for it.

"It's pretty late for a workout," my dad remarks, perusing the menu himself, as if he's not going to order the same thing he always does.

"A few of the guys are still finishing up finals, so we tried to accommodate their schedule. I could work out alone, but I like the group dynamic," I admit.

A server comes by and takes our orders: a filet for Dad, and a porterhouse for me. We order mushrooms and broccolini to share, then each request a loaded baked potato, hold the bacon.

He hands over his menu and assesses me over the rims of his glasses. "How did your classes end up this semester?"

"Really well. I'm still waiting for two exams to be posted. I barely squeaked by with a B in organic chemistry, but I'll still make the honor's list."

My dad laughs. "Apple doesn't fall far from the tree there. I hated organic chem with a passion." He clears his throat and takes a sip of water. "What else is new?"

It's not a loaded question, but it carries a bit of heft to it. He's trying to feel out my plans for next year. Surmise which medical school I'm leaning toward. Where I might end up.

What I haven't had the heart to tell him is that I'm planning to stay at South Chapel for one more year. I want to play football for one more season.

Med school can wait. My MCAT scores will keep. I haven't deferred quite yet, but I've already made up my mind about it.

"Just looking forward to a few weeks of calm before spring semester begins."

"No senioritis yet?" he jokes.

With a huff of a laugh, I bring my water glass to my mouth to avoid having to actually reply.

"Your Uncle Philip called yesterday."

Philip, who isn't actually related to us, is my dad's best friend from college. He's an anesthesiologist who lives in Ohio. He's very well connected at Case Western Reserve, which is one of the schools where I've been accepted.

"How's he doing? Did he mention the girls?" I ask, referring to his two daughters.

"They're all good." He dips his chin. "Gracie will graduate in May and is anxious to hear back from a number of schools. Makayla's about to start her residency with Cleveland Clinic. He was asking after you, of course."

I curl my hands into fists but keep them buried in my lap.

Then I sit up straighter, bracing for impact.

"So. Have you made any decisions?"

I take a sip of my water, wipe my mouth with my napkin, rearrange it in my lap.

Only then, when it's painfully clear that I'm doing everything in my power to stall, do I look up and meet my dad's gaze.

"No," I tell him truthfully. "I haven't picked a school."

With a steadying breath in, I garner all my courage and will myself to get this over with.

"I'm considering deferring and doing one more year at SCU."

His expression remains placid as he absorbs my statement.

He's always been steady—even tempered, emotionless, and practical when needed. That's why he's a damn good surgeon and has worked his way to chief physician.

"Another year at South Chapel," he repeats, rubbing at his jaw. "Because you need to? If it's a matter of making sure you have enough credit hours—"

"No, nothing like that," I assure him. "Academically, everything is fine. They offer a few electives I'd love to take while I have the chance, and I'd really like to play one more year of football."

His brows furrow ever so slightly with the admission. He looks pensive, but not at all surprised, like maybe he's seen this coming all along.

"It's your decision. If that's what you want to do, I think it's a great idea."

For a minute, all I can do is blink at him in surprise. "You do?"

"You only live once." He lifts one shoulder. "Might as well do it in a way that leaves no room for regret."

I have no idea where this YOLO mentality is coming from, but I know better than to question his opinion. I didn't expect my dad to completely reject the idea, but I was concerned that my decision would disappoint him.

Relief floods my system, followed by a sense of peace. There's a renewed determination brewing in my gut now that I have his full support.

"Selfishly, I'll be glad to have you home for another year," he admits. "Another year of dinners. A whole other season of football. Plus, now, with Hunter back in the fold—"

The server arrives then with our food.

Saved by the bell. Or in this case, a porterhouse.

Once everything is placed in front of us, we dig in.

My dad's words linger as visions of Hunter percolate in my mind. She looked so pretty when I passed her on the way out earlier. Hair down and wavy, minimal makeup and looking more at ease than she has since she reappeared.

I blink to clear my thoughts. To push her out completely would be impossible, but I need to make space to focus on something besides my stepsister. She's never far from my consciousness. Hasn't been for the last three and a half years.

An extra year of football also means an extra year at home with Hunter.

It's exactly what I need, because I'm not ready to give her up.

I'm not ready to give up on *us*.

An easy silence settles between us as we eat, though the moment my dad is done, he sets his silverware down and locks in on me. He folds his hands together and looks me right in the eye.

"There's nothing you could do to disappoint me, son. You know that, right?"

I nod and chew, ignoring the twinge in my chest. On the surface, it makes sense. But part of me does want to make him proud.

"I still fully intend to go to med school," I offer.

He smiles but shakes his head. "Even if you didn't, or even if you change your mind later, that would be okay."

The corners of my mouth ache with emotion, and pain radiates through my eye sockets as I fight back tears.

He's so understanding. Not everyone gets that. Hell, most people I know have complicated, if not downright dysfunctional, relationships with their folks.

My dad, though, has always given me his best, and more often than not, we see eye to eye.

I appreciate him so damn much.

I'm about to tell him that, but before I can, he opens his mouth and dumps a bucket of ice-cold water over my head.

"I'm especially glad you'll be home a while longer, because Magnolia's coming home for the holidays," he says, a tight smile pulling at the corners of his mouth.

My stomach sinks, along with my heart.

He knows how I feel about her. He knows how I hate her in every sense of the word.

Her being Hunter's mom.

"She's coming home, son. And this time she plans to stay."

Chapter 32

Greedy

NOW

"When?" I demand, pushing my plate away and rising to my feet. I've completely lost my appetite. I've got much bigger concerns all of a sudden.

"Garrett—"

"Answer me. When is she expected to arrive?"

I'm being rude. Disrespectful. I normally wouldn't dream of speaking to my father like this.

He probably thinks this is about my personal vendetta against Magnolia St. Clair-Ferguson.

In reality, this isn't about her. It isn't about the way she swooped into our lives and tried to erase all memories of my mom, then left my father for months at a time as she traveled the world on his dime.

Turns out Magnolia didn't want to be a doctor's wife. She just wanted the fringe benefits.

I hate how she treats him. I *loathe* that he allows it.

But this is so much bigger than them. It's so much bigger than me. This is about Hunter.

"When do you expect her to arrive?" I ask again, this time through gritted teeth. My patience is wearing thin.

Last I knew, she was in Spain. I keep tabs on her via social media. Try to make sense of her posts, her travels. Search for clues every time she unceremoniously crops back up on my feed.

She has a strange power over Hunter. One she wields with precision. Her words cut. Her actions maim. Magnolia St. Clair-Ferguson has the ability to unravel the one person I care most about in this world. That's why I hate her.

That's also why I need to know when she'll get to town. I have to get to Hunter before she does.

Phone in one hand, I dig my valet ticket out of my pocket. I have everything I need. Except an answer to the most important question.

"When is she coming, Dad?"

"She arrived this morning," he admits sheepishly. "She's at the house now."

Motherfucker.

I've got to get to Hunter first. I've got to get to Hunter *now*.

· ♥ · ♥ · ♥ · ♥ · ♥ ·

I'm going well over the speed limit down the two-lane highway, but I press it harder.

I can't get a hold of Hunter, but that isn't unusual. She sends me to voicemail or leaves me on read most days.

Levi, though, is usually better about answering. Only tonight, he's not picking up either.

Fuck, I hope they're still out somewhere together. Not at the house. Anywhere but the house.

That hope is dashed the instant I pull into our driveway. Hunter's car parked in its usual spot, next to the truck Levi's been driving. The rest of our vehicles, aside from my dad's car, are accounted for.

I come to a stop and slam my fist into the steering wheel, struggling to control my breathing.

Maybe Magnolia stepped out.

Maybe she called a car service or went out with friends.

Maybe...

Fuck.

I know in my gut none of those situations are likely. I'm not calling this game. I'm running defense with an outdated playbook.

With a sharp breath in, I will my pulse to level out and pull myself together.

Eyes closed, I focus on my breathing, but a vision floats through my mind, causing my anxiety to spike again.

I throw the car into reverse, pull halfway down the driveway, then park again, this time at an awkward-as-hell angle, essentially trapping all the other cars in the driveway.

If Magnolia is back, and Hunter was blindsided by her arrival, she's a flight risk.

Again.

I refuse to let her disappear from my life.

Not like last time.

Not ever again.

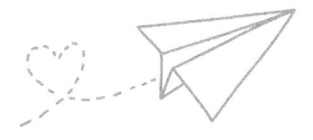

Chapter 33

Hunter

NOW

"Wait." Levi tugs on my hand, stopping me from opening the passenger door of his truck. His baseball hat is still backward on his head, his deep blue eyes piercing in the soft glow of the illuminated cabin.

I release my hold and turn to him, practically floating. Filled up with champagne and helium. Buzzing with the kinetic energy that accompanies the start of something new.

After the scary incident with the truck, then the memorable moment that followed, we stopped for dinner.

We talked and laughed the whole meal, just like we always have. Our reconnection was immediate that day in the hospital, but now? It's grown so much deeper.

I needed that release.

Finals week was a beast, and my anxiety has been flaring up big time over the last few days.

Tonight, Levi Moore gave me just what the doctor ordered.

Speaking of doctors... Dr. Ferguson's car is not in the bay where he usually parks. Greedy's truck is gone, too.

Greedy.

I've worked so damn hard to push him away, to keep him at arm's length. I make a point of acting distant and sometimes even mean just to get through the days when I have to be near him.

I hurt him every day. I know that, and I've long accepted this is how it has to be. It's the only way I can survive being in his orbit. It's the only way I can protect my heart and ultimately keep my secret.

He was peeved by the fake dating act. I can't even begin to imagine how he'll react when he learns that what Levi and I are doing doesn't seem so fake anymore.

It feels like we're hovering on the precipice of causing irrevocable damage. Levi and I have to tread lightly. Anything we do—whatever comes next—we have to consider Greedy.

"What am I waiting for?" I ask, tossing my hair over my shoulder.

He's grinning at me, his eyes locked on mine in a way so intense it makes heat creep into my cheeks.

I'm not embarrassed by what we did. In fact, I'll probably never be able to look at his forearms again without feeling all tingly and warm inside.

But with the way he's looking at me now...

"Come here," he urges, leaning over the center console and cupping the back of my head.

I let him guide me until our noses practically touch.

"Would it be okay if I kissed you?" he asks.

Sheesh. Again with the consent check-in.

Even after I rode his forearm like my own personal pony a few hours ago, he still feels compelled to ask.

What a flex. I love it.

I tilt my head slightly and part my lips, sharing his breath.

He smells divine. Like peaches and cedar.

I almost say yes.

But then I remember who's truck we're in. Who's house we're staying at. Who else is part of this equation, despite my very best efforts to hold him at bay and make him hate me.

"Daisy," Levi teases in his southern drawl, pulling my thoughts from Greedy and back to the present.

He's so close my tongue caresses his bottom lip when I wet my own.

The heat from his body soaks into mine, urging me to sink into his comfort. "Tell me I can kiss you. Please."

It's the please that does it for me. Always the southern gentleman.

"You can kiss me," I finally answer.

He presses his lips to mine in an attentive, chaste kiss. I open for him instinctively, touching the tip of my tongue to his.

A low growl escapes him as he forcefully pulls himself away.

"Dear god, woman," he huffs. "Just kissing you is a mind-blowing experience. I'm hard again." He sits back and roughs a hand over his face, as if it's truly a burden.

Smiling, I bow my head to hide the grin splitting my face. I also may or may not home in on the apex of his jean-clad thighs.

"Come on," I tell him playfully, opening the passenger door. "Let's go inside so you can calm down."

I unbuckle, then carefully step onto the running board before hopping to the ground.

By the time I've circled the bumper, he's waiting for me and reaching for my hand.

Glee washes over me when he gives me one of his dazzling Levi smiles. I grin back, interlacing our fingers and squeezing his hand.

Is this really happening?

Does he feel it too?

And if so, what does this mean for our arrangement?

As we weave through the garage, he keeps my hand in his, occasionally looking at me over his shoulder, still grinning.

"So can we count tonight as our first date?" he asks, that one dimple popping as he gives me a sheepish smile.

My body lights up at the suggestion.

We are absolutely on the same page.

Levi wants this. Levi wants *me*.

He drops my hand, then he quietly opens the door.

We make it all of three steps into the entryway before the hairs raise up on the back of my neck and I pull up short.

There's a soft voice coming from deeper inside the house. A voice I know. A voice I dread in the most visceral, stomach-churning way.

"Is someone—" Levi looks back at me, his brow furrowed in concern. Then he quickly positions himself in front of me.

As if that small gesture could protect me from the danger that has already arrived.

Ignoring the anxiety flooding my veins, I will myself to peek past Levi's shoulder.

I spot her immediately. She's striding through the kitchen, dressed to the nines. She walks with her head held high, acting like she owns the place. I guess, technically, she does.

"Hunter, darling! It's been too long."

Stunned, I stand completely still. I reel as every mental defense in my arsenal kicks in and my mind quickly works to re-erect boundaries I haven't had to worry about for years.

Levi takes a step to one side as she approaches.

My mother.

My mother is here.

My mother is in our house.

My arms dangle at my sides as she steps into my personal space and squeezes me tightly.

"Oh, let me look at you." She pulls back and smooths a hand over my hair. "I see you're going for the more natural aesthetic these days," she comments.

Except it's not a comment.

It's an insult.

It barely processes, though, because in such close proximity to her, my brain empties entirely.

I say nothing.

I do nothing.

I feel nothing as she assesses me up and down.

Levi clears his throat then. His face is marred with concern as he watches me.

Her eyes widen as if she's noticing him for the first time. "And who do we have here?"

He gives her a terse nod. "Levi Moore, ma'am."

She offers him her hand, head tilting to one side in a way she uses to trick people. "Charmed, I'm sure. Magnolia St. Clair-Ferguson."

The. Audacity.

They've met before. When Levi was younger. More boyish. Not so chiseled. He was dressed casually that day, making it obvious he didn't come from money. Of course she doesn't remember meeting him. She wouldn't have deemed him worthy of her attention then.

Levi clumsily shakes her hand, his gaze flitting from her to me and back again, brows furrowed in confusion.

My mom is here.

My mom is back in North Carolina.

I had no fucking idea she was even in the country.

Flovely.

I'm still rooted to the spot, digesting this information, when the door behind me swings open with such force it hits me and sends me barreling forward.

I put my hands up to catch myself but bump into my mom as I lose my footing, and the two of us tumble into Levi.

His quick reflexes are the only reason we don't end up on the floor. He's got an arm around each of us, his face fixed in a grimace.

A cacophony of apologies and outrage echo throughout the small room.

Levi helps my mom first, then guides me to my full height and keeps his arm wrapped around me.

Emotionless and hollow, I take in my mother. Then I turn to Levi. Finally, I force my attention to the person who just shoved into the room like a wrecking ball.

Greedy.

His eyes are frantic and his chest heaves with panicked breaths as he takes in the scene.

He looks at my mom, his face morphing into a look of disgust, then focuses on me.

His attention dips to where Levi has one arm wrapped around the front of my shoulders protectively, and his expression morphs into one of puzzlement.

Before anyone can speak, I spin out of Levi's hold, mutter something about not feeling well, and take off toward my bedroom.

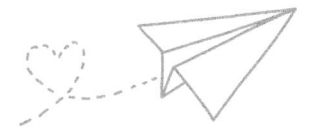

Chapter 34

Hunter

NOW

I'm numb as I enter my room. Turn on the light. Close the door.

Once I'm safely locked inside, I head straight to the French doors that lead out to the balcony and make sure they're locked, too.

Mindlessly, I walk into my closet next, pulling off clothing as I go. I rummage through sweatshirts and shift blouses and sweaters on their hangers. I don't even know what I'm seeking until I see it.

I settle on an oversized Oxford. It's ivory colored and made of the softest linen. It's so large I leave it buttoned and slip it over my head. Then I shake out my hair and pull on a pair of black leggings.

I locate my water bottle in the bathroom, fill it with lukewarm water from the sink, and then settle on the edge of my bed.

The urge to climb under the covers and stay hidden away will win out eventually—it's the safest coping mechanism in my arsenal—but for now, I fight it off.

There's one thing I need to do first.

Anxiety creeps up my neck and prickles under my skin.

The darkness buried deep is clawing its way to the surface, pulling me under inch by inch.

I'm tired of fighting. Of struggling to escape the past. Of willing the memories to die.

How long could I stay in this room until one of the guys forces their way in to find me?

My inclination is to run, but I'm so tired of running. For now, I want to burrow. I want to close my eyes and not worry about who will reappear in my life when I open them next. I want to disappear, if only for a little while. If only until this episode passes. Until she's gone. Until each breath doesn't take concentrated effort.

There's a knock at my door.

I ignore it.

A muffled voice calls out to me.

I ignore it, too.

Voices carry on in the hallway and the world keeps spinning without me. Just like it always does. Just like it always will.

My grasp on reality is slipping. *Good.*

If I sleep, I'll be safe.

If the darkness takes me and I can make it through the next several hours or even days in a state of unconsciousness, we'll all be better off.

It's easier if I'm not here.

There's peace in disappearing.

My lungs burn, forcing me to suck in a sharp breath, gasping on the inhale, then coughing on the exhale.

I wasn't purposely holding my breath.

To ensure I don't do it again, I take a long, slow breath in, then let it out.

Then I force myself to stand, to move, to make my way over to the nightstand on the left side of the bed.

I pop open the bottom drawer, then slip my hand under the lip of the latch, releasing the secret compartment.

Two phones tumble out from their hiding spot. Older models, both powered off.

I look from one to the other, then back again, waiting for my brain to catch up, then select the more expensive of the two, a deep sapphire blue device.

"Please, please, please." I hold down the power button, willing the phone to turn on. I don't remember when I charged it last. There's a good chance it's dead.

Thankfully, the backlight illuminates, and after a few moments, the device vibrates in my hand.

The SIM card isn't good in the States, so I connect to Wi-Fi and send off a message instead.

> **User 333221312:** This is Hunter St. Clair. I need an emergency session as soon as possible. You can reach me via email or at this number. I will check messages as often as I can.

I hit Send and wait. It's unlikely that I'll get an immediate response, but I leave the phone on anyway.

While I wait, I focus on steadying my breathing and double-check that I took my meds this morning. Then I walk around the room. I tidy messes that don't exist and turn the lights off, then on again before deciding I prefer the dark.

Eventually, I give up waiting for a response I know won't come and power off the blue phone. Then I stick it back in its hiding spot. I tuck away the hot-pink phone, too.

Once the cabinet is closed and my actual phone is plugged in and switched to Do Not Disturb, I pull back the covers, slip into the cool sheets, and finally, mercifully, let myself cry.

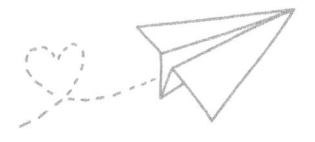

Chapter 35

Hunter

THEN

"Okay, boys. Next on the list: shower caddies." I march past an aisle filled with colorful storage containers and head for the toiletry section.

"What the heck is a shower caddy?" Levi asks, pushing one of the two carts.

I insisted they each have their own cart, and now they're dutifully following me down each aisle.

"Caddy, like in golf? Oh! Or like *Caddyshack*?" Greedy suggests.

"Dude," Levi drawls out. "*Such* a good movie."

"Let it happen," Greedy declares, then points to Levi.

"And be the ball," Levi finishes.

In unison, they break into laughter.

I would be exasperated with them if they weren't so damn cute together. Still, I don't want this to take all day.

"A shower caddy," I explain, waving my hand with a flourish like I'm on a game show, "comes in handy when you have to take your things back and forth between your room and the dorm showers."

Half the aisle is dedicated to different styles and colors. Naturally, I home in on the pink options, comparing a more compact design against a bigger model that comes with a shower cap and matching loofah.

"I'm pretty sure my dorm has an en suite bathroom," Greedy says, squinting at the rows of bins.

That makes sense. He's in the honors dorms at South Chapel. He's also a student athlete, so he'll probably shower at the field house most days.

Levi abandons his cart and comes to stand beside me. "I don't understand why I would need a container to carry my container." He picks up a dark blue caddy, frowns at it, then puts it back on the shelf.

"What do you mean by *container*? Like, all your toiletries and supplies?"

"I don't have toiletries. Or supplies." His face screws up in confusion. "I use a three-in-one shampoo–shower gel combo."

"That's two of the three, Leev. What's the third ingredient in your special sauce?" Greedy asks with a laugh.

Levi hums, genuinely considering the question. "I've never really considered what the third function is."

It's conditioner. At least I hope it is.

I poke Levi in the stomach. His abs tense in resistance, forcing me to jam my finger. "You're telling me," I say, shaking out my hand, "that you use the same product on your whole body?"

"Yep."

"Okay, fine. But you won't want your loofah or washcloth touching the gross shower floors," I argue. "A shower caddy would be useful for that."

"That's what God gave me hands for, Hunter." He holds both up, palms facing me.

I wrinkle my nose. "So you're telling me you use one single product—"

"A three-in-one product," he corrects, brows raised.

"And apply it with your bare hands? Therefore, you don't need a shower caddy?"

"Now you're getting it." He palms my head and musses my hair.

With a step back, I swat his big hand away.

"But I might get one to keep my Xbox remotes together," he muses, picking up a black utilitarian caddy.

"Oh, that's a great idea," Greedy says, snagging one for himself.

With a huff under my breath, I shake my head at their ridiculousness. Theoretically, I love back-to-school shopping. Fresh pens, new notebooks, and unopened packs of Post-its are my jam. Clearly, the boys don't share my enthusiasm.

This year, it feels like more of a chore than ever. Just one more item on the long list of things to get done before classes start, and I'm doing them all on my own. My mom and I are barely on speaking terms right now. It's not that I want her to be here for this, but it's hard not to wish that she wanted to share these kinds of moments with me.

She's officially moved out of the house and in with a man I've yet to meet. She's kept contact to a minimum, opting to text me a few times a week, mostly to tell me to tidy up the house and when to be gone for various showings.

I'm better off on my own. I know that. There's truly no coming back from our last interaction. Before that moment, she had never hit me. Yet I'm not even that shocked that it happened. If I needed a last straw, I found it. I hate that it came to this, but at the same time, I've been filled with a sense of relief since. It's finally over; the drawn-out dissipation of our relationship is done. Now, hopefully, we can both move on.

Warm hands graze over my hips, and then Greedy is hugging me from behind. He does this a lot. He gravitates to me when I'm feeling low or just lost in my own head. He's become my anchor, a safe harbor against the tempest that is my crumbling relationship with my mom.

He tightens his hold and rests his chin on my shoulder. "You okay?"

I didn't give him all the details about the altercation with my mom. He knows we had a fight. He knows our house is up for sale. Beyond that, I've compartmentalized the best I can.

For these last few weeks of summer, I want to focus on enjoying my freedom and time with Greedy. Even though we'll just be thirty or forty minutes away from each other, it won't ever be like this again. Soon, our lazy days and long nights will be replaced with two-a-day football practices and study groups.

Going to different colleges means there will be complications, but the way I feel about this boy isn't like anything I've ever experienced.

Greedy slotted into my life with kismet timing. He loves me in a way that leaves me feeling more fulfilled than anything ever has.

I wish things were different with my mom, but I don't have enough space in my heart to mourn the loss of her. Greedy lifts me up. Part of me hopes I never have to introduce him to her.

It's an unrealistic dream, but I can't stand the idea of my mom tainting the very best thing in my life.

Head tipped back, I sink deeper into his hold.

"I'm okay," I tell him. "I promise. I'm excited about my orientation overnight this week."

"I'm gonna miss you, Tem," he says, squeezing me tighter.

With a light groan, I unlace our fingers and tug on his arm so he loosens his grip around my middle. "I have the worst cramps today."

He instantly releases his hold on me, only to bring his hand to the base of my spine and knead the muscles there instead.

I practically swoon. He loves me so well.

"Do you want to come over tonight?" he asks. "I got all my stuff at Levi's packed up, and I'm planning to go back to my dad's place so I can start getting ready for school."

"Tempting," I tell him, "but I think I want to get packed up for orientation."

"Okay. Let's get this done so you can go rest." He kisses my shoulder, then takes the paper from my hand. "What's next on our list?"

With a hum, I scan the bullet points I created. "Hampers and laundry bags. This way, boys."

Naturally, they grumble about how they don't really need a laundry basket the whole way there. Greedy's clothes will be laundered as part of his student-athlete support services. Levi doesn't know the details at his school, but he insists he doesn't want to be the only guy to show up with a collapsible hamper.

"They're functional *and* fun," I assure him, perusing the options of springy mesh circles lined up on an endcap. "I'm getting pink."

"I don't know," he hedges. "I'm not convinced."

"When we come to visit you," I say, tossing my selection into the cart, "I don't want to have to wade through a sea of stinky clothes all over your floor."

He surveys me, then Greedy, his lips pulled down into a small frown. "You think you'll come out to California?"

"Of course," I tell him.

"We might not make it out until spring semester because of football," Greedy adds. "But you didn't really think we'd let you go out to California and forget about us, did you?"

A huge grin paints over Levi's expression. "You guys could come out for spring break," he suggests. "How cool would that be?"

"We could go to the beach," I chirp, already excited, though it's months away.

Greedy snags my hand and kisses my knuckles. "We have access to the beach here, Tem," he teases.

"I know." I give his chest a light smack. "But there's something dreamy about a California beach. Don't you think?"

Levi's smile widens. He selects a dark blue hamper and adds it to the cart. "All right, what's next on that list of yours?"

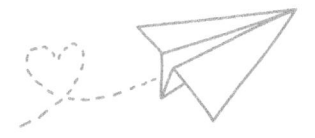

Chapter 36

Hunter

THEN

"You've got this," I whisper one last time, swiping sweat from my brow and tucking my hair behind my ears.

The AC is still out in my car, and if I sit here any longer, my makeup's going to melt right off my face.

My anxiety is rioting like it's in a mosh pit, and my stomach is taking most of the hits. I had to stop at the QuickieMart just to use the bathroom, even though I went multiple times before leaving the house.

Once I've retrieved my overnight bag from the back seat, I lock my car and scan the parking lot. There are a few people nearby, but the lot is only half-full. That makes sense. There are multiple orientation weekends offered throughout the summer, which means each orientation group is small and intimate. It's a perfect introduction to all that Lake Chapel University has to offer.

A thrill of excitement shoots through my veins as I hoist my bag onto my shoulder. I get to actually stay on campus in the dorms tonight. With a roommate and everything.

According to the agenda, we'll start the day with icebreakers, then go on a tour of the campus. Tomorrow I'll get to meet with my undergrad adviser to select my courses for fall semester.

Another wave of giddiness rolls through me, followed immediately by a period cramp.

And then comes the anxiety gas. Ugh.

Better here than in front of my new roommate, I guess.

With a slow breath out, I remind myself that this is the good kind of anxiety.

I'm branching out, creating new experiences. Even though LCU is so close to home, or what used to be my home, the campus itself is amazing.

Brick pathways and tall oak trees border the quad, and in the middle of the green space, a big white welcome tent has been set up.

"St. Clair, comma, Hunter," I tell the girl at the table under the tent when I get to the front of the line.

She looks up and rolls her eyes, clearly unamused.

Don't make *Legally Blonde* jokes on the first day. Noted.

"Hunter St. Clair?" She opens a manila folder with my name on it and leafs through its contents. "Here's your schedule and a map."

I take the proffered pages and scan one, then the other.

"Your room assignment is on the first page. The key card on top gets you into the dorms. You're in McMaster, so you'll want to head that way." She points to a stately building covered in ivy across the grassy expanse of the quad. "I suggest you wear your key card on the lanyard so you don't misplace it. You have to turn it in when you check out tomorrow, or a fifty-dollar fine will be added to your student account."

She rattles off a few more instructions, passing over another stack of papers and envelopes that I fumble to grab hold of.

With my bag on one shoulder, my pillow stuffed under my other arm, and now all my welcome papers in hand, I head in the direction she pointed.

I refer to my map, even though I've been studying one from the school's website for weeks, and eventually find McMaster Hall. With trembling hands, I swipe my key card and, miraculously, unlock the exterior door on the first try.

When I reach my assigned room on the second floor, I pause.

Should I knock?

Do I just go in?

Before I can decide the best course of action, the door flies open, and suddenly, I'm coming face to face with a tall, gorgeous redhead.

Lush, full breasts spill out of her tank top as she raises a hand to her chest. "Oh my god! You scared the shit out of me!"

"I-I'm sorry," I stammer while trying to keep my overnight bag hooked on my elbow. "I'm Hunter. And this is my room."

"*Ah*! Roomie! Here, let me help you." She takes my pillow from under my arm. "Come in, come in." With a flourish, she spins, her red hair floating around her, and moves deeper into the space. "I'm LouEllen Montbeck-Calhoun," she announces. "But you can call me Louie."

I exhale and let my bag drop to the floor. "Two first names and two last names?" I question. "I know a girl raised in the south when I meet her."

"Charleston born and raised," she confirms with a wide smile. "How about you?"

"I'm actually from here. I grew up in Lake Chapel."

"But you're living on campus?"

"Yeah, I wanted the full experience." I leave out the part where my dad has semi-permanently relocated to France and my mom recently moved in with a guy I've never even met.

"Speaking of full experience..." Louie skips to her overnight bag and pulls out two cans of hard seltzer. "We've got forty-five minutes until the first icebreaker. Drink up."

My eyebrows shoot to my hairline as she holds one can out to me. "You brought alcohol to orientation weekend?"

"Hell yes I did," she says far too loudly. "This is college, girl. I'll drink yours if you don't want it, though."

I bite my lip, considering. It's not like it's shots of eighty-proof liquor. With a shrug, I hold the can up and read the label. "What flavors are we drinking?"

We spend the next forty minutes dancing around the room, sipping sparkling peach seltzer, and unpacking the excessive number of toiletries and beauty supplies we both deemed necessary for a one-night stay.

I'm arranging my skin care routine in my bright pink shower caddy—with matching loofah, of course—as Louie goes on about her plans for fall. She's going to major in accounting and has plans to take over her family business in Charleston someday. First, though, she's going to travel. She's not actually starting classes until January because she's taking an extended gap trip to Europe this fall. She's here today because LCU doesn't offer the same pizzazz for spring semester orientation, and like me, she wants to experience it all.

I pull my phone from my pocket to check the time and discover a few unread texts waiting for me. "We should head down there in the next five minutes," I tell Louie. Then I tip back my seltzer to finish it off and set the can on my desk.

The first message is from Greedy.

> **Greedy:** Miss you, Tem. I hope you're having the best time.

The next is from Levi.

> **Levi:** Hope you remembered to pack your shower caddy. Greedy's grouchy without you around. His dad's making him do all sorts of father-son bonding.

I reply to both guys, then stash my phone and slip my shoes back on.

Louie reapplies her lip gloss in the mirror by the door, then smacks a kiss at me. "Ready?"

"So ready." Key card and wristlet in hand, I follow her out the door to my first official Lake Chapel University orientation event.

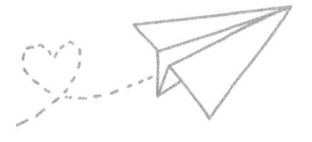

Chapter 37

Hunter

THEN

I sit up on the lumpy dorm mattress and blink, forcing my eyes to adjust to the dark room. I don't think I drifted off to sleep for even five minutes. My body aches from tossing and turning for hours.

Note to self: add a mattress topper to my next shopping list.

My head's pounding with a severity no amount of caffeine or over-the-counter meds is going to touch.

It's gonna be *such* a long day.

With a cleansing breath in, I try to center myself.

The sun hasn't even started to rise, but I might as well get up. A hot shower will feel wonderful, and this early, I'm practically guaranteed an empty bathroom.

I stifle a yawn as I stretch out my arms. I don't want to wake up Louie.

We stayed up way too late talking and laughing and having the best time. I'm genuinely bummed she won't be here until spring semester. We clicked so well. If she were moving in this fall, I would have jumped on the chance to put in a request with housing.

I slip out of my sleep shorts and tank top, then throw on a robe and step into my brand-new shower shoes.

Shower caddy in hand, I slip out of the room, smiling at the thought of the guys with their own this fall.

As expected, the bathroom is completely empty. I shuffle to the first stall and turn the knob. An icy blast shoots out more intensely than I expected, forcing me to pivot out of the way.

I turn to place my shower caddy on the floor, but as soon as I stand up, a piercing pain ricochets through my temple.

"Shit," I hiss, bringing my hand to the side of my face as tears spring to my eyes and my vision fades in and out. With my free arm, I brace myself on the wall to keep from stumbling.

My head was throbbing before, but the pain is so sharp now it feels as though someone took an ice pick to my temple.

As tears stream down my face, I slump against the wall and bow my head, focusing on steadying my breathing. By the time the pain has dulled a fraction and my heart rate has leveled out, the water's warm enough for me to shuck off my robe.

I hang it up on the little hook right outside the stall, then step into the shower. Instantly, I'm surrounded by blood swirling down the drain.

With a shuddering breath, I use my fingers to search my head, weaving them through my hairline. When I pull them away, they're clean.

More droplets of blood paint the tiles beneath me crimson. For a moment, all I can do is stare, at an absolute loss.

Then it dawns on me. My period started.

Flovely.

I groan and silently pray that I've got a tampon and a pad tucked away in my bag. My flow is always so heavy during the first few days of my cycle.

My head hurts so badly I decide not to bother washing my hair. Instead, I stand under the spray, willing it to soothe me. Once the hot water turns tepid, I quickly scrub my skin clean.

Instead of feeling rejuvenated when I'm finished, the pain in my head is so intense it's creeping down my neck.

Between the lack of sleep, the splitting headache, and the piercing cramps, a sense of malaise has settled in my bones.

I slip my robe on and trudge back to the room. Louie's still asleep, so I quietly dig through my bag for the feminine supplies I need, then put my PJs back on. I pull out an oversized Lake Chapel High School sweatshirt and pull it on, too.

I fish out a few Tylenol from my purse and swallow them dry, then I curl up on the lumpy mattress and try in vain to get comfortable.

Minutes tick by.

Then a full hour disappears.

I'm going to be useless when I meet with my adviser later.

Fresh tears prick at the backs of my eyes as my frustration mounts, only making the pain worse and sending me into a panic spiral.

My phone has only been plugged in for a couple of hours, so it isn't fully charged yet, but I unplug it anyway and send a quick text to Greedy, even though he's probably still asleep.

When I watch the clock turn to five thirty a.m., I convince myself it's okay to text Levi. Work starts at seven, so he's usually up about this time.

Daisy: Are you awake?

His response is immediate.

Duke: Yes. Why are you up?

> **Daisy:** Couldn't sleep. And then I hit my head in the shower

> **Duke:** You hit your head? How hard?

I don't even know how to answer that.

> **Daisy:** It hurts. But I'm just feeling sorry for myself because I'm tired.

> **Duke:** Do you want me to come there?

Worrying at my bottom lip, I consider. Would it really help anything to have him here? If he came, he'd have to miss a day of work.

I yawn. Then I yawn again, my body finally giving up the fight as exhaustion takes hold.

> **Daisy:** I don't know

Every inch of me aches, but I'm shutting down. Even as pain ricochets and radiates through my body, I drift off. I startle a few minutes later to find two more texts from Levi.

> **Duke:** I'm on my way

> **Duke:** Text me the dorm room number if you can

I type out 1022, then hit Send. It's the last thing I remember before I drift into a fitful, agitated sleep.

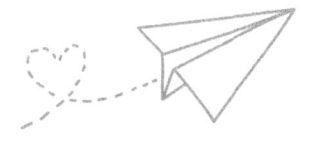

Chapter 38

Hunter

THEN

"Daisy. Hey, wake up."

Murmurs of Levi's sweet southern twang echo around my mind.

I blink my eyes open, then quickly shut them again.

It's bright. Too bright.

"Daisy. Hey, don't be mad but..."

Sighing, I force my eyes to open just enough to take in my surroundings. *Don't be mad* can't mean anything good.

I instantly recognize the vehicle we're in. It's Greedy's, but Levi's the one driving.

Instinctively, I crane my neck and look in the back seat.

"Where—"

Levi puts his hand on mine and squeezes. "We're at the hospital."

"Why are we here?" With a groan, I sit up and try to get my bearings.

Sure enough, we're in a parking lot, but I don't even remember leaving LCU.

"Greedy insisted I bring you in," Levi explains. "You were really out of it when I found you. How do you feel now?"

As if responding to his question, my lower abdomen cramps with such force I double over. It feels like a period cramp, but the pain radiates all the way to my back and even down into my thighs.

Whimpering, I tuck my legs underneath me and curl up in a ball, searching for some semblance of relief.

"I have awful cramps," I admit. "And my head is pounding."

I tenderly brush my hair back, wincing when I graze the tender spot on my temple.

"We think you hit your head," Levi tells me.

"We?"

"The girl who was with you when I picked you up. Elouise, I think?"

"Louie," I correct. "My roommate."

Levi nods. "She said you came back into the room early in the morning and she didn't know where you'd been. You passed out on the bed, but she thought you were crying in your sleep."

"I didn't go anywhere. I woke up with a killer headache, and I thought a shower might help."

I sniffle but instantly regret it when my head swims with pain.

"Where's Greedy?" I ask as another cramp rolls through me. I just want him to hold me. My head and my back ache, and my stomach is rioting. I feel that sickening hollowness that happens before I get the shakes. What I wouldn't give to curl up in the tub at the cabin or to have Greedy massage my low back right now.

"He's stuck golfing with his dad," Levi says. "They had a really early tee time, so they've already played eight holes. Greedy says he can leave after the ninth if we need him to meet us here."

I shake my head, defeated. "I just want to go home."

With a sigh, Levi takes off his ball cap and runs his hand through his hair a few times. Then he puts the hat back on his head and adjusts it from side to side. "I know, Daisy. But Greedy made me promise."

I don't have the energy to fight, and maybe he's right. Intense menstrual cramps aren't anything new for me, but I still feel like maybe I should get my head checked out.

"Will you stay with me?"

Levi nods. "Of course. I won't leave your side." He holds out my phone. "Do you want to call him before we go in?"

Thankful he thought to bring it and still in so much pain, I swipe away a tear and nod.

"Your new friend had me put her number in your phone," he tells me. "She made me swear that you would text her and let her know that you're okay."

I offer a weak smile at that. Louie was so great. Now I feel like I've ruined everything because of the stupid shower accident.

I click Greedy's name and wait with bated breath for him to pick up. I don't have to wait long before he's answering.

"Thank god," he says in way of greeting. "Tell me you're okay."

I sniffle, feeling a little sorry for myself. I'm in pain. I'm missing orientation. And Greedy's not here with me now.

"I think I'm okay. I have horrible cramps, and my period just started. Then I slipped and hit my head in the shower."

"We need to talk to housing at LCU and see if we can't get you a private bathroom or an en suite unit," Greedy grumbles.

"It wasn't the shower's fault, Greedy. It was just an accident." I yawn again, still so unbelievably exhausted. "Really, I'm fine," I assure him. I hate the idea of him worrying about me.

"Let Levi take you in to get checked out."

A wave of emotion rolls over me. He's so damn thoughtful, and I'm so damn tired. All I want is to fall asleep in his arms.

"Tem?"

"Yeah?" I sniff.

"I love you."

"I love you, too," I murmur, chest aching with sincerity. "One of us will text you when we get an update."

As I hang up, Levi exits the truck, rounds the hood, and helps me slide out. "I'll take you home as soon as they give you the all clear," he promises.

With a nod, I let him put his arm around my shoulder and guide me through the entrance of the emergency room.

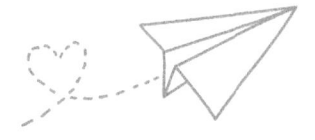

Chapter 39

Hunter

THEN

I've been to this ER once before. After I got hurt at cheer camp in seventh grade. Another girl fell during a stunt, and my body cushioned her fall. My neck and shoulder immediately ached, but I shook it off and kept practicing.

This was an elite cheer camp that was invitation only, and my mom had made a very big deal about how much it cost. My parents had no trouble affording it, I realize that now, but my mom has always made a big deal any time I wanted or needed something that cost a lot of money.

I came home from camp a few days later and diligently iced my shoulder, but by day three, I could barely use my arm.

My dad finally brought me into the ER. Turns out I had broken my collarbone, and I had a greenstick fracture in my humerus. Thankfully, the breaks weren't near growth plates, and surgery wasn't required. I didn't even need a cast because of the locations of the injuries.

We spend just a few minutes in triage in the emergency room before they take us to a more private space. People stream in and out of the room for the first twenty minutes or so, asking me to recall what happened, looking at the spot on my temple that I now realize is both scraped and bruised, and checking my vitals.

Levi has a chair pulled up so close his knees are pressed to the bed. He hasn't let go of my hand since we arrived.

Finally, a young woman breezes in and introduces herself as Dr. Jones.

She logs into the computer on the counter nearby and refers to all the notes that have already been added to my chart. Thankfully, she doesn't ask the questions I've answered half a dozen times already.

"Tell me more about the fall," she says. "What do you remember?"

"Not much, honestly. It was early, and I was still sort of out of it. My head was pounding, and I thought a shower might help. It was still dark outside, and I was in a communal shower I've never been in before."

She chuckles, keeping things lighthearted. "I remember having to shower in the dorms. Anything else?"

"I turned on the water, then sort of jumped back to avoid the cold spray. The next thing I know, I was doubled over in pain. It was..." I pause, searching for the right way to describe what I experienced. "The pain was everywhere."

"Do you think you slipped," she asks, typing away on the computer. "Or is there a chance you passed out?"

"I honestly don't remember." Everything about the last several hours is fuzzy around the edges.

"You're eighteen, is that correct?"

I nod carefully to keep from making my head pound. "Correct."

"Is there anybody else you'd like us to call for you?" she asks, glancing at Levi.

"No," I say, squeezing Levi's hand. "My dad has been in France for several months."

I'll text him later to fill him in. The last person I want to see is my mom, and Greedy promised he'd be here as quickly as he could.

"There's no one else," I repeat as a surge of sadness wells up inside.

Levi rubs his thumb over my knuckles, silently soothing me.

"I have a few more questions, and then we'll run some tests. Who's with you here today?"

I note, and appreciate, the open-endedness of the question. For a split second, I'm tempted to tell her Levi's my brother, but I don't want to catch him off guard.

"This is my best friend," I tell her.

"Hi, best friend." She gives him a quick nod, then turns back to the computer to add a note to my chart.

"Levi," he clarifies.

"Levi. Nice to meet you." Dr. Jones smiles at me warmly, then turns to him. "Would you mind giving us a few minutes?"

Panic erupts inside me at the suggestion.

If I felt alone before...

"No, Levi can stay. I *need* him to stay." I sit up quickly, wincing from the pain of the motion, and cling to his hand more securely, like I can physically hold him in place.

He shifts his chair so our forearms are touching as well as our hands.

"Easy," he tells me under his breath. "I can stay."

Then he looks to the doctor for confirmation.

"Do I have permission to ask medical questions in front of him?" the doctor asks, her tone overly professional.

I nod.

"You'll have to fill out a form saying that," she says, typing once again. "I'm going to order a number of blood tests, check your vitals,

SO WRONG

look for things like iron or vitamin D deficiency. The exhaustion you're experiencing gives me concern. Have you had mono before?"

"No," I reply.

"It's common in young adults. We've been seeing an uptick in cases this summer. It's highly contagious and can be spread by kissing or even sharing drinks."

That all makes sense. But just the thought has dread forming in my stomach. Clarissa on the cheer team had mono last year. She was out of school for a solid month, and even after she returned, she was sick all the time. Feeling this tired for days or even weeks as the semester is getting started would be rough.

"Can you tell me the date of your last period?" Dr. Jones asks.

Instantly, I blush from head to toe. This is probably one of the reasons she suggested Levi leave the room. "Can you hand me my phone?" I ask him gently.

Once he's passed it over, I open up my app and scroll to the current month. I haven't logged a single symptom in weeks, according to the calendar. I'm usually pretty diligent, but I've been preoccupied with college preparations and Greedy and the drama with my mother.

I scroll back and find the date of my last period.

It was more than a month ago—the very last week of June. I tell her the date, but then remember the blood in the shower this morning.

"No, wait. My period started this morning."

"And before that," she asks, "the first day of your last month's birth cycle was June twenty-third?"

"Yes," I confirm, double-checking my calendar. I quickly log today as day one of this cycle and set my phone down by my side.

"Have you been experiencing any nausea, vomiting, lightheadedness, or sensitivity to smells?"

"I don't think so," I hedge. Aside from feeling anxious about orientation, I've felt mostly the same.

"Are you sexually active?"

"Yes," I confirm, my cheeks heating once again.

Dr. Jones presses her lips together and regards me with an easy expression. "Hunter, when you think about your sexual encounters over the last few months, is there any chance of pregnancy?"

"No," I'm quick to answer. "I'm on birth control, and my period started today."

She bows her head and goes back to typing, this time for longer than before. All the while, I watch and anxiously await her next line of questioning.

"We need to draw several vials of blood for the tests I'm ordering. I'll put in an order for them to send up a food tray as well." She smiles sympathetically. "We don't need you passing out on us."

"Levi can stay with me?" I ask as she gathers her paperwork and logs out of the computer.

"He can stay," she confirms, looking from me to Levi. "You'll be here at least a few more hours, so if there's anybody you need to contact, you might want to do that now."

A pang of loneliness hits me once again.

Levi's here. Greedy will be here as soon as he can. There's no one else, but that's okay.

· ♥ · ♥ · ♥ · ♥ · ♥ ·

I drift in and out of consciousness for a couple of hours. The smallest sounds cause me to stir: The buzz of the fluorescent lights overhead. An alarm sounding in another patient's room a few doors down.

Each time my eyelids flutter open, Levi is here.

Holding my hand, his full attention fixed on me.

"Rest," he urges.

"You're okay," he promises.

I know I am. Because he's by my side.

He stays put, holding my hand for hours.

That is, until Dr. Jones comes back into the room wearing a tight-lipped smile.

She regards me, then Levi. When she looks at me again, sympathy shining in her eyes, my heart sinks.

"I'm going to ask you to step out of the room for a moment, Levi. If you'd like to stay just outside the door, I'll fetch you as soon as I'm done."

Though her expression is soft, her tone is firm, and this time, I don't ask him to stay.

With a kiss to my forehead, he whispers, "I'll be right outside if you need me." Then he walks out the door and pulls it closed gently behind him.

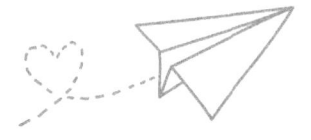

Chapter 40

Hunter

THEN

I'm numb.

So numb that the absence of pain aches more acutely than any injury I've ever experienced.

I miss the pain.

They gave me an initial dose of painkillers and sent me home with a prescription for extra-strength ibuprofen. I have instructions to rest and seek comfort care as needed in the form of heating pads and hot showers.

In three days, I'll follow up with my regular OBGYN to make sure my hCG levels continue to decrease.

I don't even know what hCG stands for.

But as soon as the words came out of Dr. Jones's mouth, *I knew*.

According to her, an ultrasound isn't necessary unless the levels don't fall and they have to look for unshed tissue. The baseline level was already lower than they expect at six to seven weeks.

I'll never get to see our baby.

A silent sob racks through me, twisting my stomach and making my chest ache so badly I gasp for air.

I'm strapped into the front seat of Greedy's truck with Levi behind the wheel.

I want to thrash and scream. Break free.

Break everything.

I'm broken.

Bleeding out and broken.

I'm still bleeding so heavily the ER nurse gave me a pair of oversized mesh panties and sent me home with a bag full of mega pads.

"I'm sorry. There's nothing we can do," Dr. Jones said an hour ago.

"*This isn't your fault,*" my dad assured me the night my mother stormed out of the house and he sat me down to tell me he had asked for a divorce.

I'm hollow. I've never felt so low. Yet the emptiness is familiar.

The good never stays.

"How about a cheeseburger?" Levi suggests, breaking me out of my doom spiral. "You need to eat. Keep up your strength."

Levi knows. He knows what's happening right now, as I cramp and bleed in the front seat of this truck.

I couldn't not tell him. I couldn't fight back the tears or hold in my sorrow.

He cried with me and held me when I told him I had been pregnant.

Had been, but wasn't anymore.

Had been, but nothing good ever stays.

At least not for me.

I hate that he knows when I haven't had a chance to tell Greedy.

I called him twice, and it went to voicemail both times.

"I'll buy you a milkshake," Levi offers, his tone soft and placating, like he's speaking to a child.

"I'm not hungry." I've told him so several times since we left the hospital. "I just want to go home."

We ride in silence through my neighborhood.

Except when we turn on to the cul-de-sac, it's clear that I can't go home.

There are two cars in the driveway, and a well-dressed woman in a pantsuit with her hair styled in sleek braids stands near the front door, a folder in hand.

Flovely.

All I want to do is curl up in my bed and sleep, but there's a decent chance strangers are standing in my bedroom at this moment, inspecting the crown molding and measuring the depth of the walk-in closet.

Swiping at a fresh round of tears, I dig through my bag for my phone. It's buried under the bag of oversized pads and the dirty blue hospital socks the nurse insisted I take with me.

I open the text thread from my mom. Maybe the showing ends soon.

There isn't any mention of the showing in our recent messages. She didn't even bother to inform me. Although I guess she thought I'd be on campus all day.

What I do find is a series of recent texts.

> **Mom:** Hunter, I need you to come to the Lake Chapel Country Club today after your school thing. Be here by 5 pm. Cocktail attire.

My "school thing" was supposed to go until late afternoon. I would have been hard-pressed to make it by five. Not that she cares.

A second text message includes the address.

A third text message comes through as I'm holding the phone.

SO WRONG

> **Mom:** Confirm you'll be here, Hunter. This is important to me.

I'm too exhausted to even roll my eyes, but I type out a confirmation. I don't bother asking about when the people will be out of our house. Not when she's obviously fired up already. Hopefully, once they do leave, I'll have time to make myself look presentable in the cocktail attire she requires.

"Have you heard from Greedy yet?" Levi asks, pulling over a few houses down from mine.

"Still nothing, but I did get this." I hand him my phone so he can read the texts from my mom.

"Wait. Greedy was golfing at LCCC today." Levi hands my phone back.

"Maybe I can catch him there. Will you go with me?" I ask softly.

"Of course." He cups my face and swallows audibly. "Daisy, I'm—"

"Don't," I beg.

I can't stand his kindness. I can't stand the idea of acknowledging the loss out loud before Greedy knows.

Levi bites down on his bottom lip and pulls back his hand. Tipping his chin toward my house, he asks, "Want me to go in there and kick them out?"

It's impossible not to smile at the offer. Levi is one of the sweetest, least intimidating people I know.

"We can wait." I sigh and rest my head back against my seat. "As long as I have thirty minutes or so, I can be ready."

"Put the seat back." Levi plucks the worn denim hat off his head and carefully places it on mine, pulling the brim low to block out some of the warm afternoon sunshine. "Sleep. I'll wake you up when they're gone."

Chapter 41

Hunter

THEN

When I woke up in the too-warm truck cab, Levi was asleep in the driver's seat, and it was already 5:20 pm. I was sticky with sweat, and my thighs were glued together with what I could only assume was blood.

I didn't have time to be embarrassed as I rushed through the house, frantically trying to pull myself together.

I failed.

I failed so incredibly badly, but the pain was devastating. Unbearable. Every time I looked in the mirror, the emotional turmoil raging inside me would rise up like bile. I couldn't even stop crying long enough to put on mascara.

As Levi weaves through row after row of fancy cars, searching for a parking spot at Lake Chapel Country Club, I flip down the visor to give myself a quick once-over... then immediately slap it back up in disgust.

My eyes are so puffy I don't even recognize myself.

My heart is shattered in a way I don't think can ever be repaired.

"Daisy. We don't have to—"

"Let's go," I say, opening my door and gingerly stepping out of the truck.

I'm wearing one of the pads from the hospital, plus two pairs of underwear and black cheer shorts under my dress. I swear fresh clots pass each time I stand, even if I've only been seated for a few minutes.

I trudge to the front doors of the country club, pushing back at the physical and emotional devastation rolling through me. I just want to get this over with.

Just as Levi catches up to me, Greedy emerges from the front doors, breathless. His eyes are full of so much heartache I worry he already knows.

How?

"Did you—"

"No." That one word from Levi is enough to clearly answer the question I didn't even fully articulate. "I would never."

Greedy strides toward me and opens his mouth to speak—but then my mother comes barreling out of the door behind him.

She charges toward me, a vision in a tight white body-con dress that hits just above the knee. Her hair is blown out in big waves, and she's wearing a gorgeous headband dotted with crystals that shimmer from the light pouring out from the entryway.

She looks stunning. I'd even say ethereal, if not for her livid expression and the vitriol oozing from her. Her scowl deepens, though not much, thanks to the Botox, as she assesses me up and down.

"Is this some sort of joke to you?" she hisses, grabbing my upper arm, her nails digging into my flesh.

On instinct, I pull back. "That hurts," I grit out, holding back tears.

"Excuse me," Levi tries to interject. "We're late because of me, ma'am. I was Hunter's ride, and I fell asleep. It's not her—"

"I don't have time to listen to your boyfriend make excuses for you," my mother hisses through her teeth without bothering to look at Levi.

Heart lurching, I look at Greedy over her shoulder. He takes another step forward, coming to my rescue.

Before he can close in on us, though, my mom is gripping my arm again, her acrylic talons digging into the already bruised skin where they drew blood at the hospital.

The reminder brings fresh tears to my eyes.

"Ow," I whimper so quietly the sound catches in my throat.

"You're hurting her," Levi grits out. He's closer. He can see the tears threatening to fall. He knows I'm barely holding it together.

"Wait—" Greedy calls out.

But I'm already being pulled through the doors.

I follow obediently. I don't have a choice. Going is easier than fighting.

·♥·♥·♥·♥·♥·

"There." My mother marches me toward a well-appointed vanity. "Fix your face. Put on some mascara and blush, at the very least." She meets my gaze in the mirror, her emerald-green irises—the color so similar to mine—meticulously lined, her eyebrows arched to perfection.

She looks beautiful.

Too bad she's so ugly on the inside.

"Stop crying, *dammit*."

If she knew, would this woman even cry with me? Probably not.

A silent sob racks through me at the thought.

I'm disoriented and desperate to get back out there. I need to talk to Greedy. He'll wait for me. He'll hold me. I need to get back out there and—

"Hunter Annalee Charlotte St. Clair, get yourself together. This isn't how I raised you."

This isn't how she raised me?

She didn't raise me at all.

My dad did.

But he's gone now.

Everything I love leaves.

"I'm going to use the ladies' room, and by the time I'm finished, you'll have it together."

I doubt that. But I reach for my bag anyway.

I pull out my phone first. The screen is black. I try to turn it on, but I'm greeted by the flashing battery sign.

Flovely.

I can't even text Greedy or Levi to ask them to wait for me. Hopefully, we can meet up after the ridiculous event my mother feels compelled to drag me to.

Mindlessly, I reapply my lip gloss. I unscrew a tube of mascara and use a magnifying mirror to run the wand over the tips of my lashes. Maybe if I don't let it get too close, maybe if I keep the makeup right on the edge, it won't streak down my face along with the tears that won't stop falling.

The toilet flushes.

I blot concealer under my eyes, which only makes them look worse.

The sink turns on.

I sweep a sparkling pink blush along the apples of my cheeks.

My mother appears in the mirror, a wide smile stretched across her face.

"Ready?" she asks, emanating pure joy. She's a completely different person from the one berating me moments ago. She's transformed or renewed somehow. A fresh wave of numbness washes over me as I struggle to understand how a person can be so cruel one minute, then so saccharine the next.

She approaches my seat at the vanity from behind, standing close enough she can probably see herself in the magnifying mirror.

I avert my attention in hopes that she won't assess me too closely.

"How do I look?" she asks.

When I lift my head, I force myself to look at her, bracing for more criticism.

A small breath of relief escapes me as I zero in on her. She's staring at herself, solely and completely focused on her own reflection.

"Hunter," she snaps.

"You look good," I reply automatically. Mechanically. "Y-you look gorgeous," I correct.

She claps and smiles coyly, clearly pleased with my response.

I exhale in relief, knowing I've passed the test.

"Let's go," she instructs.

Worried she'll grab me again if I don't get a move on, I rise quickly. Too quickly.

A small gush leaves my body, and my heart lurches. I squeeze my thighs together, panicked that the pad and all the extra layers won't be enough.

Should I duck into the bathroom to clean myself up and risk pissing my mother off more, or should I just follow her out the door?

Her exasperated use of my name—*again*—reminds me that the choice isn't mine to make.

I take small steps toward the door and meet her in the marble hall that leads back to the grand foyer of the country club.

Her heels *click-clack* on the tiles with purpose. She's two steps ahead of me the entire time.

"Come along," she encourages. Her voice is nearly an octave higher than normal. "There's someone I've been dying for you to meet."

In the foyer, a glittering chandelier throws beams of light so bright against the white and cream walls it makes my eyes burn.

Still holding back tears, I keep my head low, my gaze fixed on the red soles of my mother's shoes. When she stops and I finally look up, relief washes through me.

Levi and Greedy are here, waiting for me. Just like I hoped. They're standing in the grand foyer next to a well-dressed man.

I beeline for the boys, desperate to talk to Greedy, aching to be in his arms. Miraculously, I hold myself together. I can't fall apart. Not yet. I have to get through the event my mother insists I attend. For now, though, I can hold out. I can do this, knowing that the boys will be waiting for me when it's all over.

"Tem," Greedy whispers when I'm still a few feet away.

My mother steps in front of me, effectively cutting me off, and approaches the man next to Greedy, slinging her arms around his torso.

"Here she is. *Finally.*" The man smiles warmly at my mother, then extends a hand to me. "Hunter, I take it?"

My mom will kill me if I'm rude to her friend, so I offer him my hand and fake a smile.

"Hello." I look from the man to Greedy. Then back again, confused. The man's eyes catch my attention, the softness around them when he smiles, and then the shape of his nose…

"It's truly a pleasure." He shakes my hand eagerly. "Now that we're all together, we can finally share the big news."

"We?" I ask.

Greedy takes a single step forward. "What news?"

I focus on him again. He and Levi should probably wait outside. The last thing I want is for my mom to sink her claws into my boys, literally or figuratively.

Levi is already on her shit list since he tried to take responsibility for my late arrival. He's also dressed way too casually for a country club, and

I can't let her pick on him, too. If I can borrow a phone charger, I can get them out of here and text them when we're done—

"Surprise!" My mother claps giddily and practically bounces in her heels.

The staccato smacks of her palms against one another echo throughout the foyer and ricochet through my brain, sending a sharp pain through my temple.

"We're engaged!" she squeals.

The man is still grasping my hand, which is the only reason I don't collapse on the spot.

"I'm Dr. Gary Ferguson," he tells me. "It's a pleasure to finally meet you, Hunter."

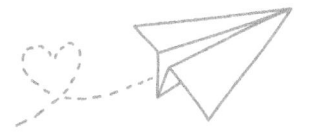

Chapter 42

Hunter

THEN

We're all seated around the table.

A singular table in the middle of a ballroom.

Where we've been summoned to celebrate the upcoming nuptials of our *parents*.

My mother's to my left, but she hasn't so much as glanced at me since we've been seated.

Gary, a.k.a. Dr. Ferguson, a.k.a. my boyfriend's *father*, is sitting to her left and hasn't taken his eyes off her.

He has a friend on his other side. Phil, I think? His best friend from college, apparently. He flew in from Cleveland for the occasion. Two girls about my age, his daughters, are next. They're both wearing pretty dresses, and they've done their hair and makeup in a way that indicates they knew they were attending a special event tonight.

And then there's Greedy.

I can feel his eyes on me.

I can feel the longing rolling off him as I do everything in my power to avoid meeting his gaze.

Levi's between us.

I've never been more grateful to have Levi by my side.

He nudges my knee under the table when a question has been directed at me or when I should acknowledge a comment. He whispers soft reminders and quiet instructions throughout the meal.

Take a sip of water.

Pick up your salad fork.

Raise your glass for the toast.

My insides are twisted into a knot of physical and emotional pain. I have to remind myself to inhale, then to let the breath out a few seconds later. I'm shocked and overwhelmed, exhausted and woozy. I'm struggling in ways I didn't know were possible.

Layers of nausea have built up inside me, both for physical reasons and because my body is working to accept what my brain refuses to acknowledge.

My mom is getting married.

My mom is getting remarried.

My mom is going to marry the father of the boy I love.

"Breathe," Levi whispers again.

I blink.

Wait, no. That's not what he said.

I exhale.

There it is.

As the carbon dioxide whooshes from my body, another excruciating cramp takes over, and I swear I can feel blood pooling between my thighs.

The pad should hold, but I've placed a napkin beneath me in case I bleed through all the layers and my dress. Wouldn't want to stain the cream upholstery, considering we'll be back here for the actual wedding.

Levi gently squeezes my thigh. Then he massages my kneecap.

"Look up and smile," he murmurs, pretending to glance over his shoulder and wave to somebody behind us in the process.

It's a ruse. He doesn't know anyone here aside from the people sitting around this table. He's wearing cargo shorts and a turquoise polo, though he's ditched his signature denim cap, the one he put on my head before I drifted off this afternoon.

Greedy clears his throat across the table. Again. No doubt trying to garner my attention.

I keep my focus fixed on the plate in front of me.

Using the tines of my fork, I create a crisscross pattern in the ranch dressing on top of each tomato. The dressing was served in a miniature silver gravy boat. Every person in the room has one in front of them.

Who has to wash each individual boat at the end of the night? It seems like a tedious task.

I'm dotting dressing on the last tomato on my plate when the conversation around me catches my attention.

"We can't wait to honeymoon in Europe," my mother says. Her voice is higher pitched than normal, with a honeyed drawl I've never heard her use before.

I snap my head to one side and stare at her. "You're going to Europe?"

It shouldn't surprise me that this is the first I'm hearing of it.

"Oh, Hunter," my mother says, using a sweet tone I haven't heard from her in years. "I've been meaning to tell you all the details. I've just been so swept up with the move, and you've been so busy getting ready for college."

I've been home alone more often than not this summer.

I didn't mind.

But our lack of quality time has nothing to do with me.

Her back-and-forth attitude toward me is giving me emotional whiplash. Usually I grin and bear it. It's easier that way. But as I sit here, detached and bleeding, desperate and dizzy with exhaustion, I can't do it. I'm done. I'm numb and I'm grieving and I want this nightmare of a night to be over.

That's the only explanation for what comes out of my mouth next.

"Does your husband know you'll be in Europe soon? Do you plan to meet up, since he's over there, too?"

"Hunter St. Clair," she hisses in a tone that turns my blood cold. "*Manners.*" Her face pinches like she's squashing the impulse to put me in my place.

I shift back on instinct, though I doubt she'll physically grab me in front of an audience.

All eyes are on her now, which she realizes a few seconds too late. She straightens and clears her throat. Then her polished mask slips into place and her voice returns to that gratingly high octave.

"Yes, your father is aware of my impending nuptials." She smooths her hair, looking shyly toward Dr. Ferguson before setting her sights back on me. "I was willing to concede on some points of our mediation to keep the process moving. Everything will be finalized by next week."

This is news to me. My dad is the one who initially asked for the divorce. She was the one dragging it out, making it exceptionally difficult.

A lot of what they've argued about revolves around me.

My college fund will cover my tuition in full, and my dad's mother left me a small inheritance. My dad has been direct depositing money into a personal savings account for me all my life.

More recently, he's been giving me an additional monthly allowance. He doesn't want me to have to worry about working while I'm in school.

The issue is that my mom can't weaponize me against him, no matter how hard she tries. There's no custody to battle over, nor can she pad her requests for spousal support under the guise of raising a child.

Greedy clears his throat again. "When is all of this happening?" His voice is even, practiced. If I didn't know him the way I do, I would assume he was making casual conversation.

When I chance a quick look at him out of the corner of my eye, the muscles in his jaw are working overtime, jumping and reacting with each passing second.

It dawns on me then that he's just finding out all these details, too.

"We're getting married Labor Day weekend," Dr. Ferguson replies. "I checked the academic calendars for both your schools," he quickly assures us. Then he turns to me, sitting straight and wearing a look of pride. "Garrett is going to South Chapel University. He's been offered a student-athlete scholarship and a spot in the honors program."

Greedy offers his dad a tense smile. "How long will you be in Europe?"

"I'll only be gone a week or so. I'll be back in town before the first football game," he assures his son. "I plan to travel with Magnolia and get her settled, then I'll visit as my schedule allows."

"I've always dreamed of an extended vacation in Europe," my mom says dreamily.

"So you'll be gone for most of the fall?" I can't help but feel jilted by the total lack of consideration and communication around this charade.

"Don't worry," Dr. Ferguson says, clearly under the impression that I can be reassured in this moment. "We'll make sure everything's taken care of before we leave for Europe. I'll set up an account with our banker for you next week. Then I'll email you the details about how to access it. You'll have a credit card, of course. Your mother and I want you to be focused on school. Your mother tells me you want to be an accountant."

"She wants to be a lawyer," Greedy corrects.

All eyes land on him. That's not something he should know about me if we've only just met. Mercifully, southern manners and niceties prevail. No one asks Greedy how he knows I want to be a lawyer. In fact, our parents don't even pause long enough to give me an opportunity to confirm or deny my own future career path.

"Maybe Garrett can help you get things situated," Dr. Ferguson suggests. "I'd like you to get to know each other, spend a little time together before you go off to school."

Without my permission, my eyes flit up to Greedy's.

For the first time since we were seated, I let him see me. I let him really see me. As I look at him, I silently plead with him to see how sorry I am about all of it. How sorry I am about what has to happen next.

Because my heart's breaking as I sit here physically and metaphorically bleeding out.

This is a nightmare I never could have imagined possible.

This is hopeless. There's no way out; no way forward.

Everything I love leaves.

Greedy's expression doesn't reflect any of the same emotions I'm feeling. He looks angry. He also looks resolved.

Pressure accumulates behind my eyes as realization dawns on me.

We're not on the same page.

We're the farthest thing from it.

I'm trying to hold it together, mourning not one, but two losses today.

He's determined, relentless, tenacious.

I can see it in his eyes.

I can see it in his posture.

I know him too well.

He loves me too much.

Greedy thinks there's a solution to this.

He thinks we're going to figure this out.

He's wrong.

I was going to love him forever, only forever isn't an option anymore. The tears well again.

I do my best to stop them, minimize them, will them away. I blink rapidly, fighting them back before they can leak out of my eyes and wreck the mascara clinging to the tips of my lashes.

"Excuse me," I breathe out. Then I stand and retreat slowly, desperate to get away from it all.

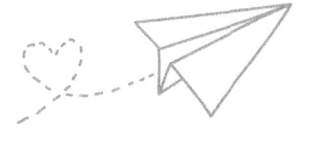

Chapter 43

Hunter

THEN

I make it all of ten steps into the grand foyer before he catches up.

"Tem, wait!"

I whip around so fast that spots dance in my periphery. "Don't call me that here," I tell him before he can get close.

I close my eyes and inhale deeply, then steel my spine and prepare for the unfathomable.

"Don't come any closer," I warn.

If I let him any nearer while I'm on the brink of hysterics, it won't end well. If he gets any closer, I'm liable to crumple right into his arms.

I wrap my arms around my torso and stand as tall as possible. Steadying my voice, I meet his gaze. "Did you know?"

"No," he insists. "I had no idea."

He runs his hand down his face, his expression forlorn. It's exactly how I feel. We were both blindsided by this—that's clear now.

"My dad's never dated anyone seriously," Greedy whispers. "Let alone mentioned getting remarried."

His eyes narrow, and I swear I *feel* the shift in his intention. Squeezing my arms around myself tighter, I brace for impact.

"Obviously, I don't think they're going to change their mind, but…" He inches forward.

I hold out one hand, desperate to keep him at bay. "Greedy, I swear to god, do *not* come any closer to me right now."

"Hunter." He whispers my name like a prayer. But there's no saving any of us now.

A cramp grips me then, and my muscles seize, forcing me to breathe deeply, just to keep my expression flat. I fight with everything I have not to outwardly react.

It doesn't work.

"Temi," he pleads. "What's wrong?"

Layers of concern coat his question. Dammit. His kindness makes it even harder to bear the tightness and the pain shooting through my lower abdomen.

"You're not okay."

It's not a question.

That's just how well he knows me.

That's just how well he *loves* me.

And yet that isn't our reality anymore.

It can't be.

"I'm fine," I tell him.

That's what people say, right?

When they're anything but.

I'm fine.

I'm the opposite of fine, but in this moment, for us, for *him*…

I'm fine.
I'm fine.
I'm fine.

To his credit, he respects my wishes and doesn't come closer. "Let's go somewhere and really talk." He glances toward the doors that lead out to the parking lot, then back at me, his eyes shining with hope.

"There's nothing to talk about, Greedy," I tell him, keeping my expression neutral and my words terse.

"*Like hell* there isn't," he shoots back. "We need to figure out how we're going to tell them."

I'm fine.
I'm fine.
I'm fine.

I'm going to do everything in my power to make sure he's fine, too.

He can't even imagine what it's like to coexist with Magnolia St. Clair. She's going to destroy his father one way or another. That's what she does.

She infects and she festers. Her love never comes freely.

She's poison.

Eventually, Dr. Ferguson will see it. He'll break, or he'll break up with her. Then Greedy will see the similarities.

My mother is the antithesis of who I am in so many ways. And yet her DNA created me. There are parallels I can't escape. In my heart of hearts, I know it's why my dad can stay away like he does. Why he doesn't call me anymore. Why he hasn't visited or invited me to come see him. We're too similar, she and I. There's too much of her in me for me to ever be free.

Eventually, Dr. Ferguson and Greedy will both hate her.

I can't bear for Greedy to hate me, too.

I won't give him the opportunity to leave.

I'm fine.

I'm fine.

I'm fine.

"Temi, listen to me. Just because our parents—"

"You are going to be my stepbrother in a few weeks. We're about to be *related*."

"That means nothing!" he shouts. Our voices are loud enough now that they're echoing off the high ceiling.

Good. I'd rather he be fuming than hopeful. His outrage serves as the fuel I need to double down.

"This means nothing," he repeats. "This changes nothing."

I grimace. "This changes *everything*."

"Tem," he says on a whisper. "I love you. I know you love me, too."

He's right. But it doesn't matter. Our connection, the idea of being with him now, trying to explain this to our parents... of giving Magnolia any part of this boy who's so kind and generous, so sweet and so good...

I can't. I won't.

I loved him. Past tense.

The only way I can move forward is if I pretend all of this is already in the past.

"We're about to be related," I tell Greedy, keeping my tone cold.

"No, we're not," he huffs, brow furrowed and lips turned down. "My dad will understand, Tem. We just need to talk to him—"

"No," I whisper harshly. "She's awful, Greedy. She'll make your life a living hell."

What I don't say is that I won't give her reason to hate him, too.

"You want to talk about a living hell, Hunter? The pain of seeing you every day would be a living hell. The idea of being in the same house and not being able to hold you is my idea of a living hell."

He strides forward and opens his arms, clearly intent on scooping me up. God, do I want that, but it can't happen.

I take a big step back, being sure not to let him touch me.

Greedy comes to an abrupt stop, his jaw ticking in frustration. It takes all my dwindling strength to resist the urge to smooth my hand along the side of his face.

"This isn't over," he whispers, both palms raised in a temporary surrender. "It's you and me, Tem. We'll figure this out. I'll stop at nothing. I won't let them keep us apart."

I close my eyes and relish the sting behind my lids. Despite the way my nose tingles and my sinuses feel heavy, moisture doesn't collect. I'm officially cried out.

The saddest part of this situation is that I believe him. He'll do everything in his power to stay with me.

It's on me to save him from her now.

"Talk to me," he urges.

Fingertips brush along my elbow, caressing inches away from where the needles were inserted just hours ago. Eyes flying open, I jump back at the contact.

He catalogs my reaction, his mouth dropping open in horror. "Baby... It's going to be okay," he assures me again. "No wrong moves, Tem, remember?"

I nod mechanically. Standing tall, I drop my hands to my thighs. "No wrong moves."

What Greedy doesn't realize is that there are no right moves here either.

No right moves, except one designed to protect him.

Nothing's wrong. Nothing's right.

I'm fine.

I'm fine.

I'm fine.

I'll do everything in my power to make sure he's fine in the end, too.

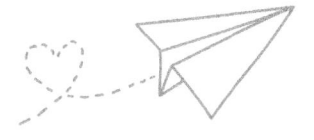

Chapter 44

Hunter

NOW

I can't sleep. I can barely remember the mechanics of breathing. When I lie flat, my lungs seize like I'm being held underwater. So I'm up. Pacing.

I shouldn't be alone. The self-aware part of me knows that.

My door is locked.

I've checked it once, twice, three times now.

My chest burns with the desire to go to him.

To sneak into his bed like I do during the dark nights.

To silently beg him to hold me, just until the morning.

But I can't.

She's here. She can't know. I can't let her hurt him.

I dig out my Kindle and try to lose myself in a book, but I can't focus.

I stretch, hoping the physical release will calm me, but just end up wandering my room instead.

After pacing like a caged animal for what feels like hours, I find myself seeking a change of scenery.

I grip the bronze handle and curl my fingers around it until my polished pink nails disappear.

Then I'm out on the balcony.

This isn't smart.

I'm far too detached from my own sense of self to be aimlessly wandering the second-floor balcony.

I stay glued to the exterior of the house as I creep away from my bedroom toward the next door, then push my way inside.

"Hunter."

Heart lurching, I zero in on the bed. Levi sits, shirtless, with his jean-clad legs stretched out long in front of him.

I freeze, holding my breath, as if I've been caught. In a way, I have. There's no hiding the tremble of my lip, the physical shaking of my hands.

"Can I stay in here with you?" I plead.

Chapter 45

Greedy

NOW

I'm pacing my dad's study when the text comes through.

This room offers the best view of the circle driveway. I need to be the first to know he's arrived.

This can't stand. Rage courses through me when I recall the way he casually dropped it on me at dinner.

Fucking bullshit.

My father knows I don't care for Magnolia.

Though he doesn't know the severity of my hatred, the depth of my ire.

Magnolia is the reason Hunter left. Hunter never confirmed it, but deep down, I've always known.

The night our parents "introduced" us and announced their engagement was the night everything changed. I stood in the middle of the foyer of a country club and witnessed her slipping out of my grasp.

We were young, and we were both scared, but I told her we'd figure it out. I promised her it would be okay, then she iced me out and left the damn country before I could prove I was a man of my word.

I'll be damned if I let the only woman I've ever loved be driven out of this house again because of my father's flighty, absentee wife.

With a long breath out, I unlock my phone and read the text.

> **Levi:** Come up to my room. It's Hunter. I think she needs help.

His room?

But if Hunter needs me...

I stalk out of the study, slamming the door closed on my way out.

"Oh, Garrett!"

I ignore Magnolia. She's sitting in front of the television. Probably still struggling to figure out the remotes like she was when I retreated to the office. She's never stuck around long enough to figure out how to work the goddamn TV. This reappearance? It has the power to drive away the person who *does* belong here. The person I'm desperate to make stay.

I take the stairs two at a time, let myself into Levi's dark room, and close and lock the door.

Instinctively, I reach for the lights.

"Don't," he rasps from the bed.

I freeze, battling to keep calm as my eyes adjust to the dark. When I can make out the details of the room, I sweep my gaze over the two people in his bed.

Him and her. Her and him.

I fucking told him where things stood with Hunter. I fucking told him she was mine.

But I saw the way he touched her earlier. It was instinctive, like it was second nature to protect her. And I saw the way she looked at him.

I recognized that look. It's how she used to look at me, always.

It's how she still looks at me on the darkest nights.

Heart pounding in my chest, I approach the bed slowly, steeling myself for the possibility of what I'm about to bear witness to.

Moonlight shines in from the French doors that lead to our shared balcony. A sliver of light is visible under the bathroom door, too.

They're under the sheets. Together.

He's got both arms wrapped around her, holding her close to his bare chest.

She's draped over him the way she used to drape herself over me.

I fist my hands at my sides, choking back the hurt and betrayal.

Hunter's breathing is soft and steady, save for the occasional hiccup. It's hard to tell whether she's asleep or awake.

"Why the hell did you—"

"*Greedy.*"

The quiver in her voice catches me off guard. It steals the words from my mouth and the air from my lungs.

Hunter peels herself off Levi and turns, reaching for me.

I react on instinct. Muscle memory. Heart recall.

Quickly, I shuck off my shirt and ditch my shoes. Then, silently, I climb into the bed on her other side.

"Greedy," she says again, shifting away from Levi, toward me.

I slot in place behind her and wrap my arms around her as best as I can. She squirms and burrows, like she can't get close enough.

When she finds a comfortable position, she lets out a shuddering breath. "My mom is here."

Her voice doesn't even sound like her own.

"I know, Tem. I'm so sorry." I tentatively pet her hair, bumping arms with Levi as we struggle to comfort her between us.

"I had dinner with my dad. He told me then," I explain. "I tried to call but couldn't get a hold of you. I rushed home as fast as I could."

"It's not your fault." She sniffs and shrinks back in on herself.

Except *it is*.

I can't ever get to her fast enough to warn her. To protect her. To be what she needs when she needs it. I've never been enough.

"What can I do for you?" I plead. It's agony to be this close, yet to not know how to help.

Does she need space? More time? If she asked me to physically remove her mother from the premises, I'd do it without a second thought. I'll do anything to take her pain away. Anything to make her *stay*.

"Just hold me," she breathes. "Hold me like the other nights."

The other nights.

The nights in my bed we don't speak of.

I look over to Levi, who's watching us silently, a frown tugging at his lips, then focus on Hunter again.

"Are you asking me to take you to my room?" I hedge.

She shakes her head a fraction. "I want to be with Levi."

The declaration slices through me like a knife. I fight back the urge to argue, to scream and rage. It was never supposed to be her and him.

It was always supposed to be her and me.

I exhale, focusing on keeping my breathing steady. Then, as calmly as I'm capable, I peel back the sheets and sit upright. "Okay. I'll go. If he's what you want—"

"Don't leave." She clutches my hand. "Greedy, *please*."

So she doesn't want to leave him and go to my room.

But she doesn't want me to leave either. I don't know what she thinks is going to happen—

"Stay."

"In here?"

"Yes. Greedy. Please stay with me. With us."

She's a shell of herself right now. I can't deny her. If she wants me to stay...

I glance back at Levi to gauge his reaction. This is his room, after all. His bed. His woman, if my suspicions are correct.

He nods hastily, shifting back and pulling Hunter to the middle of the mattress.

This time when I lie down, I situate myself as close as I can physically get. Not caring that we've already made a tangled mess out of the comforter and sheets, I hitch one leg over top of hers.

Chest aching, I seek out her soft skin, burrowing under the oversized button-down shirt she's wearing.

This isn't the first time she's let me hold her since she came back to me. Though it *is* the first time she's verbalized exactly what she wanted, and it's the first time she's told me she wants *me*.

"You're okay, Tem," I assure her, stroking one hand up and down her spine to soothe her. "I'll stay in here for as long as you need me."

She snuggles closer, like she's desperate to crawl into my skin and take up residence between the layers of tissue and muscle.

The same yearning that's always there when I'm in close proximity to her percolates deep in my gut. I ignore it and focus entirely on her comfort.

I smooth the hair away from her face. Then, without thinking, I bend low and kiss her forehead.

She leans into it, so I keep my lips pressed to her skin. When she exhales, her warm breath wraps around my neck and inspires goose bumps along my spine.

I freeze, willing my body to relax and *begging* my cock to stand the fuck down.

Her breath hitches in response to my subtle reaction.

It's just the proximity, I remind myself.

It's impossible for me to be near her—for me to fucking hold her this closely—and not physically react. She's nestled too deeply in my heart. My body remembers her too well.

The weight of Levi's arm is heavy on her hip. He keeps his face hidden in her hair, spooning her from behind.

When she inhales, it's with a shuddering breath. Then on the exhale, her hips hitch forward, and she presses into my crotch.

With a hiss, I pull back a fraction. Then I trace one hand down her spine and around her front, digging into the soft flesh stretched over her hip with a warning squeeze.

In response, she rolls her hips forward again. When she rolls them back, Levi groans.

"Distract me."

Distract her?

With pleasure.

There is no question that I'll obey her request. Every part of me is programmed to please her. She was my everything once. I'll do anything in my power to remind her of how good it can be when we're together.

"Say it again," I tell her, my lips brushing over her forehead.

She smacks my bare chest, the sound of the slap reverberating through the room.

"I'm serious, Hunter. Say it again. And tell me you're not going to regret it tomorrow."

"I want you," she says. "*Both* of you. Distract me." Then, softer, she adds, "I want to forget. I want to not think about what happened tonight. Or what happened back then."

Back then?

She doesn't offer any more context.

"Please, Greedy. Make me feel good."

My name on her lips is what does it. With a growl, I snap. Capturing her mouth with mine, I give her the first real fucking kiss she's allowed me to give in over three years.

She's sweet, just like I remembered. But the layer of sorrow beneath that taste is salty on my tongue.

I groan, desperate, wanting more, more, more. Our mouths battle for dominance, each one of us craving a different type of fulfillment from the contact.

She wants to forget. All I want to do is make her remember.

With her jaw cupped in my hand, I hold her mouth open and kiss her harshly. "You want me to make you feel good?" I ask, panting.

She nods frantically. Her eagerness fuels me.

I straddle her, one leg bumping Levi's. I'm too gone for this woman to care. I hover over her as I pepper her neck with kisses. Nipping at her ear, I tell her, "I'm about to remind you of exactly how good this can be."

She squirms beneath me, and I kiss her again. I have to. If she's finally willing to give, then I'm going to take and take and take without shame.

I need more of her. I want all of her.

We're a ravenous battle of teeth and tongues, repressed wants and desperate needs.

It takes all my strength to break the connection. I'd kiss her senseless all damn night if she wasn't demanding more. When I finally pull back, her eyes are hazy. A million memories take center stage in my mind as she holds my gaze and lets me in.

Every one plays out before me. Little moments I've almost forgotten. Big, life-changing moments I forced myself to not dwell on over the last three years.

I never gave up on us. I was giving her the fucking space she wanted. Now she's here. She's here and she says she needs me.

Moving to my knees, I glance at Levi. "Get her undressed."

"Gladly," he replies without hesitation.

Hunter is sprawled out between us, propped up on her elbows and being supported by Levi from behind.

Levi starts at the top. He unbuttons her oversized shirt with slow, deliberate movements.

I follow the path he's making for me, kissing and suckling every inch of skin he exposes.

She's bucking off the bed by the time I've reached her tummy. God, I missed the taste of her. The feel of her. The responsiveness and the way my body instinctively remembers exactly where to touch her and how to make her see stars.

I'm going to distract her so well she won't be able to think about anything else for the rest of the night.

Once her shirt's completely undone, I situate myself between her thighs.

"You know how long I've waited for this?"

She bites her bottom lip, her breath shuddering as she takes me in.

I trail one finger from her sternum down through her cleavage. Over the curve of her waist. Dipping into her belly button. I stop at the top of her pubic bone.

"Three years," I tell her.

Three years, four months, and eight days, to be precise. I keep the exact count to myself, unwilling to distract her and concerned that admitting how deep my devotion runs will scare her off.

"That's how long I've waited for you."

I rest my hand on her pubic bone, cupping her through her panties, then I dig the heel of my hand up against her clit.

"*Fuck*," she hisses in response.

"Remember that long weekend at the cabin? When I got you off by sucking on your perfect nipples and grinding my knuckles against your clit?"

"Greedy," she whines, bucking her hips.

"I know, baby. I know." I push open the panels of the button-down shirt, revealing generous mounds of supple flesh.

Fuck. I missed these tits.

Her chest is splotchy and red, from crying or from arousal. Maybe both. Her nipples are dusty pink and peaked already. They're even more beautiful now than I remember.

Bending low, I suck one nipple into my mouth, then catch the tip between my teeth and flick my tongue back and forth.

I look over to Levi, locking eyes with him as I ravish Hunter's breast.

"Suck on her other tit," I murmur, my lips brushing against her flesh.

Hunter whimpers at the loss of my mouth, clawing at my head to get me back where she wants me.

"Just wait until you see how she fucking unravels."

Levi does as he's told, taking a generous portion of her breast into his mouth.

The second he suckles on her sensitive peak, Hunter gasps and practically flies off the bed. Her back arches, and her hips crash into my pelvis with fervor.

We ravish her like that, licking and sucking, until she's a whimpering, writhing mess.

She snakes a hand between our bodies, but before she can slip it into her panties, I snag it and place it back on the mattress by her head.

"Don't even think about it," I grit out. "You made me wait three years for a taste of your perfect pussy. I'll be damned if I'm not the first one to get to touch it now."

I shift back on my knees, peeling away her panties and tossing them off the bed.

"Kiss her," I tell Levi. I know damn well she'll love the feel of his tongue in her mouth and his teeth scraping along her neck while I fuck her with my tongue.

I inhale and close my eyes as her scent envelops me. It's so heady I swear I almost come in my pants.

The first stroke of my tongue is soft, reverent. I savor every centimeter of her as I reacquaint myself with the folds of her pussy.

Hunter's already writhing, gyrating her hips and finding a rhythm. Trying to take control.

But I'm not playing nice. I'm going to take her to the edge, then pull back until she's begging for my return. I fully intend to take my time with her. I'll distract her for hours if needed.

"She needs more," Levi grunts, panting from exertion.

"I fucking know what she needs." I suck hard on her clit for emphasis. How he knows is a question for another time. "Right now, she's going to take what I fucking give her."

Despite my declaration, I double down. I suck and flick her clit in rapid succession, then slip two fingers into her pussy.

Her inner walls grip me, and my cock weeps with want. I channel all my desire into building her up, driving her higher and higher.

Hunter's nails dig into my skull, the contact searing into a secret I've kept safe for nearly three years. That connection spurs me on like nothing else can. Her fingers in my hair. Her eyes wide and wanton when I peek up from between her thighs.

Fuck edging. I'm going to make her come so hard she blacks out.

"She's close," I tell Levi. He's not the only one in this bed who knows exactly what she fucking needs.

With a finger pressed to her G-spot, I splay my other hand low on her belly and press down. I suck her clit so hard she shrieks, and I don't relent until her needy cunt milks my hand.

She's a mess of groans and praise, reaching for me and Levi both as she rides out the spasms of her climax.

I've barely caught my breath when she clutches my arms and tugs on me desperately, guiding me up.

"What do you need?" I hover over her as she arches her back and whimpers.

Her eyes have that hazy lust-drunk glaze to them still. I'll make her come over and over again all night long if this is the distraction she craves.

"I want to feel you," she begs, slipping her hand down the front of my pants and giving my cock a tentative stroke.

Fuck. I almost lose it right then and there. I haven't felt her touch in three long years, and it's even better than I remember.

"I want to feel both of you. At the same time."

Chest heaving with exertion and need, I look at Levi. We've been best friends for years, but we've never done even close to what Hunter's asking for right now.

I'm not opposed. In fact, I'm deliriously turned on and dick-drunk with desire. But it's Levi's choice.

"I'm down if you are." He cocks one eyebrow in question.

With a nod, I hastily shove off my pants. Levi does the same. Then I roll to my side and selfishly pull Hunter to face me. "How do you want us?"

"Any way I can have you," she whimpers, her breath hot on my skin.

I slam my mouth into hers and roll my hips. She's slick with her own cum, which makes her thighs feel like satin when I notch between them.

When something rubs against the length of my shaft, I bite out a curse.

"Fuck," I groan as Levi's cock nudges mine. He's right there—right fucking there—and I'm not sure I've ever felt arousal lick up my balls like it's doing now.

"Wait," Hunter whispers.

Levi and I both freeze. My heart pounds so fiercely I can barely hear her over the blood roaring in my ears.

"I'm on the pill, but don't come inside me."

I grit my teeth and nod. "I don't think we'll both fit..."

Hunter bites down on her bottom lip. "Have you seen Duke's dick in action? You definitely won't both fit."

"Brat," I snarl. I can't help but smile. There's a spark to her now that didn't exist moments ago. If this is what she wants, if this is what she needs to bring her back to life...

"Use me. Fill me up. I want to feel you both."

She slips her hand between us and guides my cock to her entrance. I hold my breath, nostalgia and desire warring inside me at the prospect of this homecoming, and give her just the tip. I hold steady, savoring the sensation.

Her.

Me.

Home.

She shifts again, reaching between her legs, and guides Levi to one side of my cock.

His crown nudges my balls while the warmth of Hunter's cunt engulfs me.

I've never felt the tingles of an orgasm start up faster in my life.

After just a few shallow thrusts, I pull out with a curse.

"You feel like heaven, Tem. Pure fucking heaven."

I press my forehead into hers, willing her to feel the depth of emotion welling inside me.

Levi takes over, lifting Hunter's top leg and notching into her pussy from behind.

"Fuck, Daisy. You take me so well, pretty girl."

He doesn't last long either. The hot, wet tip of his cock brushes mine as he retreats.

When I'm not inside her, I rub her clit. When Levi's not buried deep, he sucks on her neck and toys with her nipples. We fuck like that, our bodies in charge, seeking a chaotic rhythm, for what feels like hours.

Hunter unravels for us once, twice, and then a third time.

When it happens a fourth time, I'm buried deep inside her. The way her pussy chokes my cock is too much. I keep my thumb pressed to her clit but quickly pull out like she wanted.

"I'm gonna come," I declare.

"Thank fuck," Levi snarls.

Hunter is so wrapped up in her release that she's in her own world.

We rut between her thighs in rhythm. Each brush of his cock against mine feels like a vise grip around my balls.

Levi and I are on the precipice, chasing our respective orgasms, and using Hunter—and each other—to get there.

Instinct takes over, and I reach beyond my girl to grip Levi's head. Surprised by my own actions, I hold on tight, my fingers tangled in his hair, and sweep my tongue into Hunter's mouth.

My core tightens, and Levi moans behind us.

I don't know who let's go first, but that first jet of cum covers us both, and an explosion of warmth coats my cock as my orgasm tears through my body.

We're a mess of pants and moans, slickness and warmth.

We slow our thrusts as we come down. Hunter whimpers every few seconds as she fights to keep her eyes open.

"Sleep, Tem," I tell her, kissing the tip of her nose. "I'll clean you up once I get feeling back in my legs."

"I'll be right here, Daisy," Levi promises from behind her. "I've got you."

"*We've* got you," I correct.

"And we're not going anywhere," Levi adds.

Chapter 46

Levi

NOW

Hunter snores. It just might be the cutest fucking sound I've ever heard.

I'm still up, begging my brain to turn off and let me rest.

I can't stop thinking about what happened and about how hot it was. How I wouldn't mind doing it again.

Right now, though, I need to push those thoughts out of my mind. The most crucial issue is Hunter.

She was nearly unrecognizable when she stumbled into my room a few hours ago, shoulders sagging, hair and face a mess. At first, I thought she might be sleepwalking.

She was so out of it, both physically and mentally. I swear she wasn't fully coherent until Greedy came up and joined us.

SO WRONG

I smooth a loose strand of hair away from her face, cradling the back of her head tenderly, willing her to stay asleep. She needs the rest. When she wakes up tomorrow...

Fucking hell.

Nothing will be different, assuming her mom's reappearance isn't a weird fever dream we're all stuck in.

But I'll be here for her. I'm not going anywhere.

My knuckles caress warm skin as I stroke the back of Hunter's head. It's then I realize just how close Greedy is cuddled up to her other side.

"Shit. Sorry, man."

He grunts in response. "All good. Wasn't sure if you were still awake."

I adjust my pillow to give myself a few seconds to collect my thoughts as nerves skitter through me.

"So, that happened," I awkwardly throw out.

I swear I can hear him smirk.

"It did."

"Was that the first time you've ever, uh... you've ever been with a guy?"

Greedy knows I'm bisexual. He's never discussed his sexuality with me, though.

He clears his throat softly. It's dark and quiet, and with Hunter sleeping between us, it's best if we keep our voices low.

"That was the first time I've ever been intimate with anyone other than Hunter."

My heart stutters in my chest.

That's news to me.

Though it aligns with what he told me my first night here. That it was only ever her.

"Listen, before you say anything else, there's something you should know," I rush out.

He told me to not catch feelings, but it's too fucking late.

"I care for her, G. There's nothing I wouldn't do for her. If she wants me... if she needs me, too... I won't turn my back on her."

"I never turned my back on her," he contends, his tone low but filled with anguish.

Hunter stirs between us, and we both go silent and still.

I give it a few breaths, reconciling my emotions with what I know.

He's right. He didn't abandon her. She left him, and I know why. I'm just as guilty as he is for letting her go the first time. I allowed her to suffer alone. I allowed her to flee, to slip through our fingers when she very clearly needed us to fight for her. Or at the very least, to fight with her.

"I'm not accusing you of anything," I whisper. "I'm not even telling you to back off." I readjust my pillow one more time and wrap my arm around Hunter's bare stomach. "I'm just saying that I'm not giving her up. If she wants me, she has me."

Greedy says nothing. The only sound in the room is our breathing until we both drift off.

Chapter 47

Levi

NOW

Soft hairs tickle my chest as a warm floral scent fills my nostrils.

I'm bare-chested still. She's shirtless, too, her supple breasts pressed against my front like she couldn't stand to leave even an inch of space between us.

Awareness sparks through my limbs, and my chest tightens. I rearrange my body carefully so I don't wake her, silently extending my arms and neck, then giving my bad leg a compulsory stretch, too.

It aches this morning. I knew it would after the exertion and the angle of last night, but fuck, was it worth it.

I lower my hands under the covers to massage away the stiffness that settled in my limbs overnight. When I hit a particularly tender spot between my incision and my hip, a low grunt escapes me.

"Are you okay?" Hunter asks softly.

I don't know if I woke her or if she's been awake this whole time, but it's just the two of us now.

I also don't know how to act after what went down last night.

"Just sore," I answer.

In response, she rolls her ass back into my body and pulls my free hand around her midsection.

"Can I ask you something?" I whisper into her hair, holding her tight.

Considering all that's happened over the last twenty-four hours and what's waiting for us on the other side of that door, this may be the only chance we get to have a private conversation.

"You told me at the hospital that Greedy doesn't know... what about your mom?"

She tenses, then shakes her head. She licks her lips and meets my gaze. "I didn't tell anyone before I left town."

A surge of possessiveness shoots through me. I shouldn't feel proud that I bore witness to her darkest moment, but knowing that she trusted me then, and that she still trusts me now, lights up my insides.

I want to be good for her. I want to be more than a friend, more than a best friend, more than she's ever had. I want to be the one she relies on. The one who stays.

But I want her to want me, too.

She intertwines our fingers under the sheets, smoothing our joined hands up and down the tightness of my aching thigh.

"What are we doing, Daisy?" I ask on a whisper.

With a hum, she turns and brushes her lips against the center of my chest and keeps working her fingers into my too-tight quad. As she rubs my leg, her core occasionally comes into contact with my other thigh. Visions of how she writhed and ground against me yesterday in the truck, chasing that orgasm, soaking my arm, swamp me. With each point of contact, she squirms closer, inviting me. Enticing me.

Watching Greedy please her with his mouth lit a fire inside me. I want to be the one making her whimper and moan and beg for more as I fuck her with my tongue. But seeing the two of them together—bearing witness to how their bodies very clearly remember one another—was a wake-up call.

I'm not gonna get in the way of what they could have again. I just want to be factored into the equation, too.

"Half-naked massages aren't on the list of obligations for my fake girlfriend." I cautiously lift her hand and unwind her fingers. This is her out. Her opportunity to clarify her intentions and her feelings. I want her to make this decision now, after she experienced what she did with Greedy last night. If it's going to come down to me or him, she needs him, and I want her to have that.

I haven't even let go of her hand completely before she snatches my wrist and pulls me close again.

"I don't want it to be fake anything with you," she says into the pillow. After a heartbeat, she props her head on her hand and hits me with a sincere look. "Levi... I want this. I want us to be real."

Relief rushes my system, but—

She doesn't even give me time to ask whether she's sure. "You see me, Levi," she urges. "You see all of me, and you're not running. You fight back against my demons. You've always been there for me."

For a moment, neither of us speaks. I'm still absorbing her words, considering their meaning.

"I care about you. I'm deliriously attracted to you." She presses her breasts into me for emphasis. "Do you want me, too?"

I press my morning wood into her thigh in confirmation and kiss the tip of her nose.

"No more faking it," she whispers.

Joy floods my system. I try to temper my reaction, but it's impossible not to be elated. She wants me. She's choosing me.

Except things are so much more complicated now than they were just twenty-four hours ago. Between Greedy and now her mom, I don't see Hunter staying in this house much longer. And after last night, I don't see Greedy letting her go again. Ever.

Before I can ask about any of that, she angles up and smooths her palm down my jaw. "Be my real boyfriend, Levi Moore."

"Yes," I answer without hesitation.

Simultaneous to this euphoria, a niggle of worry worms its way into my mind.

"What about Greedy?"

Hunter sighs, her breath warming my chest as she nuzzles closer. "He's not here this morning, is he?"

He's not. But I reckon it's because he's running interference on their parents. If I know him, he had to fight like hell against his deep-seated desire to stay in bed with us.

"Good things always leave me," she confesses into my chest. "Please don't be another thing that leaves."

Those words land like a physical blow, and at the same time, tug at my heartstrings. My desire to care for this woman is unmatched. There's no denying my need to protect her. To please her the best I can. Fuck it. Greedy and I will figure it out.

If she wants me—if she needs me—who am I to deny her?

"I've got you, Daisy. I'm not going anywhere."

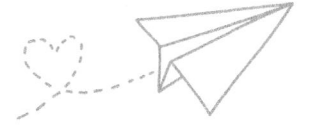

Chapter 48

Hunter

THEN

I've been hiding out for a full week, getting things in place.

I went to the follow-up with my OBGYN. My hCG level decreased drastically, meaning no additional appointments are needed. It's done. Over. They assured me yet again that I did nothing wrong. Nothing could have changed the outcome.

The bleeding has stopped, as has most of the cramping. The emotional ache is ever-present, but I've ignored my darkest feelings, choosing to power through as best I can and focus on the other worries and concerns looming over me this week.

My grief will keep. The window to make a clean break will not.

I hold my head high and refuse to let the big feelings consume me as I pass through the front door.

I've done my crying. It's time to move on to the next stage.

I roll one small suitcase over the threshold and onto the stoop, then the other, and readjust the carry-on slung over my shoulder. The rest of my belongings will stay here. Louie assures me the shopping near our new flat is top-notch.

I push up my sunglasses and use them to hold my hair back as I lock the front door of my childhood home for the very last time. Then I use the combination from the realtor to open up the key box. With a *clunk* of metal on metal, I officially turn in my key.

Without a backward glance, I grab my luggage and charge forward toward my future.

I don't make it more than a single step down the paved walkway that leads to the driveway before my foot slips ever so slightly.

Slowly lifting my leg, I shake off the white piece of paper clinging to my sneaker. It's limp from the humidity and shaped like an airplane. The nose is crushed, as if it hit a hard surface before crashing to the ground.

Greedy.

I've effectively ignored him for the last seven days.

It wasn't easy. He came by the house multiple times, called my old phone nonstop. I purchased a new phone with a new number. I needed an international SIM card anyway. I still packed my old phone, just in case. But I'm not sure I even brought the charger for it.

Thankfully, his attempts slowed as the week went on. According to Levi, South Chapel University started three-a-days, and there's a strict no phones policy when students are on the field.

I bend to pick up the airplane.

When I straighten, I catch sight of a handful more littering the yard.

One is stuck in the gorgeous dogwood tree beside the bay window of the dining room. At least two have made their way to the cul-de-sac.

I don't have to look at them to know each plane has a note for me. A confession of love. A heartfelt plea. His relentless attempts to bridge the canyon between us.

I won't be able to get in the car if I read them all.

But I let myself have just one.

With a harsh breath in, I unfold the paper, taking great care not to rip it.

> *Temi—*
> *There isn't anything I wouldn't do for you.*
> *There isn't anything I couldn't love you through.*

Holding the damp paper to my chest, I let the words sink. I allow myself to feel all the emotions I've suppressed for just a few seconds.

I envision Greedy writing the notes, searching for the words. Pouring out his heart. Folding the paper airplane just so, hoping to make the connection. Then futilely giving up, night after night, and letting the plane fly, knowing it'll crash into my window.

In my mind's eye, I watch him throw it.

I watch it soar—his words, our love.

The connection we shared, and the summer I'll never forget.

I give myself one last second to feel it all.

Then I drop the paper and watch it flutter back to the ground.

It's for the best.

It's for him.

He'll eventually move on, and his life will be categorically better without me.

There's a poetic tragedy to paper airplanes.

No matter how much care and detail has been poured into them, they all fall eventually. They're fragile and easily damaged. Their first flight is usually their one and only chance to soar.

Paper airplanes are doomed from the start, even if the few seconds of flight are full of hope and lightness and fun. Those few seconds make it almost worth the inevitable fall.

Almost, but not quite.

·♥·♥·♥·♥·♥·

I picked Levi up at the QuickieMart, then didn't tell him where we were headed until we were getting off at the exit for the airport. After a futile attempt at trying to convince me to stay, he finally agreed to support my plan.

"Thanks for doing this." I circle around to the trunk of my car to retrieve my luggage, then hand over the key to the boy who's become my best friend over the last few months.

Head bowed and lips turned down, he accepts my offering. "You know I'd do anything for you, Daisy."

He looks so defeated. Tears well in my eyes, and my lip wobbles when I meet his gaze.

Levi has quickly become the most trusted person in my life.

He knows things about me now that no one else knows—that no one else will ever know.

I'll never forget the way he helped me and held me and treated me with so much care.

I hate that this is it. That I won't be around to return the favor when he needs it. Even more, I hate that I'm hurting him by leaving.

"You're sure?" he asks for the hundredth time.

If I had to guess, he and Greedy believed some time and space were all I needed to get past the shock of my mother marrying Greedy's father.

It's so much more than that. As dramatic as it may seem, it's going to take an entire ocean of distance to move on and forget what I have to let go of here in North Carolina.

"I'm sure," I tell him, lifting my chin and meeting his eye. "I know you don't agree with me—"

"I don't," he interjects.

"Levi..." I try once more. "You don't know her like I do."

I've spent the last week telling Levi about my mom, trying to make him understand. I've never talked to anyone about her dark side before. I've always kept the worst details to myself, either because I was afraid to trust or because I didn't want to burden others. It turns out that opening up to Levi was easier than I thought.

His mom is equally awful, but in totally different ways. It was validating and eye-opening to see his reaction to some of the things I shared, especially when I got into details about the last year.

"I know you don't agree," I say, "but please tell me you at least understand."

I don't need his approval. I don't need the approval of anyone. Greedy will never forgive me. Hell, I don't think I'll ever forgive myself.

But if Levi can hold space for me or admit he understands, then maybe I can find some semblance of peace.

When Levi says nothing, I change tack.

"You know how he is."

It's the same justification I've relied on all week.

When Levi says nothing, I push harder. "He's intense. Relentless. Greedy wouldn't give up if I stuck around. Eventually, he'd wear me down."

I heave both my bags out of the car to distract myself from thinking any more about him.

"And that would be so bad?" Levi challenges, taking the bags from me.

I meet his gaze again, considering. Car horns blast, and drivers weave in and out of parked cars while people come and go. Everyone has somewhere to be. Including me.

I throw my arms around Levi's neck and hug him fiercely.

"You're leaving for California, Duke. You'll have a new state, new friends, a whole new life. Greedy has football. His honors program. His dad." I let go of his neck and drop my arms to my sides. "If I stayed, I'd have—"

"Us," he says, the word clipped. "You have us."

I dig my nails into the palms of my hands, concentrating on the sharp sting of each point to keep the tears prickling behind my eyes at bay.

"Had. I had you, Duke. Both of you." I shrug, biting down on my bottom lip. "And for one perfect summer, you two were all I needed."

I throw my arms around his torso once more and squeeze him tight, effectively ending the conversation. Eventually, he wraps his arms around me, too, and awkwardly pats my hair as we embrace in the drop-off lane of the airport.

I release him, then spin and close the trunk with a definitive *thunk*.

He shoves his hands into his pockets and rocks back on his heels. "If you ever change your mind—"

"I know. And you have my new number," I remind him. "But please, Levi, I beg you—"

"I won't share it," he promises me softly.

It's killing him to keep secrets from Greedy. I know I'm asking too much. But Levi has become important to me in a way that no one else in my life is. I hate that I'm making him pick sides and that I essentially forced him to pick me. It's a shitty situation all around.

"You've got everything you need?" he asks, nodding down to my two suitcases and the carry-on over my shoulder.

"If I don't, I've got my soon-to-be stepdad's gold AmEx in my wallet. I'll be fine. Now please go before you make me cry."

He bends low, pulls me close once more, and kisses the top of my head.

"Love you, Daisy," he murmurs.

"Later, Duke."

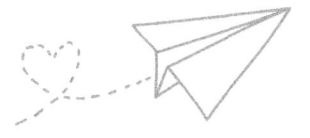

Chapter 49

Hunter

NOW

The moment Dr. Ferguson and my mom head out, I hop to my feet. I only caught the tail-end of breakfast, but they mentioned they had some shopping to do. By the time Levi and I wandered down to the kitchen, everyone else was done eating.

I clear away the breakfast dishes to give myself something to do.

"You know the housekeeper will get those," Greedy chides from his seat at the table.

He wasn't in bed when we woke up this morning. At first, I was shocked. But now I'm just angry.

I haven't allowed myself to be in a position like that for years. I assumed that after the way we connected last night, he would still be there in the morning.

Now I feel like a fool. Like it was all wishful thinking.

He was gone. Of course he was. Nothing good in my life ever stays.

"Leave her alone, G," Levi says, standing to clear his own plate. When he reaches me at the sink, he brushes the back of his knuckles against my cheek. "I'll clear and rinse if you want to load them in the dishwasher," he tells me softly.

"What the hell are you two whispering about?" Greedy sneers.

Levi eyes me warily, like he's trying to figure out the play.

Greedy's being an asshole, but I have to assume my mother's appearance has him off-kilter, like me. With a hand on Levi's arm, I clear my throat. "Levi, it's fine—"

"So it's like this, huh?" Greedy bites out.

That remark seals his fate.

"I said leave her alone." Levi turns to block me from Greedy's view, taking a wide stance and crossing his arms over his chest.

Greedy stalks across the kitchen and comes to a stop on the opposite end of the bar. He spreads his arms wide and hangs his head, letting out a humorless chuckle. Then he looks up, and his eyes lock with mine. "Really, Hunter?"

I close my eyes and rub the wrinkle between my brows. "I don't want to fight, Greedy," I whisper.

"Too fucking bad. You don't get to beg for us both in your bed, then ice me out like usual the next day."

"Last night was a mistake," I bite out on autopilot.

Levi slinks closer, pressing his warm palm to the small of my back.

"Like hell it was." Greedy shoves off the countertop like he's going to circle around it and get up in my face.

He stops short when he sees Levi stand taller by my side. Instead of approaching, he paces from one end of the island to the other.

"I've been waiting for months for you to let me in. *Really* let me in. I gave you space. I let you sneak into my bed, take what you needed from me, then sneak out the next day." He roughs a hand down his face and sucks in a sharp breath. "I told myself that, eventually, it would be enough. That if I was just patient, if I waited you out, you'd come back to me."

This is what he does. He chips away at my resolve. He says beautiful things and makes hopeful promises. I so desperately want to believe him.

"Greedy, that's not—"

He cuts me off with a jagged groan. "I thought last night—I thought last night was it."

I press my lips together and will myself not to cry. "We can't go back, Greedy."

"*Bullshit.*"

Despite what he thinks, it's the truth. What I want doesn't matter.

There's no version of reality where Greedy and I can go back *or* move forward.

Protecting him—from my mother, but also from the secrets I've kept—is paramount. I'd rather he hate me for pushing him away than ever discover the truth.

"You have to move on," I plead. "Surely there's someone—"

"No." He slaps the granite countertop. "I told you last night: I haven't looked at another woman since you left town three years ago. I haven't kissed anyone else. *Tasted* anyone else. I waited for you. I'd wait another three years if it meant you'd finally let me in and let me stay."

My already broken heart cracks further. The ache in my chest is acute, and I have to lean against the island to keep myself upright.

He... waited?

For me?

Three years of heartache swirl into a cyclone in my gut. Anxiety churns as usual, but it's mixed with something new. Something hopeful.

When I woke up and found Greedy gone this morning, I was sure he was ashamed of what we'd done. Or maybe that after he'd been with me again, he decided I wasn't worth it after all.

But knowing that he waited... that I left, but he stayed.

That he's been waiting all this time...

I'm frozen in place, mouth agape and mind reeling, as all sorts of new considerations flood my consciousness.

We're older now. Could it be different? Maybe he's right. Maybe we could try again...

Greedy interrupts my thoughts and makes his case.

"Last night? It worked. I never would have fucking imagined a scenario like that, but it worked for me." With his palms on the island, his arms spread wide, he hangs his head and breathes in so deep his shoulders heave. Then he blows out the breath. "I'm not asking you to choose. I'm not asking you to give up what you and Leev have going. I'm asking you to give me a chance. If your heart is open, then let it be open for me, too."

My head is spinning as I try to dissect his words and formulate a response. I'm ripped out of my mental reverie when the doorbell chimes. We're all frozen around the island, processing the place we've found ourselves and what comes next.

We're all silent for so long that the doorbell chimes again.

A few more seconds pass.

And then the pounding begins.

"This isn't over," Greedy whispers, looking from me to Levi and back again. Then he disappears from the kitchen.

I follow him to the front door out of curiosity, with Levi on my heels.

Greedy swings the door open wide—a bold choice based on the intensity of the pounding. Whoever's out there isn't going away until we face them head-on, apparently.

As Levi and I inch closer, a man comes into view.

He's tall and broad shouldered. Impeccably dressed in a bespoke three-piece suit. He's strikingly handsome, all sharp lines and enigmatic power. The kind of man who commands attention.

"Bloody hell, Hunter," he huffs when he sees me. His tone is softer than his appearance. The tension in his posture eases a bit as I make my way closer to the door. "I make my pilot and crew work all night to get here, and you turn off your damn phone?"

"Spence?" I ask with my heart in my throat. "What are you doing here?"

"I'm your emergency contact." He scowls at Greedy, who's standing tall in the doorway. "You really think you can request an urgent appointment with Dr. Squire, then turn off your phone and not have anyone follow up?"

Oh. When he puts it like that...

"You flew all the way from London to check on me?" My heart pitter-patters as I study him. Was the gesture over the top? Probably. But it's so genuinely on brand for Kabir Spencer.

His gaze softens another fraction. "I'd circle the goddamn earth to ensure your safety, love. You know that."

Obviously tired of being out of the loop, Greedy inserts himself into the conversation. "Who the hell are you?"

Spence straightens to his full height, then reluctantly drags his gaze away from me to assess first Levi, then Greedy. "Sir Kabir Kareem Alexander Louis Cornelia Spencer."

Neither Levi nor Greedy utters a word. I stifle a laugh. We're clearly not in London anymore.

"Of Spencer Enterprises and LC Entertainment?" he adds. As if that's going to provide clarity to the men standing in front of him.

He's met with silence. *Welcome to America, Spence.*

"Right. Okay, then." He straightens his tie, then he lifts a large bag from his feet and holds it out to Greedy. "Can I trust you to ensure my belongings make their way to Hunter's room?"

Greedy takes a step back so we're nearly standing side by side. He holds his hands up and glowers at Spence. "I'm not your butler, and there's no—"

"Of course not," Spence interrupts. "I would never expect a butler to open the door, or to be dressed like that."

"Spence," I chide.

Pissing off Greedy is not the flex he thinks it is. Especially considering this is Greedy's dad's house. I rub the spot between my eyebrows, smoothing out the furrow.

He should not have come here.

Here being America.

Here also being the house of my stepfather.

But before I have the chance to tell him that, his gray-blue eyes bore into me, tracking the nervous habit, and he frowns. Then he opens his arms. "Come here, love."

His tone brooks no argument. This isn't a request, and I don't have any fight left in me this morning. Furthermore, I *want* to go to him.

Spencer has always been my protector. My safe place. My sanctuary when the recesses of my mind become too much to bear. He traveled across an entire ocean to make sure I was okay.

I take a step forward, but before I can take another, the boys shift forward to form a wall, all but blocking me from Spence's view.

"Really?" Spence deadpans. He gives Levi a nonplussed look, then he fixes it on Greedy. "Love," he says craning his neck and locking eyes with me. "Call your henchmen off. We need to talk."

"We're not her henchmen," Levi quips. "We live here. And we're Hunter's..." He trails off, his shoulders sagging almost imperceptibly.

Kabir cocks one eyebrow, unamused and clearly unimpressed. "Do you own this residence?"

I'm growing tired of their pissing match. Either they need to let him in, or—

"This is my father's house. Dr. Ferguson's house," Greedy clarifies.

Recognition sparks in Spence's gray-blue eyes. "So that makes you—"

"Greedy." Then, standing taller, he corrects himself. "Garrett Reed Ferguson the Third."

Spence's perfectly manicured eyebrows shoot into his hairline. "Really, Firecracker?"

I try to move around Levi and Greedy. To get to Spence. To stop him. But the boys are already on high alert.

I move quickly, but they move faster.

"*Spence*," I warn.

Gritting my teeth, I grip Greedy's bicep, desperate to switch places with him. Desperate to protect him. If my gut instinct is any indication of where this conversation is headed, he'll be devastated.

Spence blinks at me, his expression one of disbelief. "You live here, with him?"

"It's not like that," I defend.

"It's not like what?" he challenges, running a hand down the front of his suit jacket. "It's not like you're in crisis and cohabitating with the surprise stepbrother who knocked you up the summer after high school? Because from where I stand..."

His words fade away. My vision blurs.

Levi curses. Then Greedy turns.

His face goes ashen, and his eyes are round with shock, seeking a truth I never wanted him to know. He zeroes in on me, and I feel it in my soul, the moment it clicks. The moment the secret I've kept for more than three years is revealed to the one person I never wanted to find out.

To Be Continued

So Real: Boys of South Chapel Book Two, coming July 2024

Afterword

Well... that just happened.

Thank you so much for reading the first book in the Boys of South Chapel series! Hunter's story is truly just beginning, so be sure to <u>Pre-order So Real</u> today!

Want even more Hunter and Greedy? <u>Sign up for my email newsletter</u> to receive two bonus chapters from the Lake Chapel University vs. South Chapel University "Shore Week" football game written in Hunter and Greedy's perspectives.

Hunter's bestie Joey has an entire (completed!!) why choose romance trilogy called Boys of Lake Chapel. The first book is <u>Too Safe</u>, and it's available now!

Acknowledgments

Thank you first and foremost to the readers, new and OG, who continue to trust me and fall in love with my characters. Special shoutouts to the following magic makers as well:

Mr. Abby—for feeding me and loving me and just getting me on a molecular, soul-deep level. No love story I ever write could possibly capture the depth of our love.

To my daughters—thank you for being my biggest cheerleaders, and for providing me with endless entertainment by way of book title ideas. I'm sorry *Too Long, Too Hard,* and *Too Deep* never made the cut. I'll keep *So Cute, So Hot,* and *So Big* in mind for this new series.

Beth—For letting me be salty when I remember that you have other friends, and for being the very best emotional support human I could ask for. My career as an author has been filled with highlights and milestones, but the very best thing it brought me is you.

Mel—For being so supportive, empathetic, and understanding throughout our journey together. You have such a knack for making my characters the best they can be. I am a better writer because you're my editor, and I'm a better person because you're my friend.

Megan—I've decided the Universe brought us together at the exact right time under the most perfect circumstances. I can't imagine doing this job or running this business without you!!

About The Author

Abby Millsaps is an author and storyteller who's been obsessed with writing romance since middle school. In eighth grade, she failed to qualify for the Power of the Pen State Championships because "all her submissions contained the same theme: young people falling in love." #LookAtHerNow

    She's best known for writing unapologetically angsty romance that causes emotional damage for her readers. Creative spicy scenes and consent as foreplay are two hallmarks of her books. Abby prides herself in writing authentic characters while weaving mental health, chronic illness, and neurodiverse representation into the fabric of her stories.

Connect with Abby
Website: www.authorabbymillsaps.com
Patreon: https://www.patreon.com/AbbyMillsaps
Instagram: @abbymillsaps
TikTok: @authorabbymillsaps
Email: authorabbymillsaps@gmail.com
Newsletter: https://geni.us/AuthorAbbyNewsletter
Facebook Reader Group: Abby's Full Out Fiends

By Abby Millsaps

presented in order of publication

When You're Home
While You're There
When You're Home for the Holidays
When You're Gone
Rowdy Boy
Mr. Brightside
Fourth Wheel
Full Out Fiend
Hampton Holiday Collective

Too Safe: Boys of Lake Chapel Book One
Too Fast: Boys of Lake Chapel Book Two
Too Far: Boys of Lake Chapel Book Three
So Wrong: Boys of South Chapel Book One
So Real: Boys of South Chapel Book Two
So ____: Boys of South Chapel Book Three
So _____: Boys of South Chapel Book Four

Printed in Great Britain
by Amazon